D1506974

Murder of a Bookstore Babe

**Center Point
Large Print**

Also by Denise Swanson and available from Center Point Large Print:

Scumble River Mysteries:
  Murder of a Wedding Belle
  Murder of a Royal Pain

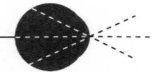

This Large Print Book carries the Seal of Approval of N.A.V.H.

Murder of a Bookstore Babe

A Scumble River Mystery

Denise Swanson

CENTER POINT LARGE PRINT
THORNDIKE, MAINE

This Center Point Large Print edition is
published in the year 2011 by arrangement with
NAL Signet, a member of Penguin Group (USA) Inc.

The text of this Large Print edition is unabridged.
In other aspects, this book may vary
from the original edition.
Printed in the United States of America.
Set in 16-point Times New Roman type.

ISBN: 978-1-61173-121-7

Library of Congress Cataloging-in-Publication Data

Swanson, Denise.
  Murder of a bookstore babe : a Scumble River mystery / Denise
Swanson. — Large print ed.
  p. cm.
  ISBN 978-1-61173-121-7 (library binding : alk. paper)
  1. Denison, Skye (Fictitious character)—Fiction.
  2. School psychologists—Fiction. 3. Large type books. I. Title.
PS3619.W36M78 2011
813'.6—dc22
                                                           2011014115

To all my Alpha Sigma Alpha sisters,
especially the
Chicago West Alumnae Chapter

Acknowledgments

Thank you to Valerie McCaffrey for helping me figure out Chase's profession and for Skye's great vintage belt. Thanks also to Melissa Kantor for allowing me to use her book *If I Have a Wicked Stepmother, Where's My Prince?* Hugs to my new grandnephew, Ethan Graham, and my new niece-in-law, Natalie Beckham Vanderhyden.

Author's Note

In July 2000, when the first book in my Scumble River series, *Murder of a Small-Town Honey*, was published, it was written in "real time." It was the year 2000 in Skye's life as well as mine, but after several books in a series, time becomes a problem. It takes me from seven months to a year to write a book, and then it is usually another year from the time I turn that book in to my editor until the reader sees it on a bookstore shelf. This can make the time line confusing. Different authors handle this matter in different ways. After a great deal of deliberation, I decided that Skye and her friends and family will age more slowly than those of us who don't live in Scumble River. While I made this decision as I wrote the fourth book in the series, *Murder of a Snake in the Grass*, I didn't realize until recently that I needed to share this information with my readers. So, to catch everyone up, the following is when the books take place:

Murder of a Small-Town Honey—August 2000
Murder of a Sweet Old Lady—March 2001
Murder of a Sleeping Beauty—April 2002
Murder of a Snake in the Grass—August 2002

The Scumble River short story and novella take place:

• • •

CHAPTER 1
For Whom the Bell Tolls

When Skye Denison saw an ad in the local newspaper announcing Tales and Treats' grand opening that weekend, she was thrilled. For a voracious reader like Skye, the luxury of having shelves and shelves of new, used, and rare books for sale just five minutes from home was nirvana. And the promise of specialty coffees, gourmet teas, and yummy pastries just added to her elation.

What she didn't realize was that the store had already managed to ruffle the fur of several of Scumble River's most vocal citizens. She should have known there'd be some kind of fuss about any new business that set up shop in her prickly hometown.

Like cats, the inhabitants of the small tight-knit community weren't partial to change, and they often showed their displeasure in spiteful and destructive ways. While the old-timers probably wouldn't pee in the interlopers' shoes, they might very well produce some obscure law that made their kind of footwear taboo.

Skye got her first inkling of the unrest on Friday

afternoon in the high school's break room. Normally she didn't frequent the lounge because the main form of entertainment there was gossip. The confidential nature of her job as the school psychologist meant she couldn't contribute, and this seriously ticked off many of the teachers. To forestall the problem, Skye usually ate at her desk.

Today, however, was different. Today, there was cake. And not just any kind of cake. It was Skye's favorite: chocolate with vanilla buttercream icing. What a shame that it was Pru Cormorant's birthday cake, and that Pru was the person Skye liked least of all her colleagues.

Still, Skye refused to let that deter her. When her conscience insisted it was wrong to eat cake honoring someone she detested, and who detested her, she promised the annoying little voice a pink-frosting rose to shut up. Once she had quieted that troublemaker, Skye continued on her quest for the delectable confection.

Since the lounge was crowded during the two lunch periods, and she didn't want to get in the way of the staff—who had only twenty minutes to wolf down their food—Skye waited until they had finished and were back in class before making her move. Her plan was to zip in, grab a piece of cake, and savor it back in her office while she started on all the special-education paperwork connected with the beginning of the school year.

Slipping through the doorway, Skye scanned the room, then darted forward. There it was, in the exact middle of the three metal tables that ran end to end down the center of the room. Intent on the double-layered hunk of ecstasy, half of which was already gone, she pushed aside one of the orange molded-plastic chairs that lined both sides of the tables and reached for the knife lying on the crumb-filled serving platter.

Just as her fingers closed around the handle, an ominous voice, the last in the universe she wanted to hear, said, "Having a late lunch?"

Skye whirled around. Pru Cormorant sat on the sofa, her arms along the back and a derisive look on her face. How could Skye have missed seeing her there? She didn't exactly blend into the surroundings. Pru's sticklike limbs stuck out at awkward angles from her egg-shaped body, and her too-small head appeared in danger of tumbling off her neck if she made any sudden moves.

"It's not late for me." Reluctantly putting down the knife, Skye felt a guilty flush creeping up her neck. "I often see kids during the regular lunch hours." Not that she had today, but Pru didn't need to know that.

The English teacher trailed a finger along the top of the couch, which was covered in a prickly plaid fabric that Skye suspected could withstand a direct nuclear hit. "We don't see you in here very often."

"No." Skye pasted a fake smile on her face. "I guess not."

"Then you must have stopped by especially to wish me a happy birthday. How sweet of you." Pru gave a malicious little laugh. "I'm sure it wasn't just for the cake." She lasered a look at the two-carat diamond on Skye's left hand. "Particularly since you're almost certainly on a diet for your wedding."

Skye's engagement to Wally Boyd, the Scumble River police chief, had been the talk of the town since June, when she had accepted his proposal and begun wearing his ring. That her ex-boyfriend, Simon Reid, was doing everything in his power to change her mind about marrying the chief wasn't helping to quell the chatter.

Simon's plea last week had been delivered in the middle of the school parking lot by a white knight on horseback, which had really stirred up the rumor mill. Skye had always liked her ex's quirky sense of humor, but she was starting to rethink that opinion. Especially since he had promised that next time he would send a fire-breathing-dragon-gram.

"I couldn't let such a big day go by without wishing you the best," Skye managed to say with false sincerity before putting her hands on her hips and staring at Pru. "But why would I be on a diet?"

Skye was well aware that ever since she'd

12

decided she wasn't willing to eat fewer than eight hundred calories a day in order to stay a size six, a lot of people thought she was too fat. But she didn't allow veiled insults to go unchallenged. If someone had something to say about her weight, let them come right out and say it.

"It's just that most brides-to-be want to look extragood for their wedding pictures," Pru said, then ruined it by adding, "And you have such a pretty face."

"For someone who needs to lose a few pounds?" Skye wasn't about to let the older woman off the hook that easily.

"Of course not." Pru's tone was completely insincere as she added, "I'm sorry if you took what I said the wrong way. I certainly never meant to offend you."

"Hmm." Skye held her tongue. "Anyway, since we haven't even set a date yet, I'm not worried about the photos."

In fact, unbeknownst to anyone beyond Skye's immediate family, the wedding was on indefinite hold. Knowing how much it meant to Skye to be married in the Catholic Church, Wally had agreed to apply for an annulment from his first wife, from whom he'd been divorced for several years. Father Burns said it might take twelve to fourteen months before the official paperwork was completed, which left them waiting on a process they had little control over.

Pru raised an overplucked brow, but before she could probe further, Skye said, "Anyway, happy birthday."

Pru nodded regally. "Thank you."

Skye felt like a bunny caught nibbling a gardener's prizewinning petunias, and she hadn't even had a bite of the darn cake. In her heart, she knew she should go ahead, cut a slice, and eat it, but she just couldn't. Not with Pru staring at her. It was one thing to stand up for herself when someone made a nasty remark, quite another to chow down in front of that same someone, who obviously disapproved of her.

While Skye tried to think of a graceful way to escape, her gaze flitted from the avocado-colored refrigerator set against the back wall to the big black trash can next to the counter, then on to the sink full of used coffee mugs. Finally, she said, "Well, I should probably get back to work."

"Don't hurry away on my account." Pru smiled meanly.

"Of course not." Skye resigned herself to forfeiting her treat and searched for a good departure line. She glanced at the old library cart holding a huge brown microwave oven, circa 1980. "But I do have reports to write, so I'll just heat up some water for a cup of tea and be on my way."

The microwave's stained exterior was gross, but using the appliance had several advantages.

14

She could turn her back on Pru, thus avoiding further conversation, and when the timer dinged, it would clearly indicate that it was time to depart.

But Pru ruined Skye's scheme by saying, "Since it's my planning period, and you can always write reports at home, I'd like to talk to you about something."

"Oh." Skye cringed inwardly. Pru had an ongoing vendetta against the student newspaper that Skye and her friend Trixie Frayne cosponsored. Many of the kids who had been on the English teacher's debate team had switched to the *Scoop*'s staff because Skye and Trixie treated them fairly. The front page got the top story, not the one written by the teenager who kissed up to them the most. Pru, on the other hand, was known for letting her pets have all the best debate topics, and the students had finally rebelled.

"What's up?" Skye asked.

"I'm concerned about that new bookstore in town." Pru ran her fingers through her greasy dun-colored hair, pulling out strands from the bun on top of her head. "I hear it will be selling romance and science fiction."

Skye bit her tongue to stop from blurting out "And your point is . . . ?" Pru was the leader of the school's old guard. No need to antagonize her further. Instead Skye said, "Romance outsells all the other genres, and a lot of the most popular YA novels are sci-fi. If those books are readily available, it might encourage kids to read more."

"Those bodice rippers are nothing but pornography." Pru's watery blue eyes scrunched into slits, and her pointy nose twitched, making her look like a nearsighted possum.

"That isn't true. They're full of love and hope and happy endings."

"Nonsense. They're obscene." Pru's lips drew together. "And I have it on good authority that those young adult books you're referring to are anti-Christian. They encourage the occult and demonic activity."

Skye clamped her mouth shut, chanting silently, *Don't, don't, don't.* It would be so easy to make a smart-alecky comeback, but she finally managed to swallow her retort and said, "I'm sure that's not true either."

"I'm surprised that you, a psychologist"—Pru's face had her *tsk-tsk* look on it—"aren't aware of the danger posed by those kinds of books."

" 'Danger?' " The word slipped out. Skye did not like where this conversation was going, and she shouldn't have allowed herself to be sucked in.

Pru's tongue snaked out as if she was about to sample a tasty morsel. "I heard that over in Clay Center some boy bit his mother in the neck and tried to suck her blood out after reading some of those vampire books."

"Really?" If that had actually happened, Skye

was sure she would have heard about it. After all, she was the police department's psychological consultant, and her mother was a police dispatcher. "Who told you that?"

Pru puffed out her cheeks. "I don't remember." Her irritation with Skye for daring to question her was obvious. "What does it matter?"

"Rumors can be so harmful," Skye said evenly. "I just like to make sure my source is reliable before I believe what I hear."

"Well"—Pru sent a quelling look in Skye's direction—"I also heard that a girl in Brooklyn sacrificed her baby after reading some book that glorified witchcraft."

"Now, that's totally unbelievable." Skye shook her head. "Surely that would have made the paper, not to mention the TV news."

Pru leaned forward and whispered, "I hear it was hushed up."

"By whom?"

"I'm sure I couldn't say." Pru got up from the sofa. "Everyone knows I never gossip."

Skye nearly choked on a suppressed "Ha!" but managed to keep her expression neutral.

"Anyway, I've started a petition," Pru went on, "and I expect you to sign it." She paused. "Unless, of course, you don't care about our kids."

Skye refused to be cornered. "This weekend, I'll talk to the owners and find out what kinds of books they'll be selling and to what age groups. I'll let you know Monday after school what I find out."

"Now"—Pru glanced pointedly at Skye— "unlike you, I have to get back to my classroom. The bell is about to ring, and the little darlings might burn down the building if they're left unattended."

Skye stared at the door after Pru Cormorant's departure, then turned and cut an extra-big slice of birthday cake. After what she'd just been through, she deserved it. Besides, if Pru planned to stir up trouble for the new bookstore, Skye would need all her strength to make sure the school's queen bee didn't sic her swarm of drones on the defenseless owners before they even had a chance to open for business.

CHAPTER 2

The Sound and the Fury

Skye watched as her cousin Hugo Leofanti, owner of Better Than New Autos, stood in his showroom extolling the virtues of a 1999 Ford Escort to Xenia Craughwell. Xenia and her mother had moved to town a little more than two years ago, after the teenager had been kicked out of several suburban schools. Much to Skye's relief, despite a rocky start, which included kidnapping a cheerleader and involving the school newspaper in a lawsuit, Xenia had managed to graduate from Scumble River High last fall.

Although Xenia had written for the *Scoop*, and Skye supervised the student paper, they had not been close. Xenia had rebuffed Skye's attempts to build a relationship and had used her incredibly high IQ to keep all the adults in the school at arm's length. Even Trixie, the paper's beloved coadviser, hadn't been able to break through the girl's defenses.

Which was why Skye had been so surprised when Xenia showed up in her office that afternoon and asked for assistance in buying a car. Skye had hesitated, wondering what Xenia was up to, but the knowledge that Xenia's father was dead and her mom acted more like a girlfriend than a parent had compelled Skye to accompany the teen. Now that she was here, Skye wasn't exactly sure what her role was supposed to be. Xenia wasn't one to take advice or need help in making a decision.

Skye had been able to convince Hugo to show them around personally, rather than handing them over to a member of his sales staff, but already she was regretting *that* impulse. She had forgotten how ruthless and underhanded her cousin could be, and she was afraid he'd take advantage of Xenia's youth and inexperience.

Flashing deep dimples, Hugo said to Xenia as he led her and Skye out of the building, "Let's get you into a car."

The early-September sun beat down on the windshields of vehicles parked along Basin Street, Scumble River's main drag. Other than the empty road, there wasn't much else to see. Ye Olde Junque Emporium was the only other business open within a two- or three-block radius.

Hugo directed them to a space a few doors down containing a small rusty hatchback with yellow block letters spelling out EZ TERMS on a side window. Skye frowned but kept silent. She'd decided to intervene only if Xenia requested her opinion, and that was about as likely as the government *truly* reducing taxes or *really* fixing the health care system.

Xenia walked around the Ford. "How many miles does this . . . this thing have on it?"

"This luxury automobile only has a hundred and ten thousand," Hugo answered smoothly, then added, "You mentioned that you're attending film school in Chicago and need transportation for the commute. This baby has a spacious interior *and* gets incredible mileage. And I can let you have her for only four thousand dollars. Let me tell you about the previous owner."

Skye studied Hugo as he talked. Her cousin had been fortunate when he took a dip in the gene pool. He had gotten a long, lean body from his mother's side of the family and a thick black mane and the Leofanti eyes from his father's. If it had been the other way around, he would have ended up short, with thinning dishwater blond hair. His dad, Skye's uncle Dante, looked a lot liked a penguin; Hugo would have probably resembled a bowling pin.

Skye had the Leofanti emerald eyes, too, but that was where the similarity ended. While Skye's shone with genuineness, Hugo's glittered with insincerity. Although he oozed charm, he was good at masking his true thoughts. This was an advantage in his chosen profession, but it did not make him trustworthy.

Xenia broke in on Hugo's sales spiel.

"Seriously, dude, fuel economy may be important, but I'm carpooling with another girl from town, so it's not totally the deciding factor. There's also acceleration and quality of the ride." She angled her pierced brow contemptuously. "By the way, FYI, four thousand is double what this piece of crap is worth, and even at a quarter of the price it would probably come back and bite me."

Hugo's expression subtly changed, and Skye felt her lips twitch. Clearly, he had looked at Xenia, outfitted in her usual Goth-punk sex-kitten attire, and thought she was an airhead on whom he could pull a fast one. He was wising up quickly.

Skye could understand her cousin's misconception. Today Xenia had on a short ruffled skirt, leggings that ended midcalf, and a pair of Doc Martens. She had layered several ripped T-shirts, all of which exposed the gold ring in her navel. A multitude of bangle bracelets worn on top of fishnet gloves on both arms completed her fashion statement. White skin and the fuchsia stripe in her hair at the temple were the only contrasts to the unrelieved black of her clothing.

"What else do you have?" Xenia shaded her eyes and looked down the line of vehicles parked on either side of the dealership. "You gotta turn it up a notch from this." She thumped the Escort's trunk. "I want something sick."

Hugo glanced questioningly at Skye, who mouthed the word *cool*.

Hugo recovered quickly. "I know just the car for you. A Volkswagen Beetle. It's hip *and* gets great mileage." He guided Xenia and Skye by their elbows. "I was saving this for Dr. Zello's daughter—she's turning sixteen next month—but since you're a friend of my cousin, I'll let you have first crack at it."

"Awesome." Xenia rolled her eyes at Skye but allowed herself to be propelled across the road to a line of vehicles parked along the curb.

"What do you think?" Hugo stopped beside a tiny yellow car that looked like an upside-down coffee cup. The lettering on its windshield read, SUPER DEAL. "She even has a cute little flower holder near the driver's seat."

"Dude, do I look like a flower kinda girl to you?" Xenia shook her head but inspected every inch of the finish, then repeated the process with the interior. Finally she asked, "What year is it?"

"Two thousand three." Hugo's smile displayed impossibly straight white teeth against his deeply tanned skin. "And she only has seventy-three thousand miles on her."

As he pointed out the car's features, Skye noticed they were in front of the new bookstore. The display window was still covered on the inside with brown paper, but the words *Tales and Treats* were painted in gold across the glass. Rumor had it that the owners had purchased the entire building and were living above the shop.

As Skye examined the second floor for signs of occupancy, the front door slammed open, and a petite woman dressed in faded jeans and a T-shirt with NEVER JUDGE A BOOK BY ITS MOVIE ~ J. W. EAGAN printed on the front came running out. "Mr. Leofanti, a word please."

"Mrs. Erwin, as you can see, I'm busy right now." Hugo hid his scowl and said, "Perhaps we can talk when I have more time. Why don't you send your husband over later?"

"It's Ms. Vaughn or Risé, as I've told you before." In an aside to Skye and Xenia she explained, "I kept my maiden name when I got married, which seems to confuse Mr. Leofanti to no end." Turning her attention back to Hugo, she said, "And for the tenth time, you need to deal with me, not Orlando, on this matter."

"Well, *Miz* Vaughn." Hugo grabbed Xenia's elbow and tried to steer her away from the woman. "I'll speak to *you* later."

"Back off! You're bruising my aura." Xenia shook off Hugo's hand, crossed her arms, and refused to budge. "I'm not in a hurry. Go ahead and talk to Ms. Vaughn."

Xenia's expression suggested that Hugo was rapidly losing any credibility he'd had with her. If Skye had liked her cousin, she would have told him that the teen was a feminist and his condescending attitude toward the bookstore woman would not improve his chances of selling Xenia a car.

"No. Ms. Vaughn can wait." Hugo made another attempt to move Xenia away. "I know just what you want."

"Oh, yeah?" Xenia snorted. "Yet, despite the look on my face, you're still talking."

Hugo's ears turned red, and he snapped, "Young lady, you have an attitude problem."

"No, I don't." Xenia smiled, clearly pleased she'd provoked him into losing his cool. "You have a perception problem." She patted the laptop case that hung from her shoulder. "Now that we have that settled, I need to check the Internet about this car." She turned to Risé. "You got Wi-Fi?"

"Yes." The bookstore owner nodded to the door behind her. "Help yourself."

"Phenomenal." Xenia fluttered her fingers at Hugo, and said, "Later."

Skye was torn. Should she go with Xenia or stay here? Since Skye was technology challenged and would be of no help with the computer, she remained where she was.

"Yes?" Hugo heaved a put-upon sigh and turned back to Risé. "What now?"

"Our grand opening is tomorrow, and you still haven't moved your automobiles." Risé gestured to the half dozen vehicles parked in front of her store, all with various messages in yellow lettering on their windows. "I asked you a week ago to put them somewhere else."

When Hugo had bought Scumble River's old

hardware store a couple of years ago and turned it into a used-car dealership, the buildings surrounding it had been vacant, which meant he'd been able to use all the parking spaces on the block to stow his inventory. The bookstore was the first business to move in since then.

"And I told you when you asked me the first time, these spots are public property." Hugo's smile was smug. "You don't own them."

"True." Risé reached into the pocket of her blue jeans and pulled out a folded piece of paper. "But I've been doing a little research."

"Good for you." Hugo leaned back on the hood of a blue Dodge Charger with ONE OWNER written across its windshield.

Skye's attention was riveted to the drama playing out in front of her.

Risé grabbed center stage by shoving the paper into Hugo's hand and saying, "According to the town statutes, no vehicle may remain parked in the same space for more than twelve consecutive hours."

"So?" Hugo's shoulders stayed relaxed under his gray pin-striped suit jacket. "Who's to say my cars haven't been moved around?"

Skye watched Risé's hands tighten into fists. Should she call the police now or wait for the woman to punch out Hugo's lights? One thing was for sure—this wasn't her fight, and she wasn't getting involved. Taking a step backward,

26

Skye put a white Mercury Sable whose sign read LOW MILEAGE between her and the possible combatants.

Risé noted Skye's movement and shook her head, causing her long brown ponytail to sway back and forth. "I'm not going to hit him," she said. "Except in his wallet."

"What do you mean by that?" Hugo sputtered.

Risé held up a finger. "The first parking offense is a fifty-dollar fine—per car." She held up another finger. "The second offense is a hundred dollars." A final finger joined the other two. "And the third is impoundment."

"Again, so?" Hugo sneered. "There's no way to prove how long my cars have been parked in the same space."

"Isn't there?" Risé smiled thinly. "Do you really want to take that risk?"

"There's no risk involved." Hugo shoved his hands in his pockets. "Do you know who my father is?"

"Santa Claus?" Risé shrugged. "The Easter Bunny?" Her lip curled. "What? There will be a lump of coal in my stocking or I'm not getting any chocolate eggs in my basket?"

"You're so funny." Hugo narrowed his cool green eyes. "My father's the mayor of Scumble River." He jerked his thumb at Skye. "And my cousin, here, is engaged to the chief of police."

Skye cringed and hurriedly said, "Not that I'd

try to influence him in any legal matters." She'd been hoping she and the bookstore owner could be friends. Besides, she really didn't want to be aligned with Hugo.

"Of course not, cuz." Hugo glanced at his watch. "Anything else? I've got to move some metal." He made an impatient face. "Some of us need to make a living from our business."

"What do you mean by that?" Risé demanded.

"Let's just say"—Hugo smirked—"you're not the only one who's done a little investigating."

A faint line dug between the bookstore owner's brows but was instantly smoothed away. "Scum-sucking bastard," she declared, then turned on her heel and marched into her shop.

"What was that all about?" Skye demanded.

But before Hugo could respond, Xenia stepped out of the building and said, "Ready to deal, dude?"

While Hugo and Xenia worked out the details of her purchase of the Volkswagen, Skye sat in Hugo's office and thought about the encounter she had witnessed between her cousin and Risé Vaughn. So far Tales and Treats was two for two. Skye had had only two encounters concerning the shop, and both times the people concerned had a problem with the new business.

All in all, it was not looking like an auspicious beginning for the bookstore.

CHAPTER 3

Remembrance of Things Past

O nce the purchase of the Beetle was completed, Skye followed Xenia home, driving the Craughwell family car, which Xenia had borrowed for her trip to Better Than New Autos. Once Skye parked the Sebring in the garage and got into the Volkswagen, Xenia suggested they stop for ice cream before she dropped Skye back at the high school.

"Sounds good." Skye fastened her seat belt. "Don't forget to buckle up."

"Seat belts are too confining." Xenia put the VW into gear.

"Not as confining as a wheelchair."

Xenia harrumphed but clicked the belt into place.

"Wasn't the warning bell bugging you on the drive over?" Skye asked, then realized she hadn't heard the irritating dinging when she got into the vehicle.

"Nah." Xenia accelerated. "I disconnected it before leaving the used-car lot."

Skye opened her mouth to ask how but realized

she didn't really want to know. Instead she changed the subject. "You were pretty rude to Hugo."

"He got on my last nerve, and I couldn't help myself."

"It's true he deserved what you said to him," Skye allowed, "but either you control your attitude or it controls you."

Xenia snorted but was silent for the next few minutes until they arrived at the Dairy Kastle. The local soft-serve drive-in was a hangout for kids, and the statue of a giant man holding a cone was often photographed by tourists on their Route 66 road trips. To Skye, he looked suspiciously like Paul Bunyan, and she often wondered what had happened to his ax and his blue ox, Babe.

Once they were parked, had given their order to the carhop, and the girl had skated away, Xenia patted the dash and said, "This is wicked nice."

"Yes. It is." Skye swept her hand in front of her. "It's much roomier than I was expecting."

"And I got a great price," Xenia bragged. "A thousand under the Kelley Blue Book Web site recommendation."

"That's amazing." Skye's tone was upbeat, but she was alarmed. It wasn't like Hugo to sell a car for one cent less than it was worth to him. She sure hoped there was nothing wrong with the

VW. Not that she had believed for a minute that he really had another buyer for it.

"Like you and Mrs. Frayne used to always say" —Xenia beamed—"it pays to do your homework."

"You did great. I'm proud of you." Skye couldn't remember ever seeing a genuine smile on Xenia's face before. "You know, I've never actually bought a car."

"Word?"

"Yep. My dad has always fixed up clunkers for me." Skye shrugged. "He and my uncle found my current one rotting in someone's barn."

"It must have taken them a long time to make a nineteen fifty-seven Bel Air so nice." Xenia's smile faded. "My mom won't even stitch on a button for me. She just hands me some money and tells me to buy a new blouse."

"Maybe she doesn't know how to sew."

"That's her excuse for everything she doesn't want to do: clean, cook, help me fill out forms for school." Xenia's lips thinned. "I think you shouldn't be allowed to have a kid until you can prove you can take care of one."

Skye silently agreed with the girl and struggled to come up with a diplomatic answer. When she couldn't, she changed the subject. "Not that I'm not happy to do it, but what made you decide to invite me to come with you to buy a car? I sure didn't contribute much to the process."

"Uh." Xenia peeled a strip of black polish off

31

her thumbnail. "My therapist says I have to start asking for help." She glanced at Skye out of the corner of her eye. "You know, quit trying to do everything myself."

"Right." Skye nodded. Xenia had been seeing a private counselor for the past couple of years. She had a lot of issues—explosiveness, impulsivity, and episodes of depression among the most serious. The psychologist seemed to be making remarkable progress with Xenia, but she still had a long way to go. "I'm glad you picked me," Skye said.

"You and Mrs. Frayne were pretty cool with stuff that happened on the paper." Xenia made a face. "Not that you let us get away with anything, but you didn't automatically freak out or blame the bad kids either."

"Well, thanks." Skye felt a glow. One of the drawbacks of being a school psychologist was lack of feedback. It was nice to hear she'd established rapport with a student, especially one she would have bet money hadn't felt a connection. "So—"

Skye's next words were cut off when a tiny brunette stuck her head through Xenia's open window and said, "Girlfriend. New wheels?"

"Got it about an hour ago." Xenia grinned. "Now I can take my turn driving to school."

"Awesome." The brunette vibrated with energy.

Since it didn't look as if Xenia planned to introduce her, Skye stuck out her hand and said, "Hi, I'm Skye Denison."

"Actually, we've met." The girl shook Skye's hand. "I'm Kayla Hines. I graduated from Scumble River High in 2004."

"Sorry," Skye apologized. "Which activity did we meet through?" She was pretty sure their encounter hadn't been in her capacity as a school psychologist. She tended to remember those kids, at least their names if not all their faces.

"You gave a talk on intelligence to my advanced English class."

"Oh." Skye was glad to know Kayla had been part of a group and she hadn't forgotten a student with whom she'd worked individually. "I hope I didn't bore you to tears."

"No. It was the first time anyone explained that there are different kinds of intelligence." Kayla's smile was radiant. "It totally made me appreciate the artistic side of myself and helped me decide to become a filmmaker. Everyone was telling me I was so smart, I should be a doctor, but I knew when we had to dissect a cat in advanced biology that it wasn't the career for me."

"I'm glad I helped." Skye settled back in her seat. This was turning out to be a good day after all. "So you and Xenia are attending the same college in Chicago?"

"It's not a college," Kayla corrected. "We're

both going to the Chicago School of Film and Photography."

Xenia added, "Kayla's a second-year student and is studying moviemaking. She's over-the-top talented."

"Xenia's no slouch either." Kayla hugged her friend. "This is her first year in the documentary program, and her teachers are already mega-impressed just from her portfolio."

"Wow. Maybe you'll both become famous and put Scumble River on the map," Skye enthused. "And you're both living at home?"

"Xenia is." Kayla climbed into the backseat as she answered. "I'm sort of between gigs. Some-times I stay at my mom and stepdad's, sometimes I crash with my boyfriend, and sometimes I hang at Xenia's place."

"Oh." Before Skye could question why Kayla didn't have a place to call home, their ice cream arrived, so instead she asked, "Do you want to order something, Kayla?"

"No, thanks." Kayla put her hand to her mouth. "I haven't been too hungry lately. Nothing sounds good to me."

Skye noticed that the girl was a bit pale and hoped she wasn't not eating because she thought she needed to lose weight. Which certainly was far from the truth.

After the carhop left, Kayla said, "Oh, I kinda almost forgot. I have good news, too."

"What?" Xenia took a huge bite of her banana split.

"I finally found a part-time job."

"Where?" Skye licked a rivulet of melted vanilla dripping down the side of her cone.

"At Tales and Treats." Kayla wiggled in her seat. "It works out perfectly since I don't have to be in class every day." She explained to Skye, "We do lots of work via computer."

"That's great," Skye agreed.

"Ms. Vaughn said I can start tomorrow." Kayla frowned. "That is, if they get the insurance and stuff straightened out."

"Oh?" Skye raised brow. "What's the problem?"

"The insurance guy told Ms. Vaughn that her policy was approved, but he stopped by this afternoon while she was interviewing me and told her that it was going to cost more than he originally said."

"Why?" Xenia asked.

"Who knows?" Kayla shrugged. "They stepped into the back room to discuss it."

"I'm sure they'll get that fixed up," Skye reassured the girl.

"Yeah." Kayla nodded. "It's the other guy I'm more worried about."

"What other guy?" Skye asked.

"The one they hired to remodel the upstairs," Kayla explained. "They're going to live up there, you know, and use two spare rooms for a B and B."

"Uh-huh," Skye encouraged.

"Well, the construction guy came after the insurance man left. At first he seemed normal, but—"

"Yeah," Xenia interrupted. "Everyone seems normal until you get to know them."

Kayla snickered, then continued. "Anyway, this creep demanded payment in cash, or he'd make sure the rooms didn't pass the building inspection." Kayla chewed her lower lip. "Ms. Vaughn really schooled him. She threatened to call his union, and he got real uptight and harsh. What a loser."

"Boy!" Xenia exclaimed. "You sure had an exciting interview."

Kayla opened her mouth, but a honking horn interrupted her. They all looked in the direction of a black BMW SUV parked a couple spaces down. A muscular blond guy was waving in their direction. Xenia and Kayla waved back.

It took Skye a second to place the young man, but then she recognized him as Chase Wren. As a senior, he'd played the prince in Scumble River High's 2002 production of *Sleeping Beauty*. Although he'd been a hotshot baseball player, he hadn't been one of the brightest bulbs on the scoreboard, which made her wonder what kind of job Chase had gotten that paid well enough for him to buy a thirty-five-thousand-dollar car.

While Skye had been thinking, Kayla had climbed hastily out of the car, saying, "That's my boyfriend. Gotta go. Bye."

"I'll see you at Tales and Treats tomorrow," Skye called after her.

"Definitely." Kayla waved, then added as she walked away, her ponytail swinging in time with her strides, "I just hope everything's ready. It would kill Ms. Vaughn if something held up the grand opening."

CHAPTER 4

Alice's Adventures in Wonderland

And then she tried to make me sign a petition against Tales and Treats." Skye sat on a bench in front of Bates Pharmacy. It was Saturday morning, and she and Trixie were supervising the school newspaper's bake sale.

"Is she out of her mind?" Trixie shrieked, jumping up and down in her seat as if she were a baby in a bouncy chair. The two students standing behind the folding table full of goodies glanced her way, and she lowered her voice. "Why would an English teacher want to close down a bookstore?"

"Because she's an idiot." Skye watched her friend fidget. As well as cosponsoring the *Scoop* with Skye, Trixie was the high school librarian and coached the cheerleading squad. To say Trixie's energy level made a hyperactive squirrel look sedate was an understatement. "She's sure it will turn our kids into vampires and porn stars."

"Oh, my . . ." Trixie had just taken a drink of Mountain Dew, and it spewed into the air.

"Yeah." Skye grabbed a tissue from her purse and handed it to Trixie. "That was my reaction, too."

"What are we going to do about it?" Trixie gazed expectantly at Skye. "We won't let her get away with it, right?"

"Well, I didn't sign her petition."

"Like that'll stop Without-a-Clue Pru." Trixie blotted the electric yellow liquid from her pale pink T-shirt. "You and I need to nip her scheme in the bud."

"What makes you think we can stop her?"

" 'Cause we're smarter?"

"Maybe," Skye acknowledged. "But she's as persistent as a smoker's cough."

"Then we'll have to find some way to persuade her it's in her best interest to back off." Trixie put her right hand over her heart. "As a librarian I'm sworn to oppose censorship of any kind."

"Really?" Skye raised a brow. "Did you have to take an oath in library school or something?"

"Nope." Trixie got to her feet and walked toward the bake sale table. "It's implied." Once she finished cajoling an older gentleman into buying a pie, two plates of cookies, and a tin of fudge, she returned to her seat. "So, what's the plan?"

"It's your pledge. You figure out the plan." Skye took the last sip of her Diet Coke and tossed the empty can toward the garbage container.

"And while you're at it, you'd better figure out a way to stop my cousin Hugo, too."

"What's he got against the bookstore?"

As Skye got up, retrieved the can from where it had landed on the ground, and deposited it in the trash, she explained about the parking situation, ending with, "Then he said, 'My dad's the mayor of Scumble River and my cousin here is engaged to the chief of police.' "

"You know I'm still mad at you about that, right?" Trixie narrowed her brown eyes. "How could you possibly not tell me that Wally proposed?"

Skye cringed. "I said I was sorry. It's just that I wasn't sure I was going to accept, and it seemed cruel to tell anyone if I ended up saying no." Wally had popped the question last November, and Skye had apologized to Trixie a hundred times since announcing their engagement three months ago, but any mention of it rekindled her friend's hurt feelings. "I was trying to save him from being embarrassed."

"Are you saying I can't keep a secret?" Trixie demanded.

"No." Skye knew she had to tread carefully. "If I had confided in anyone, it would have been you."

"I bet you told someone." Trixie dug into her jeans pocket, pulled out a miniature Butterfinger, and stripped off the wrapper. "Did you tell Vince?"

"No. Considering his profession, there was no way I would have told him." Skye's brother owned the Great Expectations hair salon, and gossip was as much part of the service he offered as an excellent haircut. "I promise you, no one knew."

"Including me," Trixie muttered. "Everyone got to see your ring before me."

"You were in Europe, and I called you the night I accepted," Skye almost screamed in frustration. "You know, one of the things I've finally accepted is that no matter how good friends you are with someone, there will come a time when they hurt you, and either you keep losing friends or you learn to forgive them."

"Fine." Trixie drew out the word. "I'll forgive you, but you have to tell me a secret. Something no one else knows."

"I don't have any secrets," Skye protested.

"Everyone has secrets."

"Okay." Skye exhaled loudly. "A few months back I had to go to a lingerie shower for one of my second or third cousins. One of the games was that as the bride opened her gifts you had to write down your first impressions. Well, my cousin is extremely flat chested and someone got her a Wonderbra, so I wrote, 'I wonder what she's going to put into it.' "

"So, what's the big deal about that?"

"When they read the slips out loud, the bride

got hysterical and that pretty much ended the party. Luckily the comments were anonymous. If Mom knew it was me, she'd never let me hear the end of it."

"Oh." Trixie was well acquainted with the Wrath of May.

"Now"—Skye frowned—"can we get back to the current problem of how to stop Hugo and Pru from shutting down the bookstore?"

Trixie ran her hands through her short faun-colored hair. "I have an idea."

"Okay," Skye's tone was cautious; Trixie was even more impulsive than she was. "What?"

"I'll dig up something on Pru, and you take care of your cousin Hugo."

"No." Skye shook her head. "Mom will kill me if I do anything to upset the family."

"You don't have to upset them." Trixie finished her candy bar and licked her fingers. "Just make sure Hugo moves his cars."

"Right." Skye sneered. "Because he always listens to me about stuff like that."

"You'll figure it out." Trixie shrugged. "You're good at that."

A couple of hours later, when the last of the baked goods had been purchased and the *Scoop* staff had packed away the table, Trixie and Skye went into the pharmacy to thank the owner for letting them use the space in front of his store.

As they waited for Mr. Bates to finish filling a

prescription, Trixie poked Skye in the shoulder. "You did too tell someone that Wally had proposed to you."

"Shh!" Skye scowled at Trixie. Several customers had turned to look at them. "Not now." Even though it was nearly impossible in a town of three thousand people, half of whom Skye was related to, she tried to keep her love life private.

Trixie ignored Skye's command for silence. "You told Simon."

"Shut up." Skye resisted an urge to put her hand over Trixie's mouth and instead dragged her behind a display of feminine products. "I thought you forgave me."

"That was when I thought you hadn't told anyone else."

"As I explained to you, I only informed him before I accepted because of . . . Well, you know." She was uncomfortable discussing Simon's vow to win her back.

"Still." Trixie sniffed. "You *did* tell someone." A tear slid down her round cheek. "And it wasn't me."

"I'm so sorry." Skye swallowed, touched by Trixie's pain. "What else can I say?"

"You can say that you'll help me save Tales and Treats."

"Of course I will. I don't want it to close any more than you do." Skye hugged Trixie. "Pick me up at two for the grand opening."

●●●

Skye was waiting on her front porch when Trixie's car roared into the driveway. Skye checked to make sure the front door was locked, then walked down the steps and climbed into the passenger seat. A lot of people in Scumble River didn't bother with deadbolts, but Skye had had a few too many close calls with deranged killers to leave her door open.

As Skye was buckling her seat belt, Trixie said, "I figured out how to find some dirt on Pru. I'll use the Internet."

"Really?" Skye asked, tucking her purse behind her legs. "How?"

"I'll Google her."

"Oh." Skye had finally begun accepting that the computer was a viable tool, but she still wasn't comfortable with some of its features, like search engines. "Every time I try to find information that way, I get a zillion hits and end up wasting more time than if I had just looked it up in a book."

Trixie flung the Civic into gear and stepped on the gas. Her prized Mustang convertible was long gone, sold to pay off a debt, but she still drove as if she were racing on the NASCAR circuit. Skye gripped the dashboard as Trixie backed out of the driveway without even glancing in the rearview mirror.

"Oh, stop flinching." Trixie slowed to a modest sixty. "You know I'm a good driver."

"How about all those tickets you've gotten?"

"The speed limits are ridiculous." Trixie tossed her head. "I've never been in an accident."

The constant acceleration and braking were making Skye motion sick, and she closed her eyes. Finally, the car stopped and Skye looked around. Trixie had parked the Honda nearly half a mile from the bookstore. "Can't you get any closer? At this rate we could have walked from my house."

"I circled twice." Trixie checked her lipstick in the rearview mirror. "All the parking spots are filled with your cousin's used-car inventory."

"Shoot." Skye got out of the Civic and tugged her black jeans into place. "I hope that doesn't keep people away."

"There was quite a crowd by the entrance, so I think today it'll be okay. During normal business hours, when they aren't giving away free refreshments, it might be a different story." Trixie linked an arm with Skye's, and they headed toward the shop. "Anyway, walking is good for you."

"If that's true, why does the mailman look like Jabba the Hutt?"

"You are so not funny." Trixie snickered. A few minutes later, she said, "Look."

"At what?" They were a block away from Tales and Treats, and all Skye could see was that the half dozen wrought-iron tables and chairs arranged in front of the large front window were fully occupied. "You knew it would be packed."

"Not that." Trixie pointed to the entrance. "That."

"Crap." Skye hadn't expected Pru to rally her troops so soon, but a small group of women holding protest signs was marching in a circle in front of the store's entrance.

"Get a load of Pru's Crew," Trixie hissed.

"Yeah, but where's their leader?" Skye asked.

As Trixie lifted her hands in puzzlement, one of the women thrust a leaflet into it. "Have you found Jesus Christ?" The picketer was a young blonde with long straight hair held back with a cornflower blue headband.

"Yes." Trixie crumpled the flyer and deliberately dropped it on the ground. "He was behind the sofa the whole time."

"If you're a good Christian, you won't go in," the blonde persisted.

Skye gripped her friend's arm, not sure what Trixie would do, but before she could say anything, an older woman with snow-white hair and a face that looked like a dried apple joined the first and said, "Now, dearies, just turn around and go home. I'm sure sweet girls like you have no idea this place is a den of iniquity."

"The hell we don't." Trixie narrowed her eyes. "Censorship is the real evil."

While Trixie was arguing with the protesters, Skye read the various protest signs. ROMANCES

ROT YOUR BRAIN. SCIENCE FICTION IS THE WORK OF THE DEVIL. DO YOU WANT YOUR DAUGHTER READING PORN? STICK TO JANE AUSTEN AND JULES VERNE.

Skye didn't catch what was said, but suddenly the Alice in Wonderland look-alike slapped Trixie in the face.

"That was assault!" Skye moved in front of her friend. "Which means if all of you don't get out of our way, I'm calling the police."

"Just try it!" Alice screamed.

The protesters linked arms and chanted, "No cash for this trash."

The picketers formed a circle around Skye and Trixie when they attempted to walk into the store. Skye blew out an irritated breath, then grabbed her cell phone from her purse, but before she could dial, two of the male demonstrators pinned her arms to her sides. Trixie seized the waist of one of the men, but another guy took hold of Trixie's shoulders.

Just as Skye was wondering if they would end up forming the world's record for a human chain, a long-legged, middle-aged redhead whom Skye knew all too well, dressed in hot pink capris, a matching spandex halter, and stilettos, barreled into the fray. She wielded her huge magenta pocketbook like a giant flyswatter, whacking protesters aside as if they were mosquitoes. A sturdily built teenage girl wearing cropped camo cargo pants, a white T-shirt, and flip-flops was right behind her swinging a backpack with the same precision.

"How can you do this?" the dried-apple-faced woman sobbed as the demonstrators scattered. "Aren't you concerned about the morals of your community?"

"I used to care about stuff like that," the red-head said, raising a perfectly plucked brow, "but I take a pill for that now."

Once Skye had stopped laughing, she thanked her rescuers, then turned to the redhead. "Bunny, what are you doing here?"

Bunny Reid, aka Skye's ex-boyfriend's mother, was a former Las Vegas dancer with a penchant for clothes from Victoria's Secret and men who broke her heart. She was the last person Skye would have expected to see at a bookstore.

Bunny enveloped her in an Obsession-scented hug. "Frannie talked me into it." Bunny was the manager of the local bowling alley, which her son owned and where Frannie Ryan, the teenager with the backpack, worked part-time. "She's got me hooked on those Harlequin romances. Those hot ones are better than a copy of *Playgirl* magazine." Bunny winked. "When I finish one of those I just want to find some stud and say, 'Squeeze me like a grape and make me wine.' "

"Do you like those, Frannie?" Frannie was one of Skye's favorite former students. They were extremely close, and Skye was surprised the teen hadn't mentioned her plans to attend the Tales and Treats grand opening.

"No." Frannie shook her head. "But I remembered you saying that in order to get people to read, it's important to give them books that will interest them, not what you think they *should* be reading, and Ms. Bunny is interested in . . ." She trailed off, her cheeks red.

Skye hadn't meant to embarrass the girl and was trying to think of a way to change the subject when Trixie came to her rescue by asking, "How did you get such a good parking spot, Bunny?" She looked pointedly at an old red Camaro, parked smack-dab in front of them.

"I've got my ways." The redhead nodded to a handsome older man sitting at one of the outdoor tables. "In fact, I'd better go thank him. When I saw you two under attack, I forgot my manners."

Skye wondered briefly whether Mr. Distinguished was Bunny's new beau, but Frannie distracted her by saying, "Let's go inside. I want to say hi to Kayla."

"Are you two friends?" Skye asked.

"Sort of." Frannie opened the shop's door. "We were both interested in some of the same colleges and went on campus visits together, but she still really wants to get out of Scumble River, and me, not so much anymore."

Skye was about to follow Frannie and Trixie into the store when she heard her name being called. Turning, she saw her mother hurrying toward her, May's four best friends bringing up the rear.

"Hi, Mom." Skye waved. "I didn't know you were coming here."

"We decided to give it a look-see at the last minute." Skye's mother reached up and pushed a stray chestnut curl off Skye's cheek, adjusted her daughter's blouse, and brushed a piece of lint off her jeans. May's own short salt-and-pepper hair was perfectly coiffed, and her brown tweed pants and matching jacket looked as if they had just left the ironing board—which they probably had. "Glory and Hester wanted to get some books, Maggie's checking out the pastry competition, and Kitty and I are here just to be neighborly."

Skye nodded. She knew her mom and aunt never passed up an opportunity to socialize.

May added, "Besides, Thea called and said there was some excitement here." Like May, Thea was a dispatcher for the Scumble River Police Department. "People wanting to close down the store."

"Someone called the cops?" Skye wasn't surprised her mother and her friends didn't want to miss the action. Gossip was better if acquired firsthand.

"The owner. She said there were protesters blocking her entrance." May frowned. "But Wally said as long as they are on the sidewalk, which is public property, he can't stop them. Some nonsense about freedom of speech."

"The police take the constitution pretty seriously," Skye confirmed. "Wally had no choice until they attacked someone, like they did me a few minutes ago." *Oops!* Skye knew she shouldn't have said that the moment the words left her mouth.

"See!" May's voice was shrill. "How can you marry someone who won't even protect you? Simon always tried to stop you from putting yourself in danger, but Wally goes and makes you the police psych consultant."

"Mother!" Emerald eyes that matched May's own blazed. Her mom didn't approve of Skye's engagement to Wally, who was older, divorced, and not Catholic. There was nothing he could do about the first issue, and he was trying to get an annulment to address the second; Skye wondered whether her mother would come around if he converted, which would solve the third problem.

"Yes?" May's expression was angelic.

"I am perfectly capable of taking care of myself, a fact Wally understands and applauds. I am *not* getting back together with Simon." Skye gritted her teeth. Why couldn't May accept that? Of course, Simon's sudden determination to win her back at all costs wasn't helping matters.

"We'll see."

"I'm marrying Wally as soon as he gets an annulment." Skye and Simon had broken up more than two years ago, when he'd refused to explain how he "forgot" to mention that the college friend he was staying with on his trip to California was a woman. By the time he finally did clarify the situation, it was too late. "Deal with it," Skye told her mother.

"Look how hard Simon is trying," May wheedled.

He had actually shown up at her parents' house last Sunday while they were all having dinner together and serenaded Skye with "Love Me Tender" from outside the kitchen window. His voice hadn't been half bad, but the Elvis outfit was a bit much.

"Drop it, Mom." Skye crossed her arms. "I mean it. Unless you want me to elope."

May looked stricken. "Don't even tease about something like that. I've been planning your wedding since you were born." She clutched her chest. "I'm going to be at both my kids' weddings if it's the last thing I do."

CHAPTER 5

All Quiet on the Western Front

When Skye finally entered Tales and Treats, she was astounded by the clever design. The main room contained the register, gift items associated with reading and writing, and a massive glass-fronted oak cupboard with an engraved plaque that read, RARE AND FIRST EDITIONS. Radiating from the central hub were the café and four areas decorated according to the genre they held.

She was immediately drawn to the mystery section. Elegant wood paneling and cushiony armchairs invited customers to relax as they made their choices. A jumbo magnifying glass hung over the fireplace mantel, and handcuffs, crime scene tape, and a variety of toy weapons were arranged on top of cherry occasional tables.

Skye looked around for Trixie, sure her friend would be attracted to this setting, but there was no sign of her. She did see her mother's pals Glory and Hester, their arms full of paperbacks. They lifted their chins in greeting.

Next, Skye tried the romances, knowing that was

Trixie's second favorite read. Here the furnishings ran to a pink velvet chaise longue and a white wrought-iron daybed stacked with frilly pillows. Oversize champagne glasses and high-heeled shoes were placed on gilt tables, and a lace peignoir hung from a brass hook on the wall. Bunny was sitting on the floor, half glasses perched on her nose, engrossed in a book with a mostly naked cowboy on its cover. A flush tinged her cheeks, and she didn't look up when Skye said hello.

Trixie had to be somewhere, and Skye doubted her friend was in the science fiction/fantasy/horror section, which was bedecked in outer-space gear, fairy wings, and vampire fangs. With Trixie's active imagination, reading anything too scary was likely to give her nightmares.

Skye was also pretty sure her friend wasn't in the literature alcove, which was decorated like a college professor's office. They both agreed that they saw enough demoralizing endings in real life and didn't need to read about them in their fiction.

On her way through the main hub to check for Trixie in the café, Skye spotted a wire cage the size of a refrigerator box behind the front counter. It was draped on three sides with dark material, and she couldn't see what was inside. Curious, she threaded her way through the crowd toward the register.

As she got nearer, Skye saw a petite figure crouching down with her head and shoulders inside the pen, and called out, "Hi, Kayla. Are you enjoying your first day on the job?"

"Sorry." After closing the door of the cage, the person turned around. She was wearing a yellow polo shirt with TALES AND TREATS stitched in black across the pocket. Beneath the store name, RISÉ was embroidered in dark green. "I'm not Kayla, but I am enjoying my first day on the job."

"Sorry." Skye felt her cheeks redden. "From the back, you two look very similar."

"No problem." The shop owner smiled. "Being mistaken for a nineteen-year-old is extremely flattering." She held out her hand to Skye. "How kind of you to come to our grand opening. I hope your being here doesn't cause a problem for you with your cousin."

"Thank you." Skye shook Risé's hand. "I'm Skye. It's my pleasure to be here, and I couldn't care less about Hugo's opinions."

"I'm thrilled that so many Scumble Riverites are here." Risé was glowing. "I was a little afraid no one would show up, and then with those people picketing in front of the door . . . Well, you can imagine."

"Of course," Skye reassured her. "But they're gone now, and at least the leader of the pack didn't show up." She paused. Why *hadn't* Pru been there, since this was her cause? "At any rate, they don't seem to have stopped anyone." She didn't mention that the protesters had probably actually attracted a larger crowd.

"Your friends told me how they fought them off." Risé straightened a stack of bookmarks. "That Bunny is my kind of woman."

"She's certainly unique. She's one of those rare, truly happy-go-lucky people who can enjoy the scenery on a detour." Skye mentally shook her head. Risé the intellectual feminist and Bunny the man-crazy flake were the original odd couple, but you never knew what circumstances would cement a friendship. "You've probably already noticed we have a lot of quirky folks around these parts."

Risé shrugged. "I've never lived in a small town before, but I imagine this is pretty typical."

"Typical isn't the word I'd choose," Skye answered, distracted by a glimpse of silver-gray fur in the cage behind Risé. "Not to be nosy, but is that a cat?"

"No." Risé laughed. "If it were a kitty, I'd let it out, but chinchillas are a little shy."

"Did you say chinchilla?" Skye asked. "Like the coat?"

"Shh!" Risé held a finger to her lips. "Beelzebub and Cherub are sensitive about that."

"Sorry." Skye giggled, then sobered. "FYI, you may want to reconsider that one name, considering what those women outside were protesting."

"Good point." Risé tapped her chin. "I'll have to think about it."

"How much is this?" A young woman interrupted them, holding up a delicate porcelain letter opener.

"Excuse me," Risé said to Skye. "I'll be right back."

While she waited, Skye wandered over to a table stacked with copies of *If I Have a Wicked Stepmother, Where's My Prince?*, a young adult novel she had read at the request of one of the girls she saw for counseling.

She was paging through one of the trade paperbacks, remembering how much she had enjoyed the story, when Risé returned and said, "Those are ten percent off."

"Thanks, but I already read it." Skye returned the book to the display.

"Well, then"—Risé motioned to Skye to follow her—"let me show you the treats part of our store."

When they entered the café, Skye noticed a table covered in cream moiré with a display of decadent chocolates in fancy gold boxes and coffee beans whose foil bags bore exotic names like RAINFOREST WINTER DARK, SEPTEMBER SUNSHINE, and MAUNA LOA SILK.

She commented to Risé, "I see you sell quite a few items other than books."

"That's true. In today's economy a store has to

be diversified in order to turn a profit. That's why we decided to have the coffee and sweets and the gift items. We even have some used books." She hurriedly added, "But we only accept ones in pristine condition, and in the three most popular genres."

"Sounds like you've really thought this out."

"Running a bookstore has been our dream for a long time." Risé's eyes shone. "Now, how about some refreshments?" She swept her arm toward the selection of pastries in steel-and-glass cases. "What can I get you?"

"These all look wonderful." Skye scrutinized the array of goodies, spotting a tray of pale tan squares. "Are those shortbread?"

"Yes."

"Yum." Skye's mouth watered. "I'll take some of those, please."

"Here you go." Risé handed Skye a plateful. "They're my husband's specialty."

"Did he make all of these?" Skye gestured to row after row of desserts.

"Yes. He was a cook in the army and loves baking."

"Was he career military?" Skye took a bite of cookie, closing her eyes to savor the melt-in-your-mouth buttery goodness.

"No." Risé's expression was hard to read. "Once he left the army he became a book scout." Risé must have seen the question in Skye's eyes because she explained, "Someone who goes to yard sales, thrift stores, estate auctions, etcetera, looking for rare and valuable books and special collections."

"Ah." Skye wiped her mouth with a napkin. "And I bet that humongous bookcase near the entrance is full of his best finds, right?"

"Yes, those are his babies." Risé wrinkled her brow, then said almost under her breath, "I just wish he'd waited to display them until the cabinet was more secure."

"I'm sure no one will steal them." Skye figured most Scumble River citizens wouldn't have any idea the books were valuable.

"That's not what I'm worried about." Risé shook her head, then seemed to put on her professional persona. "Now, what would you like to drink? We have our usual menu, plus wine and beer."

"I don't mind helping myself." Skye nodded toward the jam-packed room. "I can see how hectic things are, so don't worry about me."

"Thanks." Risé hurried away.

At the coffee bar, a short, wiry man in his late fifties was busy steaming milk and grinding beans. His pale yellow polo shirt had ORLANDO'S TREATS embroidered on the pocket. Skye got in line and waited her turn, then introduced herself and asked for a mocha latte.

"Nice to meet you." He wiped his hand on

his apron, then held it out. "I'm Orlando Erwin. My wife mentioned she met you yesterday."

They shook hands, and Skye said, "I hope she doesn't judge me by my relations." She felt warmth creep up her neck. "My cousin Hugo and I rarely agree on anything."

"Sounds like my own family." Orlando's laugh was contagious, and Skye found herself giggling for no reason.

"Where are you from?" Skye asked as he turned toward the machines to prepare her drink.

"Long Island," he said over his shoulder.

Ah, that was the accent she'd been trying to place. "How did you end up here?"

"Via the Ho Chi Minh trail." His tone was casual, but Skye noticed his shoulders tighten. "An army buddy of mine lives here. So when Risé decided to exit the rat race and wanted to open a bookstore in a small town, I remembered his stories about Scumble River and suggested we look here."

"So you're running the café." Skye noticed he said Risé had decided, not *they* had decided. "And Risé is in charge of the bookstore?"

"Risé's in charge of everything." He winked. "But since she doesn't bake . . ."

"I see." Skye grinned. "But you're the expert on old books, right?"

"I guess so." He raised a brow. "You got some you want me to look at?"

"If you have time. I inherited an old house several years ago, and I've been sifting through the contents ever since."

Skye had helped an old woman when an unscrupulous antiques dealer tried to take advantage of her, and since the woman had no relatives and had decided Skye was her reincarnated daughter, she'd left her estate to Skye. The only condition was that she fix up the house and live there. "I have several boxes." Skye's tone was apologetic.

"No problem." Orlando smiled. "Bring 'em by tomorrow around nine forty-five. Since I'm here early to do the baking, I can take a look before the store opens and we're interrupted."

"Thanks." Skye appreciated the chance to get rid of some clutter. And if the books were valuable, all the better. She could always use some extra cash. "So what do you think of Scumble River so far?"

"It's not exactly what I pictured from Ryan's description." Orlando handed her a steaming cup. "But I'm sure we'll get used to it." As he took the next person's order, he added, "At least here you don't have to worry about getting killed for the few bucks in your pocket."

"True," Skye agreed before moving away from the counter. Obviously Orlando hadn't heard about Scumble River's recent spate of murders, and she wasn't about to enlighten him.

Juggling the mocha latte, the cookies, and a spoon, Skye scanned the café for a place to sit. At first glance, all the chairs seemed to be occupied with groups enjoying the chance to socialize on a Saturday afternoon. She had seen the sign near the exit reading NO FOOD OR DRINK BEYOND THIS POINT or she would have gone into one of the other rooms.

Ready to give up and eat leaning against a wall, she saw an arm waving and heard Trixie shout, "Over here."

Not surprisingly, the table was covered with plates of pastries. Trixie had been a size four since Skye had met her their freshman year in high school. Trixie didn't exercise, ate her weight in snack food, and never gained an ounce. If they weren't best friends, Skye would hate her.

"Have you been here the whole time?" Skye demanded as she nudged aside dishes of strudel and minicheesecake in order to put down her cup.

"No." Trixie waved a book with a red high heel on the yellow cover. "I picked up this first."

"Is it any good?"

"So far." Trixie took a huge bite of lemon pound cake, then spoke around the crumbs, "Isn't this the cutest shop?"

Skye had just opened her mouth to agree when she heard a commotion in the next room.

"What's that?" Trixie craned her neck.

Skye twisted around but couldn't see anything. "Maybe they're raffling off a prize."

"Maybe." Trixie munched thoughtfully. "But I thought I heard a scream."

"The winner?" Skye guessed, when another, even louder sound reverberated. The chatter of the other diners halted as if someone had pushed the STOP button on a DVD player, and Skye turned in her seat. "Should we go see if everything's okay?"

"Yeah." Trixie half rose from her chair. "Maybe we'd better."

As Skye stood, she heard a shriek, then what sounded like a stampede. She and Trixie looked at each other. What on earth was going on?

A nanosecond later May ran into the café and yelled, "Giant rats are loose in the store. Run for your life!"

In the midst of people shouting and scrambling for the door, Skye grabbed her mother and pulled her to one side. "Calm down." It was no secret that May hated animals and was terrified of most all of them. "Stay here with Trixie, and I'll be right back."

Several women were standing on chairs. Others seemed unsure whether they should stay or go. Skye reassured them as she hurried past. "I'm sure everything's fine. Stay where you are. Keep enjoying your treats. No need to panic."

When she arrived at the front of the store, a

steady stream of screaming people was leaving as fast as they could. Risé tried to stop the tide, her voice rising above the hullabaloo, but just as it began to slow, there'd be another squeal, and the exodus picked up speed again.

Skye made a quick inspection of the remaining rooms. They were empty, with piles of abandoned books and broken ornaments strewn throughout. She returned to the central hub and found Kayla and Risé leaning against the counter. Both looked dazed. The door of Beelzebub and Cherub's cage was open, and they were nowhere in sight.

"I take it the chinchillas escaped?" Skye asked.

"I'm not sure what happened." Risé held her head. "Someone called me into the Professor's Office with a question about the last Oprah pick. I was explaining that the novel really did end that way, and no, there was not a missing last chapter, when I heard a commotion coming from the front of the store." Risé took a breath. "As I hurried in here, I saw a woman running into the other rooms yelling that the shop was infested with rats and telling everyone to get out."

"Oh, my." Skye patted Risé's arm but didn't share that the culprit was her own mother.

"I noticed that Beelzebub and Cherub's cage was empty, and I tried to explain, but no one would listen." Risé sagged. "They just all left."

"Any idea how the chinchillas got out of their

64

pen?" Skye inspected the latch. It seemed fine. "Could you have accidently forgotten to close the catch all the way?"

"No." Risé's chin went up. "I'm sure it was secure." She looked at Kayla, who was tugging on the collar of her yellow polo shirt. "Did you notice anything?"

"No, ma'am." The girl smoothed her khaki slacks. "I was in the mystery section when I heard the shouting. By the time I got up front, everyone was gone."

"Someone must have wanted to pet them and opened the door," Skye suggested.

"Beelzebub and Cherub wouldn't have run out. They would have hidden inside their house." Risé pointed to a three-sided plastic box. "Chinchillas are extremely skittish."

"Will it be hard to get them back?"

"No." Risé shook her head. "Once everyone leaves they'll come to me if I offer them raisins."

"The other rooms are cleared out." Skye offered, "Would you like me to round up the stragglers in the café?"

"There's no rush." Risé straightened. "But if you'd let my husband know what happened, I'd appreciate it."

"Sure thing." Skye patted Risé's arm again, then went back to the café.

When she explained the situation to Orlando, he shrugged and said, "It'll be fine."

As Skye made her way over to her mother and Trixie, she admired the man's calm but wondered at his remarkable serenity, which didn't seem quite natural.

Trixie had her arm around May and was saying, "Take a deep breath. Everything's okay. Maybe all you saw was a display of plush toys."

Skye kept quiet, curious to find out her mother's perception of what had happened.

"No." May shook her head stubbornly, her voice taking on an edge of determination, or maybe hysteria. "It was a giant gray rat." She held her hands twenty inches apart. "It was this big and it made the most awful sound." She shuddered. "It went *kee-kee-kee*."

Trixie eyed Skye and asked, "Did you find out what happened?"

"Yes. Risé's pet chinchillas got out of their cage. She claims that even if the door was opened by mistake or someone wanted to pet them, they'd hide, not make a run for it."

Trixie shot Skye a quizzical look. "What exactly did you see, May?"

"Well." May elongated the word by taking a shaky breath. "The crowd had finally thinned out, and there wasn't anyone in that middle room, the one with the register." Her voice strengthened as she told the tale, her love of being the center of attention overcoming her fright. "I was look-ing at the cookbook display, waiting for Aunt

Kitty and Glory to come out of the bathroom, when I heard a clink."

"Was that the cage door being opened?" Even though she knew it was useless to try, Skye attempted to shorten her mother's account. May employed the step-by-step version of storytelling.

"I suppose so." May frowned at the interruption. "I didn't actually see that part." She took a seat and ate a bite of Trixie's abandoned chocolate croissant. "You know, my throat is awful dry."

"I'll get you a coffee." Skye turned to fetch her mother a drink.

May called after her, "Black, no sugar."

Once Skye returned and May had taken a sip from the cup Skye handed her, she continued, "Anyway, I heard a clank and looked up. At first, I didn't notice anything unusual, but then the hair on the back of my neck rose and I froze. It didn't feel like I was alone anymore."

Skye stopped herself from sighing. She might as well accept the fact that there was no way to speed this up.

May wiped her mouth on a napkin, then continued, "I was about to shrug it off when I saw the rat scurrying towards me."

"It was a chinchilla, Mom."

"I don't care what fancy name you give the thing. It's still a rat, just one that has a nice fur coat."

"Fine." Skye rolled her eyes. "Go on."

"The *rat* scared me to death. It was coming straight for my throat, and all I could think about was getting away from it before it attacked me and gave me rabies."

"So you didn't see anything else." Skye folded her arms.

"Well, when I was running away, I might have seen someone crouched behind the register."

"Did you recognize who it was, May?" Trixie asked.

"No." May took out her compact and reapplied her lipstick. "All I saw before I ran in here was the top of a woman's head." May snapped her makeup case shut. "Whoever it was really needs to see Vince for a color and style. Her hair was a real drab brown, and she wore it in this ugly bun."

Skye and Trixie looked at each other. That had sounded like Pru Cormorant. Was that why the English teacher hadn't been with the protesters? Had she wanted to remain anonymous so she could sneak in and let the chinchillas loose in order to sabotage the store?

CHAPTER 6

To Kill a Mockingbird

The sun struggled to break through early-morning clouds as Skye hurried toward the church parking lot. She was considering Father Burns's concluding remark; he always ended Mass with a nugget of wisdom hidden inside a humorous aside.

This morning the priest had said, "God promises a safe landing, not a calm passage."

Sometimes she thought Father Burns could read her mind. Either that or he'd been sneaking a peek at her diary. Skye's life had never been smooth, but so far, knock on wood, she had always landed on her feet.

A voice interrupted her thoughts. "Skye! Wait up."

Skye battled the urge to pretend she hadn't heard and duck into her car. Slowing to a reluctant stop, she turned and spotted Simon loping across the grass that separated the church from the rectory.

Shoot! What kind of stunt is he going to pull this time? She hated hurting his feelings. His recent attempts to win her back had been sweet, and she was flattered, but she'd explained it was too late. She was going to marry Wally. However, convincing someone as determined as her ex-boyfriend that she had made her choice was proving tougher than she'd imagined. Simon had always been an overachiever, and he wasn't used to losing, or giving up.

As Simon got closer, the breeze tousled his short auburn hair and billowed the olive green jacket of his expensive suit, making it look almost like a cape. Everything about him was elegant, from his tall, lean physique to his long, tapered fingers, but it was his expression that struck a spark in Skye. His compelling golden-hazel eyes held a hint of sadness that hadn't been there before their breakup.

"Hello, Simon." Skye kept her voice cool. "It was a good service today, wasn't it?"

The other parishioners streaming around Skye and Simon looked at them with curiosity. Several slowed, clearly intent on eavesdropping. *Great!* News of this conversation would reach May faster than an Internet instant message.

"Yes," Simon agreed, "Father was in rare form." He twisted the church bulletin he held. "Do you have time for coffee?"

Prior to Skye's engagement, she and Simon had made a habit of having breakfast together after Mass. But that had been when she thought he only wanted to be friends. Now that he had declared his intention to win her back, she had put a stop to those get-togethers.

Skye shook her head and said, "You know I can't see you anymore."

"It's not a date. It's just coffee." Simon seemed surprised to see the shredded remains of the newsletter in his hands and hurriedly stuck them into his jacket pocket. "Mom mentioned the fuss at the bookstore yesterday, and I wanted to talk to you about it."

"Why?" Skye was surprised that (a) Bunny had told Simon about the ruckus—she usually hid her involvement in incidents like that from her son—and (b) he was interested. One of the major problems they'd had as a couple was his utter lack of nosiness.

"I really don't want to discuss it in public." Simon stepped closer and lowered his voice. "It has to do with Xavier."

Xavier Ryan was Simon's assistant, both at the funeral home he owned and in Simon's role as county coroner. Xavier was also Frannie Ryan's father.

"He's Orlando's old army buddy, right?" Skye wrinkled her brow, remembering Orlando's mention of his army buddy Ryan. She had assumed that was a first name, but now it all clicked into place.

"Correct." Simon straightened his shoulders. "I know that despite how you feel about me, you're fond of Xavier and Frannie. So please have coffee with me." He touched her arm. "I need your help."

Holy moly! Simon had never, ever asked for her assistance. "In that case . . ." Skye swallowed. There was still a spark of attraction between them, but she was determined to fight it. "Sure. But I can't be seen with you at the Feed Bag or McDonald's. You've got the gossips so stirred up they'd have us married before lunchtime."

"It'll only take a few minutes. Where do you want to meet?" Simon's lips twitched. "Guess it's hard to find some privacy when your fiancé is the chief of police. A funeral director, on the other hand, has a lot fewer minions reporting to him."

Skye nailed him with a frown before saying, "Let's meet at the Shell station by the highway. Park in back. I need gas anyway, so I'll grab a couple cups of coffee when I pay and we can sit in your car and talk."

"Fine," Simon said as he got into his Lexus. "But if we're seen, this will look more suspicious than if we just went to a restaurant in town."

He was right. Skye chewed her lip as she drove toward I-55. Except she'd promised Wally no more Sunday breakfasts with Simon, so doing it this way felt like less of a betrayal. She only hoped Wally felt the same way when she told him about it this afternoon.

When Skye arrived at the station, she found

Simon already parked by the Dumpster. After filling up her Bel Air and getting the coffee, she moved her car next to his sleek white luxury sedan and climbed into the passenger seat.

Handing him a Styrofoam cup, she said, "Let's hear it."

"As you guessed, Xavier and Orlando were in Vietnam together." Simon gave Skye his full attention. "They did two tours of duty and kept in touch once they got home."

"Okay." Skye took a sip of coffee, wincing as she burned her tongue.

"And the reason Orlando and his wife chose Scumble River for their bookstore is because of Xavier's description of the town."

"That surprises me, since Xavier has always struck me as not having much connection to Scumble River. I kind of thought he only stuck around for Frannie's sake." Skye tilted her head. "Was he born here?"

"Yes," Simon answered slowly. "And after he got out of the service, he came back here and married his high school sweetheart. They'd been trying to have a baby for over ten years when Frannie was born. His wife died shortly afterward, and my uncle said Xavier was never the same. Said he just withdrew until his whole life was his daughter, his job, and his Vietnam Vets group."

"I see." Skye nodded. Simon had inherited the

funeral home from his uncle. "But how is Xavier being responsible for Risé and her husband settling in Scumble River a problem? Surely they don't hold Xavier responsible for what happened yesterday."

"That I don't know. But . . . ," Simon started, then seemed to change his mind. "You have to promise to keep what I tell you confidential. That means from everyone. Including Wally, Trixie, and your mother."

"If it's not something illegal." Skye couldn't keep that from Wally no matter how fond she was of Frannie and her father. "Then I promise."

"No. Nothing criminal." Simon grimaced. "Just foolish." He forestalled Skye's question by saying quickly, "Xavier invested money he shouldn't have in the bookstore."

"Yikes!" Skye brows puckered. "By money he shouldn't have, you don't mean . . ." *Please, God, don't let Xavier have stolen to get the money he'd invested.*

"No." Simon blew out a tired breath. "Worse."

"What could be worse?"

"As well as his own savings, he used the treasury from his Vietnam Vets group."

"Hell!" Skye choked on the coffee she had just drunk. "Embezzling *is* stealing."

"He didn't misappropriate the funds." Simon took a swallow from his cup. "He just convinced the group it was a great investment."

"Phew." Skye exhaled, realizing she'd been holding her breath. "Then there's no problem."

Simon didn't respond.

"Is there?" Skye didn't like the look on Simon's face. "What aren't you saying?"

Simon fiddled with the plastic top on his cup, flipping the little tab up and down. "Xavier promised the group that if anything happened, he'd refund their capital."

"Crap!" Skye slumped against the window. "If he invested his own nest egg, where will he get the money to reimburse them?"

"Frannie's college fund is the only thing left." Simon shook his head. "And he'd rather slit his throat."

"Isn't it premature to think the bookstore will fail just because of one little protest?" Skye narrowed her eyes. "Unless you're holding something back."

Simon stared out the windshield.

"What aren't you telling me?" Skye demanded.

"That's the problem." Simon groaned. "I don't know. But Xavier's been acting strange ever since Orlando and Risé moved to town."

"I know there are some other issues with people like my cousin Hugo, but . . ."

"I don't think it's that." Simon tapped his chin. "Look, I'll try and find out more from Xavier, but if you could help make sure the Scumble River rabble-rousers don't shut down Tales and

Treats, and keep your ears open for anything else, I'd appreciate it."

"I'll do what I can. Trixie is bound and determined to keep the bookstore open, too, so she'll help." Skye glanced at her Timex and grimaced. "Sorry, but I've got to run."

"What's your hurry?"

"Do you remember me mentioning the boxes of books I found when I moved into my house?"

When Simon nodded, Skye continued, "As it happens, I've got an appointment with Orlando at nine forty-five. He'll take a look at some of the books to see if they're valuable, and if they are, he'll sell them for me."

"I thought I read that the store doesn't open until one on Sundays." Simon took Skye's empty cup and stacked it inside his own, along with her crumpled napkin.

"That's right. He's meeting me beforehand so we won't be interrupted." Skye fumbled for the door handle.

"Thank you for listening to me." Simon got out of the Lexus and hurried around the hood. He helped her out, then kissed her cheek. "I appreciate it."

"You're welcome." Skye waved as she walked toward her car. "Call me if you find out what Xavier is hiding."

She watched Simon turn out of the gas station, then got into her Bel Air and started back to town. The road into Scumble River had once been lined with acres of corn and soybeans, but several housing developments had sprung up in the last few years. The occasional old farmhouse looked oddly forlorn sprinkled among the cookie-cutter homes huddled on handkerchief-size lawns. Skye felt sorry for the farmhouse owners, who were often harassed by the newcomers to either sell or make improvements they couldn't afford.

Heading east, she spotted the remains of an old barn that had been allowed to disintegrate until its roof now sat on its foundation. The only thing left standing was the silver silo, which rose out of the ground like a missile ready to launch. A deer munched on a row of stray cornstalks.

It was a beautiful fall day, but during her drive Skye saw no one in the front yards, and all the garage doors were closed. How many children were glued to their video games inside? It seemed that often people moved to the country for the fresh air and open spaces but then never took advantage of either one.

As she approached Tales and Treats, she saw that Hugo's used cars were still parked out front. She was surprised that Risé hadn't taken further steps to get rid of the vehicles. The store owner hadn't struck Skye as someone who gave up easily. There must be something she was missing.

Skye braked and scanned the area. After a

couple of minutes, she spotted two tiny security cameras aimed at the parking spots directly facing the shop. *Aha.* It looked as if Risé was following through after all on her vow to prove that Hugo's inventory was there for an illegal length of time.

Giving up on finding a close space for the Bel Air, Skye double-parked, blocking in a green Chrysler selling for only two thousand dollars and a blue Hyundai that was a steal at nine hundred and ninety-nine dollars. Since the used-car lot was closed on Sundays, she figured her Chevy would be okay while she unloaded her cargo.

As Skye got out of her car, she noticed that a shade was pulled down over the bookstore's front window and no sign of lights peeked around its edge. Had Orlando forgotten their appointment? She checked her watch, then shook her head. It was only nine thirty, on time for Scumble Riverites but early for everyone else.

Hmm. Should she move her car while she waited? No. First she'd drop off the books near the building; afterward she'd find another spot for the Chevy. Skye unlocked the trunk and reached for the first two cartons. She heaved them into her arms and struggled to the sidewalk, her purse banging heavily against her thigh.

Skye rested for a second, then made her way to the entrance. As she lowered the boxes to the concrete, she noticed that the door was slightly ajar. It took her a second to come to the conclusion that Orlando had probably left it like that so she'd know it was open and would come inside. If he was working in the café, he'd never hear her knock.

Boosting the cartons back up to chest level, Skye used her toe to nudge the door open a little more, then hip-checked it, widening the gap so she had room to enter. As she stepped into the unlit shop, she called out, "Yoo-hoo, Orlando. It's Skye Denison."

Between the boxes she could barely see over, and the lack of illumination, Skye felt like she was in a cave. She paused just over the threshold and tried to get her bearings.

Intent on recalling whether there was anything between her and the counter, Skye took one tiny step, shouting, "Mr. Erwin? Orlando? Are you here?"

There was no answer. As far as Skye could tell, there were no lights on in any of the store's rooms. What in the heck was going on? Why would the door be open if no one was around? Where was Orlando?

Getting no response to her third yoo-hoo, Skye inched ahead. She stopped to listen, but all was as silent as outer space. *Yikes!* This was starting to remind her of a haunted house, and she hated haunted houses.

"Anyone here?" Skye's voice quavered. She'd

never realized how spooky a dark, empty book-store could be.

No answer. Taking a deep breath, Skye forced herself to shuffle forward. If she could just get to the front and put these boxes down on the counter, she could go wait in her car until Orlando showed up.

By her estimation, she was only about three feet from the register. As she took another step, her foot slid into what felt like a melon. What was a piece of fruit doing in the middle of the floor? Moving to the right, she encountered a wooden barrier. There had definitely not been anything like that in the shop yesterday.

Sighing, she finally gave up and eased the boxes to the floor. Still unable to see in the darkness, Skye crouched. Tentatively, she reached out and touched the obstruction, then ran her hand down its length. It felt like a cabinet. Had it fallen over during the night?

Making her way back toward the entrance, she trailed her fingers along the adjacent wall until she found a light switch and flipped it on. Bright-ness flooded the store. Skye blinked rapidly, blinded by the sudden glare.

When her eyes finally adjusted, she gasped, "Risé!" and rushed forward.

The huge, heavy rare-book cabinet that had been set against the wall was now lying across the floor. Sticking out from under it, facedown, were a head and shoulders. The shiny brown ponytail splayed against the yellow polo shirt looked vibrant and alive, but the instant Skye touched the store owner's neck, she knew the woman had been dead for quite some time.

CHAPTER 7

The Picture of Dorian Gray

A squad car squealed to a stop in front of Tales and Treats, but its lights weren't flashing and its siren was silent. Wally Boyd jumped out and sprinted toward Skye, who was slumped in one of the shop's outdoor wrought-iron chairs. As the chief of the Scumble River Police Department, Wally worked days Monday through Friday, but knowing he'd want to be first on the scene involving a death, Skye had called him directly rather than dialing 911. Evidently, he'd stopped at the police station to pick up a cruiser before coming to the store.

Wally's warm brown eyes held a hint of concern as he gathered her into his arms, but his tone was light. "You can't even visit a bookstore without finding a body, can you, darlin'?"

"Guess not." Skye buried her face in his muscular chest, not wanting him to see her tears. Unfortunately he was right; she'd stumbled across several corpses in the past, and it never got any easier. At least this time it appeared to be a tragic accident rather than a murder.

Wally settled her back into her chair and handed her a starched white handkerchief. "I'll go take a look and be right back."

Skye nodded, blotting under her eyes and blowing her nose.

Wally returned a few minutes later. He tucked his cell phone into his shirt pocket and said, "Reid is on his way. He was on I-55 heading to Joliet when I called him, and he had to find a place to turn around."

"Okay."

"Are you up to telling me about it while we wait for him?"

"Of course." Skye took a deep breath. "Yesterday, at the grand opening, I mentioned to Orlando Erwin that I had inherited a bunch of old books."

"The boxes you have stacked in one of the upstairs bedrooms?"

"Right," Skye confirmed. "Anyway, Orlando is an expert in rare books and first editions, and he offered to take a look at what I had, to see if there was anything valuable."

"Is that why you were here when the store was closed? You were meeting him for an appraisal?"

"Uh-huh." Her teeth caught her lower lip and worked it for a moment. "But there weren't any lights on and he wasn't around."

"How did you get inside the building?" Wally

ran his fingers through his short black hair, ruffling the silver strands at his temples.

"The door was off the latch," Skye said. "I thought Orlando had left it open for me, so I went inside."

"I take it he wasn't there."

"No. And the main room was dark." Skye crumpled Wally's white linen hanky. "I figured he was in the café since he does all the baking."

"So you went in there?"

"Not exactly." Skye straightened the hem on her black skirt. "The boxes of books I was carrying were really heavy, and I didn't want to put them on the floor since it's so hard to lift them from there, so I headed towards the counter."

"In the dark?"

"Yeah." Wally's dubious tone made her recognize how silly her reasoning sounded, and she rushed to explain, "You see, I'd just been in the store yesterday, and I knew there wasn't anything blocking the path between me and the register."

"But . . ."

"But then my foot bumped into something." Skye swallowed hard, realizing that what she'd thought was a melon had actually been a human head.

"Is that when you called me?"

"First, I put the boxes down and felt the barrier, trying to figure out what it was. Then I found the switch and turned on the lights."

Skye blanched. "When I saw that the humongous rare-book cabinet had fallen and crushed someone underneath it, that's when I called you. Once you were on the way, I came out here to wait."

"Which was exactly the right thing to do," Wally reassured her.

"Thank you." Skye's smile was halfhearted. "I aim to please."

Wally got up.

"Are you going back inside?" Skye asked.

"Yes." Wally leaned down and kissed her cheek. "I need to take a walk through the rest of the store to see if we have a second victim."

"You don't think it's an accident?" Skye asked, chewing on her thumbnail.

"I have no idea, but the question is, where's Orlando?" Wally walked toward the open door. "And if that's his wife in there, why hasn't he come looking for her?"

"Oh, my." Skye followed Wally and peered inside. "I hadn't thought of that, but it's the million-dollar question, all righty."

Skye paced up and down the sidewalk, thoughts ricocheting through her mind like pennies in a clothes dryer. Where was Orlando? How had the cabinet fallen over? She paused in midstep, another worry popping up. How would this affect Xavier's investment? Scanning the street in both directions, she was relieved to see that the police car hadn't attracted any onlookers.

For once she was thankful that there were so few businesses left in this part of town. But could Orlando run the store without his wife? Would he even want to?

The minutes ticked by as if each was an eternity, and Skye was getting nervous. Maybe Wally should have radioed for backup before going inside the store. Before she could decide whether to check on him or call the PD for help, Simon pulled his Lexus behind the squad car. He jogged toward her carrying a black doctor's case. She knew the bag contained a camera, stethoscope, flashlight, rubber gloves, and liver thermometer. The body bag would arrive with Xavier in the hearse.

"Are you okay?" Simon's brow was furrowed and his knuckles were white. "What happened?"

Skye explained, adding, "Do you know where Orlando and Risé are living?"

"I thought they were living above the store." Simon glanced at the second-story windows. "But I must be wrong, because if they were upstairs, surely they'd have come down to see what's going on."

"That's what I thought, too." Skye hadn't mentioned who the victim was or that Orlando was MIA. "But I did hear that they were having some problem with the carpenter who was handling the remodeling, so maybe the apartment isn't done yet."

"That's probably it."

"Why do things like this happen?" Skye tilted her head, regarding Simon with an anguished expression. "Every time something good comes to Scumble River, something bad seems to follow."

As Simon put an arm around Skye, Wally walked up to them. "No one's in there except the vic. So whenever you're through hugging my fiancée, feel free to do your job, Reid."

"Oh, put a sock in it, Boyd." Simon gave Skye's shoulder one last squeeze, then pulled on a pair of rubber gloves. "Let's see what we have."

Glaring at Simon, Wally followed him into the store.

When Wally returned, Skye was once again sitting in the wrought-iron chair. It seemed like hours since the two men had gone inside, and she was staring at her cell phone thinking she should call someone. But who? The chief of police and the coroner were already on site. The only one missing was Xavier with the hearse.

Wally sat down beside her. "Do you have any idea where Risé and Orlando are staying?" It was getting warmer as the sun grew stronger, and Wally rolled up the sleeves of his denim shirt. Since he'd been off duty when Skye called, he wasn't in uniform and wore jeans and sneakers.

"The emergency number the police station has for Tales and Treats is disconnected—it must have been for their house in the city—and there's no other phone listed."

"No, I don't know where they're staying."

"How about employees? Does anyone local work for them?"

"They have one clerk," Skye answered, then shook her head. "I could try to get in touch with her, but she doesn't exactly live in any one place."

"Great." Wally shook his head. "Any other ideas before we start trying to track her down?"

Skye opened her mouth to suggest asking Xavier but instead said, "Can I go inside?" Even though she couldn't see why Simon would care if she told Wally that Xavier and the store owners were friends, she had promised not to reveal *anything* he had told her yesterday. So letting him know that she was going to disclose that relationship seemed like the right thing to do.

"Why? Nothing's going on in there right now." Wally absently rubbed the muscles in his tanned forearms. "I had to call for help to lift the cabinet. Even though it weighs a ton, I could slide it off, but Reid insists it has to come straight up."

"I . . . uh . . . need to tell Simon something." Skye made her voice sound casual.

Wally raised an eyebrow. "What?"

"I'll tell you after I talk to him." Skye tilted her head and tried to look innocent. "Okay?"

"Fine." He jerked his head toward the store. "Don't touch anything."

"Sure." She got up, then hesitated. "I'll be back in a second."

"Go." Wally's tone was irritated.

Simon was taking pictures of the cabinet from various angles when Skye approached him and said, "I need to tell Wally about Xavier's connection with this store."

"No." Simon stopped what he was doing and turned toward her. "You promised not to tell anyone, particularly Boyd."

"We need a phone number for Orlando." Skye ignored the accusation in his voice. Simon knew the situation had changed, and he was being unreasonable. "The emergency contact info at the police station must be old."

"Then you don't have to tell Boyd about the investment, just that Xavier and Orlando are old army buddies, right?"

"Yes." Skye thought for a moment. "That's all I'll say as long as this is an accidental death." She gestured to the cabinet without looking at it. She really didn't want to see poor Risé again. "But if the situation changes . . ."

"Right." Simon sighed. "I know."

Xavier was getting out of the hearse when Skye walked outside. His normally pale complexion was even pastier than usual, his expression was apprehensive, and he was wringing his hands.

She should have realized that when Simon called him for a pickup at Tales and Treats, he'd be worried the victim was one of the store owners. Poor guy. The loss of Risé would hit him hard. He didn't have many close friends.

As soon as Skye explained Xavier's friendship with the store owners, Wally hurried over to the hearse.

The two men spoke quietly for a couple of minutes; then Skye heard Xavier say, "They're staying at the Up A Lonely River Motor Court. They're supposed to move into their apartment above the store Monday afternoon after the building inspector green-lights the remodeling."

Darn! Skye exhaled loudly. Her godfather, "Uncle" Charlie Patukas, was the owner and manager of the motor court, president of the school board, and Scumble River's most influential citizen. He was also one of the biggest gossips in the county. They'd have to be cagey if they didn't want news of the fatality to be all around town by nightfall. It would be even worse if Skye's mother were the dispatcher on duty, but May didn't work on Sundays.

Before Wally could make the call to Orlando, Anthony, one of the part-time police officers, parked his truck behind the hearse and jumped out.

He waved a fistful of bright orange straps and said, "I brought these. Dad uses them to move appliances when he's on a job alone."

"Good thinking." Wally smiled. "Glove up. Then go on inside and get things set with Reid. I'll be there in a second."

Anthony touched his finger to the brim of his baseball cap. "Sure thing, Chief." He nodded to Skye, then rushed past her into the store.

While Xavier got the gurney and body bag from the back of the hearse, Wally joined Skye on the sidewalk. "Would you mind calling Orlando at the motor court?"

"Not at all." Skye powered up her cell phone. "What should I say?"

"Just tell him there's an emergency and he's needed here immediately."

"Okay." Skye started punching in the number to the motor court, one she knew by heart. "Should I mention our missed appointment if Uncle Charlie wants to know why I want to talk to Orlando?"

"That's a great idea." Wally squeezed her free hand. "The longer we can keep the death quiet, the better."

As Wally strode over the shop's threshold, Skye turned her attention to the phone.

A second later, Charlie answered, "Up A Lazy River Motor Court."

"Hi, Uncle Charlie. It's Skye. Could you put me through to Orlando Erwin's cottage?"

"Why do you want to talk to him?" Charlie was nearly as bad as May in wanting to control Skye's life.

Skye explained, ending with, "Have you seen him around today?"

"Can't say as I have," Charlie said, his voice thoughtful. "Not real good business to miss appointments with customers."

"Maybe he forgot." Skye kept her tone light. "But I do need to talk to him to reschedule."

"You going to your ma's for supper tonight?" Charlie was in no hurry to forward the call.

"Probably not." Skye resigned herself to a few minutes of chitchat. "You?"

"Sure." Charlie chuckled. "I never miss one of May's Sunday dinners if I can help it."

"They are good," Skye agreed.

"So you want to talk to that book fellow?"

"Yeah. I'd really like to get rid of these old books." Skye crossed her fingers. "And I'm in sort of a hurry."

"Okay. I'll ring his room now. Take care, honey."

"Thanks, Uncle Charlie." *Phew.* She'd made it past the first hurdle.

"Hello?" A woman's voice answered on the first ring.

Skye frowned. "May I speak to Orlando Erwin, please? Skye Denison calling." Had Charlie put her through to the wrong cottage?

"Hello, Skye. He's not here right now. This is Risé."

Oh. My. God! Skye stared at her cell as if it had turned into a rattlesnake. If Risé was on the phone, that meant that . . . Oh, no—she'd made the same mistake yesterday, but this time she'd assumed that the tiny brunette was the store owner when it was really Kayla.

"Skye, are you there?" Risé's tone was brusque. "Why did you want to talk to Orlando? I'm sorry if he missed an appointment or something, but this isn't a good time. Try him later on at the store."

"Uh, wait. Don't hang up." Skye wasn't sure what to say, and she knew she had to tell Wally immediately that Risé was not the woman who had been crushed. "I'm sorry to bother you, but there's an emergency at Tales and Treats. You need to come down here right away."

"What—"

Skye cut her off. "I'll explain when you get here."

"But—"

Flipping the phone closed, Skye cut off Risé again and rushed inside the shop. She heard, "One." The men had threaded moving straps under and around the cabinet. "Two." Wally held one end and Anthony held the other. "Three."

Skye waited to speak while Wally and Anthony heaved the cabinet to an upright position and Simon and Xavier steadied it against the wall.

Once she was sure the cabinet was secure, Skye pointed to the body. "That's not Risé Vaughn."

"Then who is it?" Simon asked.

"It's Kayla!" a voice cried from the doorway. "It's my Kayla!"

CHAPTER 8

The Strange Case of Dr. Jekyll and Ms. Hyde

C hase Wren wailed, sounding like a wounded wildebeest, then charged toward Kayla's body, tears running down his chiseled cheeks.

"Stop." Simon stepped into his path. "I'm sorry to tell you she's dead." He grabbed the distraught young man by his shoulders and attempted to turn him around. "You have to leave immediately."

Chase shook him off like a bull with a rodeo rider, and when Simon hit the floor, Anthony stepped in front of Chase. The hulking ex–baseball player stumbled but quickly regained his footing.

"Whoa there, son." Wally got behind Chase, grabbed both his arms, and twisted them up his back. "Let's all calm down. We can talk outside."

Chase continued to lunge toward Kayla's body, struggling to break Wally's hold. Wally tightened his grip, then shot Skye a meaningful look.

She immediately said in her most soothing tone, "Come on, Chase. I know it's awful to see Kayla like that, but there's nothing you can do for her, and she wouldn't want you to get into trouble."

Chase went rigid when Skye spoke Kayla's name. Then he slumped and started to sob. "What am I going to do without her? She was my whole world."

"I know." Skye moved closer and patted the young man's biceps. "Let them finish in here while we go sit outside and talk about it."

"Okay, Ms. Denison." He hiccuped. "I can't stand seeing her like that."

"That's right." Skye took his hand and led him toward the door. "Try to forget, and remember her the way she was the last time you two were together."

"She was so beautiful. All the guys were jealous of me." Chase's blue eyes glazed over in pain. "I was so proud of her."

Wally had followed them to the exit, and Skye jerked her chin up, signifying that she had everything under control, as she seated the young man at one of the outdoor tables. Wally sketched a question mark in the air, indicating she should interview Chase, then went back inside.

Skye nodded and turned her attention back to the sobbing young man. He gulped a couple of times, took out a large hanky, and blew his nose. She waited, content to let him establish the pace of their conversation.

Finally, he said, "Kayla's the only girl I ever loved. We were going to get married next month."

"I'm so sorry." Skye leaned forward. "When did you two start dating?"

"Our freshman year in high school." He gazed over Skye's head.

"That's a long time to be together," Skye said in a comforting voice. "I'm sure it's a shock."

"I just can't believe it." Chase buried his face in his hands.

Skye searched her mind. What would Wally want her to ask Kayla's boyfriend? "What made you come here this morning?"

"I was worried about her." Chase rubbed his eyes with his fists. "She never showed up at my place last night."

"Were you expecting her?" Skye asked, wondering why it had taken him so long to check the store for her.

"Not exactly." Chase shook his head. "She spends most nights with me, but she technically still lives with her parents."

Skye nodded, remembering Kayla's explanation of her living arrangements. "So you called her folks this morning and found out she wasn't there either?"

"Actually," Chase admitted, "I called them around midnight, after I tried her cell a few times and it went straight into voice mail."

"And when she wasn't there . . . ?" Skye trailed off, confused. Why hadn't Chase come to Tales and Treats at that point?

"The thing is"—Chase frowned—"sometimes she spends the night with Xenia. She has all the latest filmmaking gadgets, and I knew that Kayla had a big project she was working on for school, so I thought she might have crashed at Xenia's."

Skye nodded again. That, too, fit in with what Kayla had said. "Did you call there?"

"I tried, but the machine picked up, and Xenia didn't answer her cell."

"Is that unusual?"

"Not really." Chase's neck turned red. "Xenia doesn't like me."

Skye tucked that information away and was considering what else Wally would want to know, when a silver Toyota Prius zoomed up and parked behind Chase's SUV. It was beginning to look like a parade lineup with all the cars double-parked bumper to bumper.

Risé threw open the driver's door and exploded out of the car. She was wearing a short pink T-shirt with the words PARDON ME WHILE I SLIP INTO A GOOD BOOK emblazoned across her chest, and she tugged at it as she tore toward Skye and Chase.

She skidded to a stop inches from Skye's chair and demanded, "Okay, I'm here. What's the big emergency?" Her tone was stiff, but her expression was worried.

Before Skye could answer, Chase howled and lunged at Risé, shouting, "This is all your fault."

It took both Wally and Skye to subdue Chase, but he finally calmed down enough to be sent to the police station with Anthony. Wally had decided they would continue questioning the young man after they were finished at the scene. Soon afterward, Xavier and Simon left with the body, and now Skye, Wally, and Risé were staring at the shards of glass and scattered books on the shop floor.

"That poor, poor girl." Risé's skin was ashen, and she blinked back tears. "I should never have left her alone yesterday to close up."

"What time did you leave here?" Wally asked.

"We close at eight on Fridays and Saturdays," Risé answered mechanically. "I left about fifteen minutes later. Kayla wanted to finish vacuuming, so I told her to lock the door when she was finished. I took Beelzebub and Cherub and headed for the motor court."

"Her pet chinchillas," Skye explained when she noticed Wally's puzzled expression.

"Oh." Wally made a note on the pad he took from his breast pocket. "Did you and your husband leave here together last night?"

"No." Risé's mouth twisted. "He couldn't wait

for me to count the cash drawer. He had a meeting to attend over in Laurel and took off right behind our last customer."

"Where is he now?" Wally looked up from his notepad.

"I have no idea." Risé's tone was tart. "He never made it back to the cottage."

"Is that usual for him?" Wally raised a brow.

"No, not anymore. It used to be, a long time ago, but he's been sober for nearly fifteen years. He's never slipped and taken a drink in all that time."

"But he used to get falling-down drunk?" Wally asked.

"He preferred to call it becoming accidently horizontal." Risé sighed. "But yes."

"Was he going to Laurel for an AA meeting?" Skye asked quietly.

"Yes." Risé nodded. "He attends meetings a couple times a week, and they have one especially for vets over there."

"And when he failed to return to the motor court, you didn't look for him or try his cell phone or call someone to find him?" Wally's tone was skeptical.

"He refuses to carry a cell. And I didn't know where to go or who to call." Risé shrugged. "Everything in AA is confidential, and since we only recently moved here, he hasn't found a sponsor in the new group yet." She whispered half to herself, "I should have known the recent stress about my previous job and then opening up a business might push him over the edge."

"I'm sure it's not your fault," Skye said.

"Excuse me a minute." Wally pulled out his phone and dialed. "Silvia, get ahold of the Laurel police and the county guys, and ask them to be on the lookout for Orlando Erwin. Pull his description from his driver's license." He listened a minute, then turned to Risé. "What was he wearing and driving?"

"He had on jeans, a navy T-shirt, and a leather jacket," Risé reported. "And he was on his motorcycle. A 'sixty-eight Harley."

Wally relayed the information, hung up, and said, "Now, Ms. Vaughn, without touching anything, do you see any sign of a burglary?"

"Not at first glance." Risé looked around. "Can I go into the other rooms?"

"Yes, but keep your hands in your pockets."

After she made the rounds, the store owner shook her head. "It seems as if everything is just like I left it. I took the cash." Risé paused, then said thoughtfully, "The only things that anyone could get some real money for are the first editions and rare books." She pointed to the smashed cabinet that Wally and Anthony had leaned against the wall. "And they were in there."

"Could that cupboard have fallen on its own?" Wally asked. "Maybe if it were bumped?"

"I doubt it." Risé's voice was bitter. "I told Orlando that it wasn't fastened to the wall securely enough because I was worried about an earthquake. But otherwise, it's so heavy, someone would have had to shove it over on purpose."

Skye touched her arm. "Do you have an inventory of the valuable books?"

"On my laptop." Risé gestured with her chin. "It's in my car."

Skye and Wally waited while Risé fetched her computer, booted it up, and compared the list to the volumes scattered on the floor. Wally had supplied her with a pair of rubber gloves but cautioned her not to move anything from where it lay.

Finally, Risé straightened and said, "At least seven books are missing."

"Are those missing the ones that are worth the most?" Skye asked.

"Not all of them." Risé tapped the laptop's screen. "But this one, a nineteen twenty-two first edition of *The Velveteen Rabbit*, is worth eight thousand dollars."

Wally had been inspecting the place on the wall where the cabinet had been fastened, but when he heard Risé's claim, he said, "Okay. Everyone out. I'm requesting the county crime scene techs."

Skye, Wally, and Risé trooped outside. While Wally made his call, the women sat at an outdoor table. Skye thought how lucky they were that the weather was still mild. Early-September temperatures in Illinois could range from eighty degrees during the day to freezing at night.

A few minutes later, Wally joined them. "It'll take the techs forty-five minutes to an hour to get here." He turned to Skye. "Sugar, if you want to take off, that's fine."

Skye nodded and started to rise, but before she got to her feet, Risé grabbed her hand. "I'd appreciate it if you stayed." Her cheeks reddened. "But I understand if you can't."

"Of course I'll stay if you want me to." Skye looked at her watch; it was only a little past twelve thirty. "No problem."

"Thank you." Risé slumped back in her chair. "I'm not usually this needy."

They were sitting silently when Skye's stomach growled. "Hey, I just had an idea." She realized the only thing she'd had to eat all day was a cup of gas station coffee. Now she sort of wished she'd taken Simon up on his offer of breakfast. "How about I go get takeout from McDonald's? I'm starving, and I bet the chief is, too. How about you, Risé? Could you do with some lunch?"

"Well." Risé hesitated. "I did skip breakfast, hoping Orlando would show up."

"What would you like?"

"I try to eat vegetarian, but I think considering the past twenty-four hours, today I'll call a Big

102

Mac a vegetable." Risé smiled for the first time. "What the hell, get me fries and a chocolate shake while you're at it."

"Wally?" Skye looked at him.

"Sounds good." He took out his wallet and handed her a twenty. "Chow's on me."

When Skye arrived back from her food run, Wally had cordoned off the block. She rolled down her car window and said to Anthony, who was watching the south entrance, "What's up?" It was unusual to barricade a whole section of street for anything less than a hostage situation or a shoot-out.

"When I got back from the station, the chief told me to set up the barricades. He wants to keep out any onlookers." Anthony was a nice-looking young man with sandy brown hair. He worked part-time for the PD and part-time for his father, who owned an appliance repair business. "The bookstore is scheduled to open any minute."

"What are you supposed to tell people who show up?" Skye was trying to figure out what story would cause the least amount of harm to Tales and Treats' reputation.

"Chief Boyd never mentioned that." Anthony puckered his brow. "Any idea what I should say?"

"Hmm." Skye tapped her chin. "Will everyone have heard it on their scanners?"

"No." Anthony gave her a shy smile. "We kept it off the radios."

"Excellent!" Skye wrinkled her nose. "Then you can just say a possible gas leak is being investigated."

"And the real truth is?" a sharp voice asked.

Skye turned and stared into Orlando Erwin's bloodshot eyes. "Mr. Erwin, am I glad to see you." Skye had been half afraid he was lying dead somewhere.

"And why is that?" Orlando sat astride his motorcycle, pulled up next to the Bel Air's rear passenger door.

"Because—"

"Shit!" He cut her off. "I was supposed to look at some old books for you, wasn't I? Sorry. I was chemically inconvenienced."

"Yes, but that's not what's important now." Skye said to Anthony, "This is the missing store owner we've been looking for. Let him in."

The young officer moved one of the sawhorses so she and Orlando could get past the cordon. They pulled in behind Risé's Prius. Skye got out of her Chevy, balancing the cardboard drink carrier and three white McDonald's bags. Squinting, she could see Zelda Martinez, the newest Scumble River police officer, guarding the other end of the street.

Curious as to where Orlando had been, Skye hurried to catch up with him as he strode over to where his wife and Wally were sitting.

She arrived in time to hear him say, "Sweetheart, I'm so sorry."

Risé remained seated. Ignoring him, she thanked Skye, who had handed her a paper cup and a sack of food.

Skye looked at Wally, who shook his head. He wanted to hear what the couple might say in the heat of the moment.

"I slipped." Orlando took a deep, harsh breath. "The pressure got to me."

Risé unwrapped a straw and stuck it into the opening on the milk shake's plastic lid.

"With our grand opening ruined, it suddenly hit me that we didn't have the cushion of your salary or a fat savings account anymore. I couldn't take it." Orlando's tongue darted out, and he ran it over his chapped lips. "I thought after fifteen years I could take just one drink, but I woke up this morning in the drunk tank at the county jail, with no memory of how I got there."

Skye whispered in Wally's ear, "Why didn't County report that Orlando was in their jail when you told them to be on the lookout for him?"

"They don't formally process the drunks," Wally said in a low voice. "They just let them sleep it off and then release them once they're sober."

"Oh." Skye turned her attention back to the store owners.

Orlando was still trying to explain. "They let me out about an hour ago." He shoved a hand through his brown hair. "I tried to call you, but your cell is off, and you weren't answering at the motor court or at the store, so I came straight here."

"Shut up!" Risé's face was set in hard, tight lines. "Just shut up! We'll talk about this later. Kayla's dead, and we've been robbed."

"Oh, my God!" Orlando sank to his knees. "Poor thing. She was such a sweet girl."

"Yes, she was." Risé blinked back tears. "She really was."

For a long moment no one spoke; then Orlando broke the silence. "That's it, then." He uttered a string of vivid and anatomically detailed invectives. "We're ruined. We'll lose everything. Who'll want to come to a store where someone has died?"

Skye caught her breath. Was Orlando right? Would people hold the death of a local girl against Risé and Orlando, as Chase had? Would they boycott the shop out of fear or revulsion or just plain spite? Was this the end of Tales and Treats before its story even got started?

CHAPTER 9
Look Homeward, Angel

When Skye arrived home, her lights were on and vehicles of every description filled her driveway. *Crapola!* Just what she needed— her family must have heard the news about the body in the bookstore and descended on her to find out the details. Once Wally put up the barricades and sent Chase to the police station, it was inevitable that the Scumble River grapevine would kick into high gear—and Skye's mother was one of the biggest grapes.

From the cars parked in front of her house, Skye knew exactly who was inside. The white Oldsmobile belonged to her mother, the blue pickup to her dad, Uncle Charlie drove the Cadillac, her brother owned the Jeep, and Trixie's Civic rounded out the group.

Shoot! She really didn't want to have to deal with any of them right now. When the crime scene techs had finally arrived from Laurel, it had taken the team a couple of hours to go through the store. Meanwhile, Wally had sent Risé and Orlando to the police station, left his officers in charge at the store, and he and Skye had driven to Kayla's parents' house to inform them of her death.

Afterward, Wally and Skye had taken the bookshop owners' reports, along with a statement from Chase Wren. It was now past five, and Skye craved quiet and solitude. And maybe a sandwich, since she had never gotten to eat her Big Mac.

She sat unmoving in the Bel Air. What would happen if instead of getting out, she turned around and headed to Wally's? A moment's reflection reminded her that if her family thought she was missing, their ensuing actions would be worse than facing their questions now. May and Charlie were not above calling in the National Guard, not to mention the cadaver dogs and the FBI.

Blowing out an exasperated breath, Skye dragged herself out of the Chevy and trudged up the sidewalk. She wasn't surprised that her family was inside her house instead of waiting on the front porch. Her mother had a key, and although she was supposed to use it only for emergencies, May would definitely classify her quest for the most recent buzz as urgent.

As Skye stepped through the front door, the smell of roast beef and the hum of chatter greeted her. She crept forward and peeked into the kitchen. The men were gathered around the table, while May and Trixie bustled from stove to refrigerator to cupboard. Bingo, Skye's black cat, gazed at her from beside his food bowl. He nudged it in her direction, and when she made no move to fill it, he meowed unhappily.

Bingo's mew drew May's attention to Skye, and her shriek alerted the others. In the blink of an eye, they all descended on Skye like shoppers on a Black Friday door-buster sale item.

Skye braced herself for the onslaught. May won the race, which was nothing short of remarkable considering that Trixie was twenty-five years younger and had come in third in the Stanley County marathon a few weeks ago.

"Are you all right?" May swept Skye into a hug, pulled her into the room, and whirled her around, all the while talking so fast she nearly stuttered. "What kept you so long? What happened? Who died?"

Skye stood still and let her mother fuss. When May worked herself up to this state, she resembled an overly caffeinated telemarketer, and there was nothing you could do but let her get through her spiel.

The others gathered around them, and Skye spotted Loretta Steiner grinning at her from the doorway. She was Skye's sorority sister, sometimes her attorney, and possibly her future sister-in-law. At six feet tall, with coal black hair and mahogany skin, she looked like royalty from some exotic land, a queen wearing Manolo

Blahnik sandals and a Cartier ruby pendant.

Loretta found Skye's family vastly entertaining and didn't try to hide her enjoyment. Skye wondered whether she'd still be as amused if she and Vince became engaged and Loretta replaced Skye as the target of May's attention.

Skye's father, Jed, interrupted her thoughts by awkwardly patting her shoulder. "You okay?" His faded brown eyes peered anxiously from his tanned, leathery face.

"I'm fine, Dad." Skye kissed Jed's cheek, hugged her mom, and led the brigade back toward the table. "Wally and I had to wait for the crime scene techs to finish. Then we talked to the owners. I don't think they know what happened yet. Kayla Hines was the victim." Since the next of kin had been notified, Wally had said it was okay to reveal who had died.

There was a split second of silence while everyone absorbed the information; then Uncle Charlie said, "I knew those new people were going to be nothing but trouble from the minute I met them. He's some old hippie still 'scarred' by the war, and she thinks she's so freaking green, she might as well be Kermit the Frog."

Charlie was an imposing figure, weighing in at more than three hundred pounds and standing six feet tall. He was also opinionated, manipulative, and he disliked change. But he would do anything for May, whom he thought of as a daughter, or Vince and Skye, whom he considered his grandchildren.

"Really, Uncle Charlie." Skye blew a curl out of her eyes. "Trying to conserve our natural resources is a good thing, and Orlando fought for this country and doesn't deserve to be called names."

He harrumphed but didn't argue. After a moment, he, Jed, Vince, and Loretta sat down, and May and Trixie went back to the stove. As soon as everyone was settled, they all started talking and asking questions at once. Skye's head was spinning, and she swayed, unable to focus on what anyone was saying. She felt like she might pass out.

Suddenly, Loretta put her fingers in her mouth and let out a piercing whistle. Everyone fell abruptly silent, and Loretta said, "People, give her a chance to talk." She turned to Skye. "Start at the beginning and tell us what happened. Don't leave anything out."

Charlie and May frowned, but Vince and Trixie nodded. Jed shoved back his John Deere gimme cap and scratched his head, his expression hard to read.

May said, "Is that the way to behave in front of your maybe, I hope, future mother-in-law?"

"Sorry." Loretta's expression was neutral. "Too many years dealing with unruly clients, I guess." She turned her head toward Skye and winked. "So . . . ?"

Skye walked over to the fridge and retrieved a can of Diet Coke. After popping the top and taking a healthy swallow, she described her day, skipping her coffee with Simon. She ended by saying, "Which means, it looks as if the store was robbed, and poor Kayla was unfortunately in the wrong place at the wrong time."

"What aren't you telling us?" May aimed her laserlike truth-finding glare at Skye.

"Nothing that's relevant to the situation." Skye could have kicked herself. Why had she added those last five words?

"How about what isn't relevant? Come on, Skye. You're the police consultant and engaged to the chief. The girls expect me to tell them stuff everyone else doesn't know."

Skye opened her mouth, but Jed spoke first. "Ma, gossip's not very Christian of you."

May's cheeks reddened. "I can't help it. I got RLS."

"What's that?" Trixie asked.

"I saw it on that talk show," May explained. "That one with the Hollywood psychiatrist. He says people like me have Restless Lips Syndrome."

For a nanosecond the group was silent; then they all chimed in with their opinions regarding TV hosts and their medical qualifications. As the voices reached a peak, Skye caught a blur of black fur out of the corner of her eye and rose from her chair.

With everyone distracted, Bingo must have decided this was the perfect time to make a move on the roast. He ran past the people seated at the table, crouched, and launched himself at the counter. They all watched as at the last moment he apparently realized he couldn't make it and flailed all four legs as if he were trying to fly, then dropped to floor. Everyone roared with laughter, and Bingo stalked out of the kitchen.

"Poor kitty," Trixie murmured. "Do you think he's hurt?"

Skye shook her head. "Just his pride." She sat back down. "A cat's irritation rises in direct proportion to his embarrassment times the amount of human laughter."

Bingo's antics had served to sidetrack the conversation, and May remembered that supper was ready. Which was a relief. Skye was starving. As the others discussed the burglary, the new store owners, and Kayla's death, Skye devoured several slices of juicy roast beef, a mountain of creamy mashed potatoes, and heaping spoonfuls of corn casserole, then finished it off by using one of May's homemade Parker House rolls to sop up the rich, dark gravy.

Once her hunger was appeased, she tuned back into the conversation just in time to hear Charlie say, "I don't think it was a break-in at all. I bet you six ways to Saturday someone meant to kill that Risé woman."

Skye asked, "What makes you say that, Uncle Charlie?"

"That woman and her husband have rubbed a lot of people the wrong way." Charlie took the last swallow of his Budweiser and held up the can, jiggling it to indicate he was in need of another. "They're sticking their hands into a lot of people's pockets, and you mess with someone's livelihood and you're likely going to get burned."

"Who?" May hurried to replace Charlie's beer. "Anyone important?"

"Me, for instance." Charlie reached for the bowl of Waldorf salad. "Flip Allen told me they're fixing up rooms above their store to rent out to tourists. That's going to cut in on my business at the motor court."

"How did Flip know they were going to use that space as a bed-and-breakfast?" Skye asked. Flip was married to her cousin Ginger Leofanti Allen.

"He was the one who did the remodeling for them." Charlie emptied the remaining potatoes onto his plate. "Said they tried to stiff him."

"How?" Trixie asked.

"Wouldn't pay him after he did all the work." Charlie ladled gravy over the snowy mound.

Skye was silent for a moment, remembering that Kayla had mentioned overhearing that argument; then she said, "I thought Flip worked

114

for that big builder who's been putting in that development west of town. When I talked to him about doing some stuff at my house last summer, he told me he signed a contract with them not to do any independent jobs."

"I don't know anything about that." Charlie shrugged. "He must have gotten some kind of dispensation."

"Who else, Uncle Charlie?" Vince's green eyes gleamed with interest, and he absentmindedly smoothed back the sides of his butterscotch blond hair. He was an extremely handsome man who had dated most of the single women in Scumble River and its surrounding counties at least once.

"Tomi over to the Feed Bag's not too happy at the prospect of them siphoning off her morning-coffee-and-donut crowd." Charlie forked a piece of beef into his mouth, then spoke around it. "That, and people stopping in the afternoon for a piece of pie, is a good chunk of change for her. With Erwin baking fresh stuff all day, folks might go to Tales and Treats instead."

Skye wondered whether Charlie was aware of Hugo's and Pru's grudges against the store owners, so she asked, "Anyone else you can think of?"

"Your cousin Kevin Denison had a run-in with them about their insurance." Charlie gestured with his knife. "They gave him a hard time about the premium he quoted being different from the actual amount they had to pay."

Great! Another cousin was unhappy with the bookstore owners—that made two from the Denison side and one from the Leofantis. "But why do you think they'd want Risé dead versus Orlando?" Skye asked.

"Because she's a bi—witch." Charlie finished eating and wiped his mouth. "Her husband is just an idiot."

"Why do you think she's a bitch?" Loretta asked. She ignored Charlie's and May's frowns when she uttered the *b* word, and continued, "Was it because she was assertive? If her husband had been the one acting that way, would you have called him a bastard or admired his grit?"

"I don't know what you're implying, little lady—"

Trixie cut Charlie off. "Of course you do." She smiled at Loretta before telling him, "She's implying you're a chauvinist, and you have to admit you are."

Charlie's face turned magenta, and Skye was worried he might go into cardiac arrest. He was a prime candidate for a stroke since he was over seventy-five, drank, smoked, and didn't exercise at all. "Uncle Charlie was born in a different time," Skye explained. "Besides, he's just not a warm and fuzzy kind of guy. Actually, he pretty much treats everyone the same."

"Okay." Loretta nodded. "But I still want to know what Risé did to make you think she's so bad."

"I can't rightly put my finger on it." Charlie ran his hands through his thick white hair. "It's mostly an impression she made, that whatever she did before opening that bookstore, she was the boss, and no one messed with her. Once she gets something up her butt, she never lets it go." He narrowed his bright blue eyes. "Take Hugo and those dang used cars of his, for instance. She is bound and determined to make him move them, or die trying."

Skye gulped at Charlie's words and sent a silent prayer to the heavens. *Please, please, God, let Kayla's death be a burglary gone wrong.*

After everyone had finished, the dishes were done, and the leftovers were distributed among them all, everyone got up to leave. As the group made its way to the foyer, Skye noticed that Vince and Loretta hung back, bringing up the rear. She crossed her fingers that there was a good, not bad, reason for their wanting to talk to her alone.

Just before walking out the door, Vince said, "One second, Loretta; I need to use the john." The others hesitated, but he waved them off.

Once May, Jed, Charlie, and Trixie had gone, Skye asked Loretta, "What's up?"

"Let's wait for Vince to get back." Loretta's face was glowing.

"I think I can guess, but why the secrecy?"

Vince emerged from the hall bathroom and came up behind the two women in the foyer. He put an arm around each and beamed. "Because we wanted you to be the first to know, Sis. Loretta and I are engaged."

"That's wonderful!" Skye's voice bubbled with pleasure. "I'm so happy for you both."

Loretta reached into her pocket and slipped a large emerald-cut diamond set in platinum on her left ring finger, then held out her hand. "Isn't it beautiful?"

"It's gorgeous," Skye assured her friend. "Did you pick it out by yourself, Vince, or did you help him, Loretta?"

"He completely surprised me." Loretta clung to Vince's arm. "He proposed last night."

"You done good, bro." Skye hugged Vince, then embraced her friend. "This is so wonderful."

"It is," Loretta exulted. "Now we'll be both Alpha Sigma Alpha sisters and sisters-in-law."

"I'm flattered you wanted me to be the first to know, but why do I think there's a catch?" Skye looked from Vince to Loretta.

"Let's sit down." Vince led them toward the back of the house and into the sunroom. "So, do you remember the promise you made to me last June?"

"Yes," Skye answered cautiously, taking a seat on the wicker chair. "I said I'd run interference with Mom next time you were in trouble."

118

Vince and Loretta snuggled together on the matching love seat, and he said, "I'm calling in that marker."

"Why?" Skye became instantly wary. "Mom will be happy about you getting married. Won't she?"

"The marriage part, yes." Vince picked up one of Bingo's catnip toys and tossed it from hand to hand. "The wedding part, not so much."

"What kind of wedding are you planning?" Skye didn't hide her look of consternation.

"Small." Loretta took the felt mouse from Vince and gave it to Bingo, who was pawing at his knee.

The cat immediately dropped it and sauntered away.

"Oh." Skye felt relieved. Yes, May would prefer a huge affair, but she'd be okay with a small wedding for her son. Now, if it were Skye, it would be a different story. "She'll be fine, as long as the family's included."

"That's the thing." Vince spun the TV remote on the glass-topped coffee table. "When Loretta said small, she really meant intimate."

"Like just Mom, Dad, me, Loretta's parents, and her siblings?" Skye offered, thinking she could probably sell that to May without too much drama.

Vince shook his head. "Even tinier."

Skye cringed. "What's teenier than that?"

Vince's and Loretta's expressions told Skye that something really bad was coming.

"Me, Loretta, you, and Wally." Vince's gaze slid from Skye's.

"Oh, my God!" Skye screamed. "Please, tell me you aren't eloping."

"Technically, we aren't." Loretta gave Skye a calculating look. "Since we're telling you and asking you and Wally to stand up for us."

"Mom is going to kill you both." Skye glared at them. "And I'm not going to be collateral damage."

"You promised," Vince insisted. "You pinkie swore." He thumped the back of her head lightly with his thumb and forefinger.

"Shit!" It was times like this when Skye wished she used the *f* word.

"Yes, it'll hit the fan, all right." Vince made a face.

"Why? Tell me why you want to elope," Skye demanded. She turned to Loretta. "Won't your mother be disappointed? You're her only daughter."

"That's the problem." Loretta's right eye gave a single twitch; then not a muscle moved in her face. "Although my parents like Vince, he's not exactly the husband they'd choose for me."

"What's wrong with my brother?" Skye's voice was knife-edged.

"Let me count the ways." Vince spoke without rancor, but there was something in his eyes that made Skye think he was more upset than he let on. "I don't live in Chicago. I didn't go to college. I'm not a professional. I don't have a lot of money. And . . ."

"And?" Skye hated to ask, afraid she already knew the answer.

"He's Ca—"

"Caucasian, right?" Skye said half defiantly. "They want you to marry an African-American."

"Nope." Loretta's eyes glinted with equal parts amusement and irritation. "I was going to say he's Catholic. They want me to marry a Christian."

"Sheesh. We are, too, Christians." Without waiting for a response, Skye went on, "Which reminds me, why is Mom okay with you marrying a non-Catholic when she's having a hissy fit because Wally isn't Catholic?"

"She likes me better," Vince teased. "Seriously, I think once Wally's annulment comes through, she'll be all right with him."

"Getting back to you two." Skye pressed her fingers against her temples. "You're really going to elope?"

"Yes." Loretta nodded.

"Neither of us wants a big, fancy wedding." Vince's voice was firm. "Especially after what went on with Cousin Riley's last June."

Riley's over-the-top platinum wedding had inconvenienced everyone, caused oodles of hard feelings, and ended in murder.

"You have a point," Skye conceded. "But you don't have to go to the other extreme."

"Look." Vince drummed his fingers on the coffee table. "It'll be so much easier this way."

"We'll have a party at Christmastime," Loretta joined in. "It'll give everyone a chance to get used to each other without the pressure of a wedding."

"Without a lot of nosy people watching our two families' every move," Vince added.

"Okay." Skye held up her hands in surrender. "I give up. What do you want me to do?"

"We'd like the four of us to fly to Las Vegas the first weekend in October," Loretta explained. "You and Wally can spend the weekend, or longer if you want, but we'll come back the following Sunday."

"And until then," Vince added, "we need to keep our engagement and the arrangements for the wedding a secret from both families. Which should be easy with Loretta's folks, probably a little harder with Mom and Dad."

"You two do realize that if a robin falls within fifty miles of Scumble River, Mom knows about it before its wings quit fluttering?" Skye tilted her head. When they didn't react, she sighed. "What else do you have on your evil minds?"

"Before Loretta and I come back from the trip, you need to break the news to Mom." Vince tried to sound casual. "In person."

"No way." At that instant, Skye knew that she might as well rejoin the Peace Corps. The only thing that would save her from May's fury would be living in a foreign country with poor phone service.

"Look, if Mom starts to get suspicious, just give her a whiff of Lysol and tell her your house needs cleaning." Vince's eyes gleamed with mischievousness. "That should throw her off the scent for a while."

"This is so, so much bigger than the favor I had you do for me," Skye whined.

"You agreed to the deal."

"And you knew all along what you were going to ask in return, didn't you?"

"Of course not." Vince shook his head.

"Right." Skye didn't believe him for a second. "I don't know how and I don't know when, but I'm getting back at you both for this."

Vince and Loretta snickered.

"That is, if I live through the experience," Skye muttered.

"Mom'll get over it." Vince patted Skye's cheek. "You worry too much about her."

Skye shook her head. Her brother was excellent at existing in the here and now, but he had never been very good with the concept of future consequences. This time, he might regret that. If May missed her only son's wedding, she wouldn't let any of them live it down for a long, long time.

CHAPTER 10

Catch-22

Skye had been back inside her house for less than a minute after escorting the newly engaged couple to their car when she heard knocking. Thinking her brother had forgotten something, she ran into the foyer and flung open the door. Instead of Vince demanding his Tupperware container full of leftovers, Simon stood on her porch holding a pizza box.

"What are you doing here?"

"I thought you might not have had a chance to eat today," Simon explained.

"I do keep food in the house and am able to cook." Skye let the sarcasm roll off her tongue. Simon wasn't here just to feed her, and he didn't have that cute, slightly goofy look he wore when he was trying to romance her, so something was definitely up.

He glanced over his shoulder, then said, "I need to talk to you in private."

"I live alone on a fairly deserted road." She made a show of sticking her head out the door and gazing around. "I'm pretty sure no one is eavesdropping."

"Can I come in?" Simon juggled the flat cardboard box. "It's important."

"No." Skye gave him a speculative look. "I don't think that's a good idea."

"How about we sit out here?" Simon gestured to the porch furniture. "The weather's nice. Just flip on your outside lights."

"Okay." Skye tipped her head. "But this better not be about winning me back."

"I promise it's not."

"You wait right there," Skye ordered. "I'll go get some plates and napkins. Do you want anything to drink?"

"I'd love a scotch, but I'm guessing you don't have the bottle you used to keep for me anymore, so how about a glass of wine?" He put the pizza down on the wicker table.

She nodded, closed the door, and after a second's thought locked it. Hurrying to the kitchen, she worried about what her ex wanted to discuss. None of the subjects that came to mind was encouraging.

Simon had made himself comfortable while she'd been gone. The citronella candle Skye kept on the table was lit, and he had taken off his suit jacket and tie and was settled in one of the pair of matching wicker armchairs with his feet up on the ottoman.

Skye put down two glasses of Zinfandel, plates, and a stack of paper napkins, then took a seat. "Go ahead. Eat while it's still hot."

"Thanks." He flipped open the box. "I haven't had anything since coffee with you. I was on my way to brunch when I got the call from Boyd."

While Simon devoured three slices of pizza, she nibbled on one. She may have eaten a huge dinner a couple of hours ago, but who could resist Aurelio's pepperoni and mushrooms on a crispy thin crust?

Finally, Simon wiped his mouth with his napkin. "You sure aren't eating much." He sneered. "Has Boyd got you on a diet for the big wedding?"

"Of course not. He likes me the way I am," Skye snapped. "Do you really think I'd lose weight because some *man* told me to?" She was tired of hearing about weddings, and she was especially tired of discussing what she should look like by the time hers rolled around.

"Oops! Sorry. That was just my jealousy getting out of hand." Simon's expression was contrite. "Let me rephrase that. Don't you like the pizza?"

"If you must know, Mom and the gang were waiting for me with a complete Sunday dinner ready to be served when I got home." She made a wry face. "I wonder how many other thirty-five-year-old women have mothers who break into their houses to cook for them."

"May is one of a kind." Simon's tone was fond. "If my mother broke into my house, it would be to steal the silver in order to finance some get-rich-quick scheme."

"Bunny's not *that* bad." Skye took a sip of her wine. "She would never steal from you."

"You're right." Simon picked up another piece of pizza. "She'd just try to con me out of the money."

They both laughed; then Skye sighed and said, "I'm not going to like why you're here, am I?"

"Probably not."

"Shoot!" She took a deep breath. "I'm ready. Tell me your news."

"The medical examiner's preliminary findings are that Kayla's death was not an accident."

"Because the rare-book cabinet was deliberately pushed over?"

"Not only that." Simon finished chewing and swallowed. "Because it appears she was hit over the head before the cabinet was yanked on top of her."

"How can he know that so soon?"

"Her skull was smashed in, but the bookcase only hit her from below the shoulder blades."

"Still." Skye's chair squeaked as she leaned forward. "It was most likely a crime of circumstances. The thief didn't realize Kayla was there, and when she caught him, he hit her, shoved the cabinet over, and ran."

"Maybe." Simon twisted a gold signet ring on his right hand. "But I'm concerned about Xavier."

"His investment?"

"That, although I don't think that poor girl's death will keep business away for long—people have short memories." Simon struggled to explain his reasoning. "More, I have a bad feeling that this wasn't—how did you put it?—a crime of circumstances."

"Why would you think that?"

"Something isn't adding up." Simon adjusted the crease on his trousers, then picked up his glass. "Xavier was really upset when he first came into the store and he thought Risé was the woman under the bookshelf, and he rarely expresses any emotion."

"I can see why he'd be distressed. After all, he, Orlando, and Risé have been friends for years." Skye wasn't sure what Simon was trying to say. "Not to mention that Xavier doesn't have many people he's close to. He's always struck me as an extremely lonely man."

"That's true." Simon stared at his black wing-tips, wiping a smudge from the toe with his napkin before continuing. "But I think it has something to do with what he's hiding."

"Then you'd better find out what his secret is." Skye sipped her wine. "Not to be mean, but what does any of this have to do with me? If Xavier's going to open up to anyone, it would be you."

"True." Simon tented his fingers under his chin

and spoke over the tips. "But if Boyd is going to confide in anyone, it's you."

"Are you afraid that Xavier is somehow involved in that girl's death?" Skye's tone was incredulous. "You've got to be kidding."

"I don't think he killed her." Simon leaned back in his chair and laced his fingers over his flat abdomen. "But he might know who did."

Standing on the sidewalk watching Simon get into his car, Skye blew out an exasperated breath. What a day. She'd stumbled across a dead body, muddled the victim's identity, handled Chase's meltdown, learned the missing Orlando was actually in the drunk tank, and helped Wally notify Kayla's parents of her death. Then she'd faced her family's interrogation, Vince and Loretta's demands, and finally Simon's request.

Skye had agreed not to inform the police about Xavier's investment in the bookstore, but she'd cautioned Simon that if Kayla's death was anything other than the result of a burglary gone wrong, she *would* tell Wally. Skye also had assured Simon that she would keep her ears open for anything that might reveal what Xavier was hiding. Before he left, she'd made him promise not to show up at her house uninvited again— no matter what wonderful food he brought.

She climbed the steps to her porch, stopping midway to stare at Simon's Lexus disappearing down her driveway. She was relieved to see him go. She really needed some time alone to process the events of the day and get ready for work tomorrow. A distracted school psychologist was a careless school psychologist, and that never ended well.

Before claiming her well-earned solitude, Skye reached a hand inside the front door and flicked on the halogen light that was mounted on a pole in her yard. It took her only a moment to clear up the debris of the impromptu pizza party, and as she balanced the box stacked with plates, wine-glasses, and used napkins, she glimpsed a flash of yellow behind her garage. What in the world was back there? The only thing she could think of that might be that particular shade was a piece of Caterpillar equipment. But what would an earthmover be doing on her property? Surely, her father hadn't bought her a backhoe.

Skye was stumped for a second until she remembered the VW she'd helped Xenia Craughwell purchase. But why would the girl be hiding on Skye's land? Had she heard about Kayla's death? And if so, how would she react to the news? Xenia's response to any given situa-tion was a crapshoot, and Skye had long ago given up betting on it.

Before Skye could stash her armload of trash and go investigate, the VW zoomed out from in back of the garage and screeched to a stop at the foot of Skye's steps. Xenia jumped out and ran up to the porch.

"Seriously. You have more people in and out of here than a crack house."

"And how would you know that?" Skye arched an eyebrow. "It had better be from TV."

"Don't freak." Xenia opened the front door and gestured for Skye to go inside. "It's just an expression."

"Good." Skye led Xenia down the hall toward the kitchen. "How long have you been spying on me?"

"I wasn't spying." Xenia crossed her arms, her expression more embarrassed than defiant. "I had just driven into your driveway when the Macy's Thanksgiving Day Parade arrived, so I pulled behind the garage to wait. I wanted to talk to you in private."

"I see." Skye put the dishes and glasses in the sink and, after scraping off the dried cheese and scraps, threw the box in the recycle bin.

"What was Mr. Reid doing here?" Xenia pursed her lips disapprovingly. "I thought you were hooked up with that buff police chief." She shrugged, answering her own question. "I guess I should know by now that everyone cheats and there is no happily ever after."

"That's not true. Simon was just—" Skye heard herself stammering and closed her mouth in order to gather her thoughts. "Mr. Reid had some information he needed to share with me."

"Over dinner?"

"Not that it's any of your business, but Mr. Reid is the county coroner, and—"

Xenia cut her off. "Kayla's dead, isn't she?"

"I'm so sorry—"

"I knew it. I just knew Kayla was dead."

"Did you hear it from someone in town?" Skye asked, but wondered why Xenia would have come to her for the information if she'd already been told.

"People were talking, but I didn't want to believe what they were saying." Xenia bit back a sob. "When Kayla didn't show up at my house last night to work on her project and she didn't answer her cell and her boyfriend kept calling me, I knew something was wrong."

"Did you go looking for her?" Skye had a sinking feeling. "Xenia, did you go to Tales and Treats trying to find her?"

"Yes," Xenia whispered, then sobbed, "It's my fault. Kayla's dead because of me."

"Shh." Skye put her arms around the girl. "Tell me all about it." *Ay-yi-yi!* What had Xenia done? Had her anger issues finally resulted in her killing someone?

"If only I had gone inside." Xenia leaned into Skye and whimpered, "Why did I just drive away? Why do I always do the wrong thing?"

Phew! That was a relief. Xenia's crime was one

of omission, not commission. "When were you there?" Skye asked, pulling out a chair from the table and easing the girl into it. She didn't know whether the ME had been able to pinpoint the time of death, but Xenia's information might help narrow it down if he hadn't.

"Around eleven."

"Did you see anything or anyone?"

"No. The window was dark and no one was around, so I figured they were closed and Kayla had already left. So I did, too." Xenia drew an unsteady breath. "What if she was still alive and if I had gone in I could have saved her?"

"You mustn't beat yourself up for acting in a reasonable manner." Skye felt her heart break for the girl. When she'd moved to Scumble River, Xenia had had difficulty fitting in, and Kayla was the first real friend she had made. "It was after hours, the lights were off, and there was no sign of trouble. Why would you try to go in?"

"Because Kayla was missing." Xenia's voice cracked. "I should have done a better job looking out for her."

"In those circumstances, there was no reason to have gone inside." Skye scooted her chair closer to Xenia and took her hand in both of hers. "Was Kayla really missing? Did she tell you that she was coming to your house for sure?" Chase had made it seem like Kayla often decided at the last minute where she was spending the night.

"Not exactly." Xenia brushed a long black pigtail back over her shoulder. "I just figured she'd be over since she had a big project due Monday and I have better equipment than she does."

"And did she always answer her cell phone?" Skye probed, determined to alleviate the girl's guilt.

"Well . . ." It was clear from Xenia's expression that she wasn't sure whether to tell the truth. "No, not always." She added grudgingly, "Especially when she was with Chase. Kayla liked to keep her love life separate from her school life."

"So there's no way you really could have known she was in trouble."

"I guess not." Xenia looked relieved for a moment, then stiffened. "But with Chase calling and calling, I should have known."

"He'd never done that before?"

"Not in a long time." Xenia stubbornly held on to her feelings of culpability. "He knows I don't like him, so I should have realized that he'd only call me if he'd tried every other way to find Kayla."

"I respect the fact that you're taking responsibility for your actions, but in this instance, there is no way you could have guessed Kayla was in trouble unless you're clairvoyant." Skye stood. "The only guilty one in this case is the person who committed the crime."

"I suppose." Xenia slumped further in her seat and picked at a hole in her fishnet gloves.

The good hostess in Skye kicked in. "Would you like some tea or hot chocolate?"

"I'd rather have coffee."

"Okay." Skye shrugged mentally. Xenia was eighteen, and it wasn't as if she was asking for a shot of bourbon. "I have some wonderful pumpkin cake. My mother made it. Would you like a piece?"

"Sure." Xenia reached down to stroke Bingo, who was sniffing her Doc Martens. "I'm sorry to burst in on you like that, but I didn't know who else to go to."

"I'm happy to talk to you anytime, but"—Skye finished preparing the coffee maker and toggled the switch to the ON position—"how about your mom?"

Xenia thrust out her jaw. "You've met my mother. She can barely manage to focus on me long enough to order takeout for dinner. She usually just gives me a twenty and tells me to get what I want."

Skye nodded reluctantly. Raette Craughwell was extremely young and, from what Skye had heard, maintained an active social life. Xenia was left pretty much on her own. The only time Raette paid attention was when Xenia got into trouble, which was one of the reasons Xenia got into trouble so often.

There was a moment of silence while Skye tried to think of something comforting to say, but Xenia was too sharp for platitudes, so after a second, Skye put a slice of cake and a cup in front of the girl and asked her, "Do you take cream or sugar?"

"I drink it black, one sugar."

Which said a lot about Xenia, Skye thought as she took a sip of her heavily sweetened and lightened coffee. "Would you mind going over your experience at Tales and Treats? There might be a clue as to who attacked Kayla."

"You mean killed her." Xenia took a gulp of her coffee and stared coolly at Skye. Apparently, Xenia's hard shell was back in place. "You don't have to mince words with me."

"Understood." Skye picked up the pen and paper she had taken from a drawer. "Can you be any more exact about the time you arrived at the store?"

"Let me think." Xenia dipped a finger in the cream cheese frosting and licked it clean. "The clock on the bank sign read eleven eleven when I drove past. I remember thinking my grandma used to say that seeing a number like that was good luck and telling me to make a wish."

"Good." Skye made a note. "I take it you drove there in your Beetle?" When Xenia nodded, she went on. "Did you pass anyone on your way, either walking or driving?"

"Not after I went through the stoplight at Basin and Maryland." Xenia forked a bite of cake into her mouth, then mumbled, "That end of the street was deserted."

"Were there any vehicles parked along there that you recognized?"

"There were all those used cars from the Better Than New dealership."

"Hmm." Skye chewed the end of her pen. A memory was tickling at the back of her mind, but she couldn't quite scratch the itch yet.

"I stopped my VW in front of the store, saw the lights were off, and drove away."

"You didn't get out and try the door?"

"No." Xenia's voice was bitter. "For once I was worried about getting in trouble, and I didn't want to leave my car double-parked."

"Was there a police cruiser anywhere in sight?" Skye was happy the girl was becoming more law-abiding but curious as to why.

"No. But those security cameras Risé installed Saturday morning were aimed right at me."

Eureka! Skye shot out of her chair. The security cameras. That was what she had been trying to remember. Had Wally noticed them? It wasn't as if it was common for Scumble River businesses to have them.

"Chief Boyd is going to want to talk to you about all this. I'd be happy to come with you to the police station."

"That sucks!" Xenia jumped up and headed for the door.

Skye blocked her exit and said with a straight face, "Gravity sucks, too, but we'd be in trouble without it."

CHAPTER 11

The Sun Also Rises

Grateful to be finally alone, Skye slowly climbed the stairs to her bedroom, stripped off her clothes, and crawled into bed. Wally had still been at the station when she'd called to share Xenia's information, and he'd asked her to accompany the girl to the PD.

While Skye and Xenia were driving into town, Wally had contacted Risé and Orlando and asked about the security cameras. Risé told him that they were hooked up to a recording device in the store's back room. She claimed that she had forgotten about them in all the shock and confusion.

While Wally was interviewing Xenia, he sent an officer to retrieve the security recordings. Once Wally had finished questioning Xenia, he and Skye viewed the footage. Someone had double-parked outside the store at eight thirty Saturday night. Unfortunately, the image was fuzzy, and the vehicle was an unrecognizable dark blur. Wally had had to send the recording to the crime lab in Laurel to see whether the techs there could enhance the image.

139

By the time all the loose ends had been tied up and Wally had driven Skye home, it was past midnight and she was exhausted. Not only had it been a long, stressful day, but it was way past her usual ten o'clock bedtime.

So why wasn't she in dreamland? Skye lay on her side, watching the red digital numbers of her clock radio change as the minutes went by. Maybe she should have gone home with Wally. At least missing sleep while in his bed had other benefits. But he had been even more worn-out than she was, and since she had an early meeting at school the next day, she hadn't wanted to disturb him at five a.m. when she got up.

Sighing, she flipped over onto her back, laced her fingers behind her head, and stared at the ceiling. The problem with this case was that they weren't sure what the intended crime had been. Was it a burglary gone bad, or had the criminal been intent on murder? And if that was the case, who was the intended victim? Charlie seemed certain that if anyone had given someone a motive for murder, it had been Risé.

Monday, as Skye pulled into the high school parking lot, a red Hummer roared past her and squealed to a stop in the no-parking zone at the front entrance. The driver hopped out of the vehicle and hurried to the door, where he repeatedly jabbed the intercom button. All schools were kept tightly locked down since 9/11. Too bad the only people inconvenienced were the staff and the parents, as evidenced by the unending spate of school violence. The bad guys got inside no matter what precautions were taken.

The Hummer driver looked somewhat familiar. Who would be there more than an hour before classes started? Oh, yeah. Now she remembered. He was the magazine sales rep. Scumble River High had decided to sell magazines for its annual December fund-raiser. She wondered how many subscriptions the kids would talk her into buying.

As she got out of the car, a warm breeze blew across her face, and she smiled. It had been a nice fall so far. The temps had been in the high seventies, with lots of sunshine and no sign of an early winter. She crossed her fingers that the weather would continue to be warmer than usual and that it would snow only a couple of inches on Christmas Eve and melt completely away by New Year's Day.

After pushing her windblown hair out of her eyes, she grabbed her purse and tote bag, then strode across the asphalt and used her key to get inside. Homer Knapik, the high school principal, was standing in the school's foyer, his gaze fastened on the door. He was squarely built with an excess of body hair and a permanent frown. He reminded Skye of Bigfoot with a bunion.

As soon as he caught sight of Skye, he boomed, "You. In my office immediately!"

Yikes! What did Homer want? Skye followed the principal past the front counter, down a dark narrow hall, and into his lair.

He shut the door and marched over to the coffee machine on the credenza beneath the window. Homer had been the principal at the high school for as long as most people could remember. In fact, he'd been there when Skye was a student, which made the whole colleague/equal-footing relationship a bit hard to pull off.

For the last couple of years Homer had been threatening to retire, but much to the disappointment of his staff, those had been empty promises. The teachers were convinced that even if Homer died, the board would just stuff and mount him in the chair behind his desk. If that happened, Skye was pretty sure no one would be able to tell the difference, at least as far as the running of the school went.

Without turning around, Homer barked, "I heard you found another stiff."

"That stiff, as you so eloquently put it, was one of our students not too long ago"—Skye's voice was rebuking—"so I'd appreciate it if you referred to her in a respectful manner." Skye wasn't good at standing up for herself, but she didn't let anyone denigrate the kids, even after they were dead.

"Don't take that holier-than-thou tone with me." Homer faced her, holding a steaming cup. "When you've been around here as long as I have, see if you're still so protective of the little brats."

Skye paused. Changing Homer's mind was probably impossible, but she'd keep after him about how he treated the students.

Her lack of response seemed to irritate him, and he moved on to another complaint. "What are you, some kind of pied piper for the dead? When you walk through a cemetery, do the corpses rise up and follow you?"

"Are you nuts?" Skye was beginning to worry about Homer's sanity. "No one outside of a horror novel can do that."

"Everything I say can be entirely validated by my own opinion."

Skye kept her expression neutral. There was no way to respond to a statement like that. Heck, she wasn't even sure what he'd actually said.

"What do they call your affliction, anyway?" the principal jabbed at Skye.

"I'd tell you, Homer, but it's too hard for you to pronounce. And you don't have to worry. Someone like you certainly can't catch it."

"Are you being smart with me?" He slammed his cup down on the desktop, hot liquid sloshing over the sides.

"Of course not." Skye barely stopped herself from rolling her eyes.

"I've told you before"—Homer's tone was that of a salesman speaking to an unreasonable customer—"I want you to quit finding corpses."

"Okay." They'd had this conversation before, and it never ended well. It was hard to defend yourself against an accusation you were afraid might be true. "I'll put that on my to-do list."

"That's what you said last time." The hair growing out of his nose bristled. "But you did it again."

"And how do you suggest I carry out your order?" Skye was trying to remain calm, but he was starting to seriously tick her off. Did he think she got a bounty for every victim she found?

"Staying out of police investigations would be a good start." Homer's face turned a mottled red. "Quit poking your nose where it doesn't belong."

"You are aware that I was hired to consult for the police department?" Skye knew he was, because although her school contract allowed her to moonlight, it stipulated that she inform the principals and the school board, which she'd done.

"Everyone knows the only reason you got that gig was because the chief was hot for you." Homer plunked into his chair, which groaned in protest. "Now that you're engaged to him, give the man a break and stop interfering."

"I do not interfere." Skye refused to let someone who resembled a Yeti disparage the assistance she provided the police. "I help."

Homer snorted. "Quit finding dead bodies. Quit finding murderers. Quit bugging the crap out of me." Homer pointed a hairy finger at her. "Do what we pay you for."

"What are you talking about?" Skye always got her work finished, even when it meant staying late and taking reports home to finish. "What haven't I done?"

"Straightened out Pru Cormorant." Homer pretended to search for something in a drawer, not looking at Skye when he muttered, "She's gone a little off."

"So, what's new?" Skye retorted. "She's been past her sell-by date for years."

The English teacher had been at Scumble River High for as long as Homer had and was a law unto herself. Every once in a while she did something so atrocious that Homer was forced to take some action, like the time she wrote on a report card, *Since our last conference, your child has reached rock bottom and started to dig.*

Unfortunately, Homer usually delegated the task of doing something about Pru to Skye. This was the beginning of Skye's sixth year at Scumble River High and at least the third time Homer had ordered her to "fix" Pru.

"She's got her panties in a bunch over that new bookshop." Homer pushed a clipboard across his desktop to Skye. "She wants the whole school to sign this petition and boycott the store." He turned his back. "You've got to get her under control."

Skye cringed. "That isn't *my* job. It's *yours*."

Homer ignored Skye and continued, "Worse yet, she's already sent petitions home to some parents. I've been getting calls all weekend asking if what Corny is saying is true and wanting to know what the school is doing about this matter."

"I discussed this with her last Friday." Skye pushed the clipboard back toward Homer. "There's absolutely no merit to her accusation that the bookstore is selling porn or books advocating devil worship."

"And this was all before that girl was killed in the break-in." Homer's two oversize front teeth gnawed on his bottom lip. "I hear now Corny is claiming the wild animals they keep as pets are really the reason for the murder. Which doesn't even make sense."

"Holy moly." And Skye had thought nothing Pru did could surprise her. "That's ridiculous. The 'wild animals' are chinchillas, and they didn't get loose. She, or one of her minions, let them loose."

Oops! She had forgotten to tell Wally about that episode, as well as what Charlie had said about Risé. She'd have to call him as soon as she was out of her meeting.

"I don't give a damn." Homer swept his desktop with his arm, sending the offending clipboard along with various other items, flying to the floor. "Just make Corny stop, so the parents quit calling me about this shit."

"Why don't you order her to stop?" Skye made a scornful noise and answered her own question. "Oh, yeah, she's tenured, so you can't, because you don't have much to hold over her head, right?"

"So what?" he snapped. "It's your job to convince her to quit being a pain in my crack. You're the shrink. Counsel her about her evil ways."

"Right." He'd tried using that tack before. "The fact that you blatantly don't believe in all that 'psychobabble,' as you put it, makes it pretty obvious your real motive is to pass the buck."

"Have it your way." Homer folded his hands across his paunch and leaned back. "Do it because I'm ordering you to, and because, unlike that lunatic English teacher, *you* do not have tenure."

Skye opened her mouth to protest but closed it without speaking. He was right. Since she was considered a part of neither the teaching faculty nor the administration, she had none of the protections most of the staff enjoyed. She'd tried to join the union, as many of her fellow school psychologists in other school systems had, but so far the matter was still being considered.

"Any suggestion on how I can prevent Pru from acting within her constitutional rights?" Skye asked. Not that she didn't want the teacher to cease and desist harassing the bookstore, but she had no idea how to make her stop.

"Nope." Homer scratched behind a hairy ear.

Skye wondered whether she should get him a flea collar for Christmas this year.

"Just don't mention I told you to do it." Homer pointed his finger at her.

The ringing of the phone saved Skye from responding.

Homer snatched up the handset. "Yes?" He paused, then said, "No. No. Tell him I'm not here. . . . Hello, Shamus. What can I do for you?"

Skye flinched, hoping this call wasn't about her. Dr. Shamus Wraige was the superintendent of the Scumble River School District, and not one of Skye's biggest fans.

She unashamedly eavesdropped and heard Homer say, "No, I didn't sanction that petition." He listened, then whined, "Pru Cormorant sent it to her students' parents without telling me." He listened again before bleating, "I *do* have control of my staff. In fact, I just asked our psychologist to talk to Mrs. Cormorant about her concerns and suggest she not involve the school in her personal issues." After a long pause, he said, "Ms. Denison assures me there is no merit to Mrs. Cormorant's fears. Yes, sir. She'll take care of it today." He banged down the receiver and told Skye, "Dr. Wraige does not want to get one more call about this matter." Homer dug a roll of antacids out of his desk drawer.

"And you told him I could stop Pru?"

"Yes, so hop to it." Homer threw a handful of Tums into his mouth.

The white fizz around his lips made him look like a wolf with rabies. Normally Skye might have found that amusing. Not now. Not considering that he had just offered her up to the superintendent as a sacrificial lamb.

"You know"—Homer suddenly froze, and beads of sweat popped out on his forehead—"if Corny finds out I told you to stop her, she'll hound me to hell and back."

"I promise not to mention your name."

"You'd better not," Homer warned, then threw two more antacids into his mouth. "Because if that happens, I'm making you twice as miserable as she makes me."

"I'll do what I can, but truly, I have no idea how to get her to quit."

Homer appeared to make a sudden decision. "I've got to make a call." He picked up the phone. "You can go now."

As she was gathering her things, Skye heard part of Homer's conversation. "It's me. I've decided we should go to the cabin this afternoon. Start packing now. I'll be home in a couple of hours. I'll call in sick for the rest of the week."

Apparently, Homer wasn't taking any chances

149

that Pru Cormorant would turn her attentions to him.

He looked up from the file he had opened. "Are you still here? I thought you had an appointment at seven fifteen." He looked pointedly at the clock on the wall behind her. "You're late."

Great! Skye yanked open the door and dashed out of the office. As she jogged down the hall toward the library, where the meeting was being held, she ran through Homer's list of commands: Stop finding bodies, stop finding murderers, and stop Pru Cormorant from riling up parents against the bookstore. Nope. She had as much chance of doing any of them as she had of winning a million dollars.

CHAPTER 12

Crime and Punishment

After the meeting, which went well despite her tardiness, Skye spent a few minutes talking to Trixie about the murder, then retreated to the relative safety of her office. She sank into the chair behind the desk, let her tote bag fall to the floor, closed her eyes, and murmured to herself, "I totally take back all those times when I was a kid and I said I'd never need a nap."

Shaking off her fatigue, Skye turned on her computer and found the document containing the teachers' schedule. The first of Pru Cormorant's two planning periods was second hour. Skye had forty minutes to figure out how to tame Scumble River High's own Cruella De Vil. Too bad Skye felt more like a Dalmatian puppy than the Teacher Whisperer Homer expected her to be.

After some thought, Skye decided the best way to approach Pru was unofficially, which meant she needed to run into the mulish woman by chance rather than appear to have sought her out. Unfortunately, there was one major obstacle to that scheme.

Pru had one of the nicest classrooms in the school. Not only did it have actual walls instead of folding curtains—it had windows and an exterior door. So, when the weather was pleasant, the best place to find Pru when she wasn't teaching was right outside her room sitting in a lawn chair. This made casually bumping into her difficult.

Concentrating, Skye tried to come up with a plausible reason for being outdoors and near the English teacher's room. A few minutes before the second bell rang, the solution came to her. She could claim to be exercising. In fact, she could credit Pru with motivating her to work out, saying that after their chat about wedding pictures in the faculty lounge last Friday, she'd had a change of heart.

Skye hated to encourage the older woman's narrow-minded idea of beauty, but if it helped the bookstore and got the principal off her back, she was willing to do so—but only this one time. After all, a man may have to do what a man has to do, but a woman has to do what he can't. And clearly, Homer couldn't handle Pru.

Having decided on a plan, Skye exchanged her black pumps for the tennis shoes she kept in her bottom drawer—a good school psychologist was prepared for any occasion—tied her hair back into a ponytail, and took the bottle of water from her lunch bag. At the last minute, thinking it might add an air of authenticity to her disguise, she grabbed the stopwatch from her WISC-IV test kit and put the lanyard around her neck. She just hoped she remembered to put it back when she was finished, as it was impossible to administer the Wechsler Intelligence Scale for Children without a timer.

When Skye walked out of the building, she turned left and saw Pru in a lounge chair with a copy of *Cosmopolitan* tented over her face. Skye wondered how the teacher could consider romances porn, yet buy a magazine with a cover that contained a scantily clad woman and a promise of an article inside titled, "Six Sex Positions for the New Millennium." Not that Skye cared what the older woman read, but it did seem a tad two-faced. Of course, being hypocritical had never bothered Pru in the past.

A snore drifted out from under the periodical, and Skye wondered how she could wake Pru without making it obvious she wanted to talk to her. Shrugging, she decided she'd have to "accidentally" run into her chair.

Backing up out of sight, Skye started to jog. As she rounded the corner, she increased her speed and banged into the lawn chair. Pru snatched the magazine from her face and gazed up at Skye, an angry expression twisting her features.

Before the older woman could yell at her, Skye said, "I'm so sorry. Enjoying some fresh air?"

"Yes, I was." Pru's pale blue eyes were malicious. "What are you doing out here, dear?"

"Just jogging during my morning break."

"Really." Pru raised a drawn-on eyebrow. "I thought you told me that you weren't going to lose weight for your wedding pictures."

"True." Skye forced herself to look contrite. "But I considered what you said and decided you might be right, so I'm trying to run a couple of miles every day."

"How energetic of you." Pru's tiny pointed teeth appeared in her version of a smile. "Well, all I can say is that I hope you keep it up."

"Me, too."

"So many young people have no follow-through these days." Pru tucked a greasy strand of hair behind her ear. "When I was your age we were expected to stick to our decisions, not change course every five minutes."

Skye nodded silently, a firm believer that you rarely learn anything valuable if your mouth is moving.

"Look at those two over at the bookshop."

Eureka! Just the subject Skye wanted to talk about. "Risé and Orlando? How are they not sticking to their plans and following through on their decisions?"

"They're prime examples." Pru pursed her thin lips. "I heard that they both had completely different careers before coming here and opening that store." She *tsk*ed. "All this hopping from job to job is what's ruining America. It used to be you stayed in your position until you retired, and it was a disgrace to get fired or quit."

"Still"—Skye tried to steer the conversation into a more positive light—"now that you've seen Tales and Treats, surely you don't still think it's full of porn and how-to manuals on the occult, do you?"

"Maybe not," Pru admitted. "After the unfortunate incident of her pets escaping and emptying out the store, I went back and spoke to Ms. Vaughn about my concerns."

Skye had to bite her tongue to stop herself from blurting out, "You mean after *you* let the chinchillas loose." Instead she asked, "And what did Risé say?"

"She assured me they wouldn't be selling the racier romances or the darker science fiction to anyone under eighteen. And they do have that lovely café. She gave me a card for free coffees for a year to show her appreciation for my concern."

"I guess that means you can stop gathering signatures for your petition and disband the protesters." Skye wondered whether the complimentary beverage card was a bribe. More important, had it worked?

"Yes." Pru thrust out her bottom lip. "Hardly anybody signed anyway," she muttered, then brightened. "But clearly, something is wrong with that store and its owners, or there wouldn't have been a murder, so I'm still going to keep my eye on them."

"Being robbed is not their fault," Skye pointed out. "That could happen to any business."

"Not in Scumble River." Pru shook her head. "I can't remember the last burglary around here. I believe that everything happens for a reason. And more often than not the reason is someone's past goof-ups. Thus, there has to be a reason that store is attracting violence. And I think it has to do with that couple's previous life."

"What did they do before?" Skye asked. Risé had mentioned her husband's prior occupation but not what she had done. "I thought Orlando was a book scout, which should be pretty harmless."

"Maybe." Pru twitched her shoulders. "But *she* was some hotshot executive."

"I wonder why she'd give that up," Skye mused. "Her salary had to be a lot more than the money they can make from the store, and she's got to be within five or six years of retirement age."

"Exactly." Pru's tone was predatory. "They're hiding something, and I won't rest until I find out what."

"So then, after I jogged out of her sight, I went and told Trixie she didn't have to try to dig up any dirt on Pru after all." Skye was sitting with

Wally in the hall outside of Father Burns's office at the rectory. "She seemed almost disappointed."

They were waiting for the priest to arrive for their late Monday afternoon appointment to discuss Wally's annulment. They'd met with him briefly once before and had been given paperwork to complete, but today he was going to discuss the entire process with them.

"That sounds like Trixie. She likes a good fight." Wally chuckled, then asked, "What did Homer say when you told him?"

"He agreed that although Pru might still be harassing the bookstore, it didn't sound as if she was going to pursue the petition angle."

"I'll bet he was relieved."

"You sure couldn't prove that by me." Skye made a wry face. "He just grunted, told me to get back to work, then picked up the phone and ordered his secretary to get his wife on the line and cancel their trip."

"Homer sounds like our mayor." Wally ran his thumb down Skye's cheek. "Your uncle isn't too happy that we have another murder. The city's in negotiations with new businesses for several of those empty storefronts on the same part of the street as Tales and Treats."

"I wonder if Hugo knows that." Skye leaned her head on Wally's shoulder. She was so tired. She hadn't slept well last night, and the stress of the last couple of days was catching up with her.

"I just told you my cousin and Risé are in a big fight over parking spaces."

Skye had been unable to reach Wally all day, so she was using this time to fill him in on what she'd forgotten to tell him the previous evening.

"Right." Wally put an arm around her. "You mentioned she had disagreements with Flip and Kevin, too. I'd say it was odd that so many of your family members are somehow involved with that woman, except that you're related to half the town."

"Maybe more. Mom keeps coming up with new branches on the family tree." Skye nestled closer. "It's a good thing it was a burglary. If Risé was the intended victim without any other motive, a lot of my relatives would be suspects."

"It's pretty amazing that Risé has managed to tick off so many people in such a short time," Wally commented.

Before Skye could respond, Father Burns walked in the front door and ushered them into his office. He was a tall, ascetic-looking man who had been the priest at St. Francis, the Scumble River Catholic church, for as long as Skye could remember. He had to be close to sixty, but he had an ageless face and a gaunt body that hid his age.

Once Skye and Wally were seated on the leather wingchairs facing Father Burns at his desk, the priest said, "As I warned you the first time we spoke, the annulment process isn't usually smooth or quick, and I'm sorry to tell you, yours seems to have already hit a snag."

"Oh?" Wally tensed.

"What's the problem, Father?" Skye took Wally's hand and gave it a squeeze.

"I'm afraid the address you furnished for your ex-wife isn't any good." He looked at them to see whether they understood the gravity of the situation. "Although declaration of nullity is still possible, without her input, the proceedings will be even more drawn out."

"In other words"—Wally narrowed his eyes —"it would be best if I found her?"

"It would speed things up. Her involvement isn't essential, but the Church does like to give both parties an opportunity to present their views of the marriage." Father Burns sat motionlessly. "How long has it been since you've had contact with her?"

"A couple of years." Wally's hand tightened on Skye's. "Since we didn't have children, and the prenup she signed precluded her from claiming any of my assets or asking for alimony, or what-ever it's called nowadays, there was no need to keep in touch."

"Fortunately, your line of work should assist you in locating her." Father Burns smiled. "I'm sure God will guide you in your search."

"Thank you, Father." Skye was afraid this setback would cause Wally to try to persuade her to marry him without the process, so she asked, "Could you explain to us why the Church requires an annulment?"

"The Church's stance is that matrimony is life-long." His dark, serious eyes studied them for a long moment; then he continued. "The annulment procedure is used to determine if an essential element, which prevented the sacramental union promised, was missing when the couple entered into the marriage."

"And what are those elements?" Wally asked, glancing at Skye to see whether she knew.

"The most common is insufficiency or inadequacy of judgment," the priest explained. "There is also psychological incapacity, and absence of proper intention to have children, be faithful, or remain together until death."

"Since Darleen left me for another man, we should have that last one covered," Wally said drily. "Not to mention her psychological problems, which I found out about during the divorce."

"That will help." Father Burns looked down at the rosary in his hands. "But the real question is, can you honestly state that you knew there was something missing, something radically wrong, right from the start? Did you have second thoughts prior to the nuptials or have serious difficulties in the early years of the marriage?"

Wally didn't hesitate. "Yes. I knew I didn't feel

the way toward Darleen that I had toward someone previously." He gazed into Skye's eyes. "I wanted to back out of the wedding the night before, but I couldn't humiliate Darleen in front of all her family and friends." He stared at the priest. "We fought almost from the first day of our marriage. We were never a team."

"I'm sorry to hear that." Father Burns's voice was gentle. "However, it will help your case."

"But I should still locate Darleen." A flicker of impatience crossed Wally's eyes, but his voice was unruffled. "Right?"

"It would help." A corner of the priest's lips turned up.

"Even though Darleen and I weren't married in a church and I'm not Catholic?" Wally wrinkled his brow.

"Yes," Father Burns answered. "The Catholic Church views all marriages with respect and presumes that they are valid and binding. Consequently, it requires even non-Catholics to have any previous marriage annulled."

Wally's expression was skeptical.

"I understand that this must seem like a lot of nonsense, but without it your marriage to Skye will not be valid in the eyes of the Church. And I know Skye well enough to say without a doubt that this will trouble her greatly, now and in the future. For you to do this is a great act of self-giving love."

Both men turned to Skye, and she nodded.

"I've waited a long time for her." Wally gave Skye a loving look. "If this is what it takes to make her happy, I can wait a little longer."

"Thank you." Skye caught her breath at the raw emotion in his voice.

Wally squeezed her hand, then asked the priest, "Is there anything we can do in the meantime?"

"Make sure the people you've chosen who are familiar with your marriage to Darleen have filled out and returned the questionnaire you gave them." Father Burns rose from his chair and ushered them to the door.

"I'm sure praying wouldn't hurt," Wally teased gently.

"True." The priest nodded. "But God has three answers to your prayers, and people generally like only the first one, which is 'yes.' The other two—'not yet' and 'I have something better in mind'—take a little more faith."

"They certainly do," Skye murmured.

"Just remember, the nicest thing about the future is that it always starts tomorrow."

As they walked out to the parking lot, Skye asked Wally, "Was what you said about knowing you didn't feel the way toward Darleen that you felt toward someone else, and wanting to back out of the wedding, true?" All that he'd told her previously was that his and Darleen's marriage had been rocky from the start.

He stopped. "Every word." Tugging her under a huge old oak tree that hadn't started losing its leaves yet, he pulled her to him.

As she gazed into his warm brown eyes, Skye saw the heartrending tenderness of his gaze, and a tiny part of her blew out a sigh of relief. She had always wondered what he felt for Darleen and whether she had been his true soul mate.

"And was that person you felt more for . . . Was that me?" Skye slipped her arms between his jacket and shirt, caressing the planes of his back.

"Yes, it was you," he whispered. "It's always been you, since I first saw you."

His breath was warm against her face, and her heart raced. "Is it awful of me to be glad?"

"No." His lips brushed against hers. "Not if you love me as much as I love you."

"Once I turned eighteen, I always wondered if you'd ask me out sometime." She could feel the heat of his body pressed against the length of hers.

"I was twenty-four years old and you were still in high school. It wouldn't have been right." He rained tiny kisses all over her face. "Then after you went to college, you rarely came home."

"A huge mistake on my part." She raised herself on tiptoe, cradled his cheeks between her two hands, and pressed her mouth to his.

Wally gathered her closer, and his tongue stroked the soft fullness of her lips.

Skye shivered in delight, and at first she didn't hear the sound of a throat clearing. Then abruptly she stiffened and stepped out of Wally's embrace. He gave her a puzzled look, then blew out a sigh of resignation.

Officer Zelda Martinez stood a few feet away, her olive complexion a dusty pink. "I'm sorry to bother you, Chief, but you've got your cell switched off and we've had a break in the case."

CHAPTER 13

Brave New World

At approximately four forty-five p.m., a Ms. Judy Martin, who claimed to be the director of the Scumble River Public Library, phoned the PD." Zelda stood at attention and focused her gaze over Wally's right shoulder. "Ms. Martin stated that she had important information regarding the Tales and Treats burglary but refused to give the dispatcher any details and insisted on speaking directly to the chief."

"And when she was told I was unavailable?" Wally asked when Zelda didn't continue.

"Ms. Martin declared that she would wait for you at the library."

"Thank you." Wally nodded, dismissing the officer. Once Zelda was gone, he said to Skye, "This has got to be about the stolen books. We sent out a list to other rare-book dealers in a three-hundred-mile radius and to Internet brokers, but why would a librarian be involved?"

"I don't have a clue." Skye put both hands up in a "who knows?" gesture. "But Judy isn't prone to exaggeration or drama." As a frequent patron of the library, Skye knew the librarian well. "If she says her info is important, I'd bet it is."

"Then we best get over there and hear what she has to say."

Since Skye and Wally had each driven from work directly to the rectory, she followed him in her own car. The library was on the second floor of city hall, in the same building as the PD. So while Skye drove around to park in the public lot, Wally pulled his squad car into the garage.

They met at the entrance and climbed the stairs together. It was almost five thirty, a half hour after the library was supposed to close, but the door was unlocked. Skye and Wally stood at the chest-high counter and looked around. There was no sign of Judy.

The library was divided into two main rooms, both of which were jam-packed with shelves. There were a few wooden chairs and a couple of study carrels, but the rest of the space was crammed with books and magazines. A small office was wedged into a corner.

"Anybody here?" Wally raised his voice. "Ms. Martin, it's Chief Boyd."

There was no answer.

The town had needed a bigger library for years, but somehow the funds never materialized. Lack of resources also meant limited hours. Currently, on the weekend the library was open only from ten to four on Saturday and noon to three on Sunday. Judy and two high school students on a work-study plan were the sole employees, although the Friends of the Library provided a couple of volunteers.

"I'll check the office," Skye offered.

"Good. I'll see if she's anywhere among the shelves." Wally headed into the other room.

Skye walked over to the tiny cube and stuck her head inside. It was empty. As she returned to the circulation counter, she noted how threadbare and depressing the surroundings were. With most of the budget reserved for acquisitions, the paint on the walls had faded to a sickly goldenrod, and the carpet was somewhere between a tumbleweed tan and mouse-droppings brown.

Someone, presumably Judy, had attempted to brighten the space by adding lacy green plants to the tops of the shelves and hanging colorful mobiles from the ceiling. But they just added to the clutter and highlighted the shabbiness.

Skye and Wally met back at the entrance, and he said, "No sign of her among the shelves."

"She wasn't in her office either." Skye felt a prickle of concern. "I hope nothing's happened to her. If she had some knowledge of the crime, and the criminal found out, maybe he kidnap—"

"We don't even know what she wanted to tell me," Wally cut her off. "Let's not borrow trouble."

"I'm not." Skye's voice had an edge to it. "But she specifically said she would wait for you here, so where is she?"

167

Wally stepped into the hallway and yelled, "Hey, anyone around?"

He had just taken a deep breath to call out again when Judy came rushing up the stairs, still drying her hands on a paper towel. She wore her shiny brown hair to her shoulders and had a light dusting of freckles across her button nose. Her wholesome good looks reminded Skye of the old TV show character Gidget. And the pink and black polka-dotted skirt and pink cotton T-shirt she wore reinforced that girl-next-door image.

Skye stepped out from behind Wally and raised her hand in a small wave. "Hi, Judy."

"Hi, Skye." After ditching the paper towel in the trash can, Judy apologized. "Sorry to keep you waiting, Chief Boyd. I was in the bathroom. It sure would be nice if there was one up here. Oh, well. As my grandma used to say, if wishes were horses, we'd all be in the Kentucky Derby." She smiled at them both. "I'm so glad to see you two."

"What's up?" Wally took his notepad from his pocket. "Officer Martinez said you had something urgent to discuss with me."

"I do." Judy fished a key ring from her pocket, then walked around Wally and Skye. "Let me lock up and I'll show you. It's easier than trying to explain."

"Sure." Skye glanced at Wally. What did she need to show them?

After Judy secured the library's entrance, she motioned for them to follow her. "They're in my office." Once they had squeezed into the tiny space, she pointed to a pile of books. A paper grocery bag was pushed down around them. "These do not belong to the library."

"Oh?" Wally's voice was neutral. "Then how did they get here?"

"They were deposited into our remote box sometime between four p.m. on Saturday and noon Sunday," Judy explained. "You know, the one in the parking lot that people can drive up to and return books without getting out of their car."

"Right." Wally nodded. "When did you realize these weren't library books?"

Skye guessed these were the stolen books, but she couldn't tell what Wally was thinking.

"I didn't have a chance to go through the returns until this afternoon," Judy said. "I'm on my own on Sunday, and my part-timer doesn't come in until one on Monday. But as soon as I saw them, I knew." She pointed to a small volume on top of the pile. "This is a first edition of *The Velveteen Rabbit*." Her finger hovered over the cover. "Usually if there are books that aren't ours, I assume they are donations for the yearly used book sale the Friends put on, but this book is so rare, I knew . . ." She trailed off.

"What did you know?" Skye asked. Why was Judy taking so long to get to the point?

"My first thought was to return it to the owner. Then I saw the other titles"—Judy's voice held a note of excitement—"and figured that they must be the rare books stolen from Tales and Treats this past weekend."

"Let's see." Wally flipped a page in his notepad and without touching the books compared them to what he had written there. "Yep, these are the ones." He made a checkmark next to each item on the list. "They're all here."

"Which makes you wonder." Skye tapped her chin. "Why bother to steal a bunch of valuable books, then dump them in the library return bin within twelve hours of taking them? It's not as if the thief had a chance to find out he couldn't sell the books."

"My thoughts exactly." Judy gave her a beaming smile. "Our usual donations are worn-out paperbacks, encyclopedias, and *Reader's Digest* condensed sets."

"So you don't think our thief was altruistic?" Skye's lips curled upward.

"I seriously doubt they were meant as a donation." Judy grinned back.

"Did you touch the books?" Wally asked.

"No." Judy shook her head. "I pushed the sack down, and the top book tipped me off."

"How did you hear about them?" Wally frowned. "I left orders that the details be kept quiet. The list was only to go to other dealers."

"Oh." Judy's cheeks turned red, and she studied her pink ballet flats. "I'd rather not say."

Skye put her hand on the other woman's arm. "You're dating Anthony, aren't you?" She figured pillow talk was responsible for the leak.

"Yes," Judy whispered. "But it's not his fault. I saw his notebook and kind of . . . uh . . . took a peek. I was curious about the new bookstore." She glanced quickly at Skye, then away. "I was a little afraid that people would sell Risé and Orlando their used books instead of donating to our sale. Or that our readers would buy from them rather than borrowing from us."

"And if your circulation goes down, so does your budget," Skye guessed.

Judy nodded. "I just wanted to see what kind of books they were interested in."

"Anthony shouldn't have left his notes lying around." Wally scowled.

"True," Skye agreed. "And I'm sure if you explain that to him, he won't do it again."

"Maybe." Wally's frown didn't lessen. "But I should suspend him."

"No!" Judy cried. "He's such a sweet guy, and it was my fault."

"Besides"—Skye shot Wally a pleading look—"his goof actually ended up being helpful."

"Well . . ." Wally hesitated.

"Everyone deserves a second chance," Skye cajoled. "Even a police officer."

"Okay." Wally stared sternly at Judy. "But no more snooping."

"Cross my heart," the librarian promised, making an emphatic X on her chest.

"Good." Wally ended the matter. "You both stay here while I run next door and get Martinez."

The two women made small talk until Wally returned with the officer and an evidence collection kit. He put on rubber gloves, inserted the paper sack along with the books into a plastic bag, then tied it off. After sticking a signed evidence tag on the outside, he handed it to Zelda and instructed her to take it to the county crime lab for testing.

After saying good-bye to Judy, Wally and Skye headed toward the parking lot. When they reached her car, she said, "I suppose you have to go back to the station. With this new lead and all, you probably have to work."

"There's nothing to work on until we get the lab results." Wally brushed a curl out of her eyes. "Did you have something in mind?"

"Actually, I had a surprise planned." Skye took his hand and kissed the palm. "For being such a good sport about the annulment."

"I'm glad to get it if it makes you happy." Wally traced her lips with his fingertip, then trailed it down her neck. "You know I'd do anything for you." He grinned. "But a surprise sounds nice."

"Good." Skye opened the door of the Bel Air. "Get in and leave everything to me."

"Lead on." He unbuckled his utility belt and took off his tie, throwing both in the backseat before sliding into the passenger seat. "You're full of surprises lately, but I'm ready for anything you got."

Skye smiled mysteriously, jumped into the car, and started the engine. She refused to answer his questions as she drove, but when he guessed correctly, she finally admitted they were going to the Scumble River Recreation Club. It had been such a mild fall, the board had decided to leave the club open for the month of September. It was usually closed after Labor Day to everyone but hunters and people wanting to go sledding.

Skye tuned the radio to 94.7 FM, her favorite oldies station. She would always be a country music fan, but lately she had been in the mood for something different, and WLS played the best variety.

Although when "Right Back Where We Started From" poured out of the speakers, the irony wasn't lost on her. Judy's news had put them back to square one in the investigation. Skye opened her mouth to comment but stopped herself. She knew she couldn't resist talking about the case for long, but she'd hold out as long as possible. Wally deserved a reward for all she was putting him through in order to marry her.

When they arrived, she handed Wally her key and he unchained the barricade barring their entrance into the private club, then chained it back up once she drove through. From ten in the morning until six in the evening, a guard was on duty. He or she checked membership identification, punched guest cards, and unlocked the gate, but after hours, members had to fend for themselves.

Once Wally was back inside the car, Skye drove a short way up a narrow gravel road bordered by grassy areas dotted with trees and picnic tables —all empty at this time of day. Just before the main beach area, which had locker rooms and a pavilion, Skye turned down a dirt path that led to a small lake at the back of the club. She parked on the grass and hopped out of the Bel Air.

Popping the trunk, she handed Wally a cooler and grabbed a basket and an old bedspread, then led him toward the lake. It was a short, steep hike down to the water, but that slope provided them with privacy from the gaze of anyone casually driving by. As she had hoped, the beach was deserted. They were alone at last.

Wally helped Skye spread the quilt on the sand, then sat down and took off his shoes and socks. "Too bad you didn't tell me we were coming out here. I'd have brought my swimsuit."

"Don't worry." Skye's expression was poker-faced as she kicked off her sandals. "We have everything we need." She handed him a Beck's and a bottle opener before unpacking their picnic supper.

"When did you arrange all this?" Wally took a swig of the ice-cold beer.

"I swung by the supermarket before meeting you at the church."

"So that's why you didn't want me to pick you up," Wally deduced.

"Yep." Skye put a paper plate heaped with fried chicken, potato salad, and biscuits in front of him, along with a napkin wrapped around a plastic fork and knife. "You're always doing such nice things for me. I thought it was about time I reciprocated."

"Sugar"—Wally's voice deepened—"you have no idea all the nice things I'd like to do for you."

"We should probably talk about that, now that we're engaged."

"What do you mean?" Wally bit into the chicken leg he'd picked up.

"There's a lot of stuff I haven't asked you about and probably should have." Skye stared at the smooth blue water. "For instance, I had no idea you hadn't been in touch with Darleen since she left here two years ago, or that you two had had a prenup."

"Oh." Wally wiped his fingers on a napkin. "What else?"

"Money." Skye took a deep breath. "I know

your father is wealthy, but I'm completely in the dark about what your financial situation is like." Her stomach felt queasy. She hated discussing issues like this, but she summoned up a smile. "You know I pretty much live paycheck to paycheck and plow anything extra into my house."

"Money never seemed that important to you." His tone was cautious.

"It's not the cash per se," Skye hurried to explain. This was what she'd been afraid of. Growing up rich, Wally had probably been pursued by a lot of women. "It's how money affects people."

"Ah, now I understand your concern." He scooted nearer. "Okay. I don't have a trust fund. I do have a small inheritance from my mother, which would be about enough for us to pay cash for a really nice house. As for my father's empire, I don't know who's in his will or what he's done about the company, but I doubt my name is mentioned." He took her hand. "Does that make you feel better?"

"Yes." Skye kissed his cheek. "I'm not crazy, and I like being comfortably well-off as much as the next girl, but the thought of being insanely wealthy scares the heck out of me."

"Me, too." Wally hugged her. "Anything else you want to know?"

"Not at the moment." She had considered asking him whether he wanted children but could handle only one big life-changing question a day. And considering the annulment might take a year or more, she had time to work herself up to that topic.

"Good. I don't want us to have any secrets." Wally kissed her. "I want us both to go into this marriage with our eyes wide open, so ask away anytime."

"You, too," Skye said. Wally had worked with her mother for more than fifteen years, and even though May did not want him as a son-in-law, there was no way she had kept her mouth shut on her favorite topic—her kids. Which meant Wally already knew everything about Skye, so she felt pretty safe offering complete disclosure.

After they finished eating, Skye brought out a plate of chocolate-covered strawberries. "Are you ready for dessert, or would you rather wait a bit?"

"Definitely wait a while." Wally patted his flat stomach. "I'm stuffed."

"Me, too." Skye crawled over and sat between Wally's legs, resting her back against his chest. "So, what do you think about this latest development with the bookstore case?"

"Probably the same as you." Wally pulled her closer and rested his chin on top of her head. "Burglary was *not* the motive for the murder."

"I agree, but what makes you so sure?"

"The victim was hit over the head. Then the

bookshelves were pushed over on top of her."

Skye contemplated that piece of information for a moment, then said, "You're inferring that if the thief had already knocked her out, thus enabling his or her escape, why also crush Kayla? The crook would only do that if he or she wanted her dead."

"Exactly." Wally nodded. "And even if the criminal killed Kayla so she couldn't identify him or her, then why attempt a robbery in the first place when it was clear someone was still in the store? The lights were probably still on. And since we didn't find any evidence of forced entry, the door was still probably unlocked, too. Which means anyone could have walked in and caught the bad guy in the act. Most thieves wait for the place to be empty."

"Hmm." Skye bit her lip. "Good point."

"Those pieces of information, along with the books turning up in the library return box, make me think we're after a murderer, not a thief who killed someone in the course of a burglary." Wally's voice was confident.

"Great." Skye's tone was resigned. Should she mention Xavier's involvement with the bookstore? No. If Kayla was the intended victim, the fact that he had invested in the business wasn't relevant.

They were silent for a moment before Wally mused, "The county crime scene techs have finished with the store, so I gave Risé and Orlando the go-ahead to open up tomorrow. Maybe I should stop them." He paused, then said, "No." He trailed his fingers lightly up and down Skye's arms. "The techs already gathered all the evidence, and if the criminal was after Kayla, not the books, Tales and Treats probably doesn't have anything to do with the case. And if it does, better to let it open up and allow whoever murdered that girl to think he got away with it."

"Yep, keep an eye on the store and see what happens," Skye agreed. "But what I can't figure out is, who would want to kill a young girl like Kayla?"

"The usual motives are money, vengeance, and obsession." Wally covered her hands with his. "What do you know about her?"

"She doesn't seem to have any money. Her family is lower-middle-class and she needed that job."

"How about revenge or passion?" Wally asked. "Anyone mad at her, or does she have a jealous ex?"

"Not that I've heard. She seems well liked and dated Chase Wren all through high school. They were engaged to be married. You saw how broken up he is about her death." Skye twisted to look at Wally. "Do you want me to see what Xenia has to say?"

"That's a good idea. And I'll work on the

forensic side." Wally got to his feet. "Now, let's stop worrying about criminals and concentrate on us."

"Good idea." Skye took his hand and pulled herself up. "Want to take a dip?"

"Sure." Wally looked around. "Did you say you brought our suits?"

"Nope." Skye unbuttoned her ecru blouse, revealing a cream lace bra. "Is that a problem?" She twitched her shoulders and the top dropped onto the sand.

"Guess not." Wally grabbed the tails of his shirt and skimmed that garment along with his white T-shirt off over his head.

Skye shimmied out of her nut brown skirt. "I didn't think so." She fingered the top of her ivory satin panties.

He unzipped his uniform trousers and kicked off them and his Jockeys. "I'm ready."

"Yes. I would say you definitely are." Skye unhooked her bra and wiggled out of her under-wear. "Race you to the raft."

CHAPTER 14

The Turn of the Screw

Skye was still smiling when she arrived at work Tuesday morning. Her night with Wally had been fabulous. They'd gotten a lot of issues between them cleared up, and the rest of the time they'd spent together was better than she'd thought possible. Even the ominous note she found in her mailbox from Neva Llewellyn, the junior high principal, couldn't wipe the grin off her face.

"Why are you so happy?" Ursula Nelson, the school secretary, watched her with suspicious beetle brown eyes. "Didn't you see that message from Neva?"

"I saw it." Skye refused to give the older woman the satisfaction of appearing concerned. "Please tell her I'm available anytime she's ready to see me."

"Go right in." Ursula rose from her chair like a bird of prey and flapped her wing toward the principal's closed door. "She's been waiting for you."

Skye glanced at her watch. It was barely eight o'clock and the staff wasn't required to be at the school for another half hour. What in the heck had gotten Neva in such a state? She searched her mind for any recent offenses, but the first few weeks of classes had gone smoothly. Surely Neva didn't share Homer's aversion to Skye's work with the police.

When Skye entered the principal's office, Neva, seated at a gleaming cherrywood writing table roughly the size of a cruise ship, looked up and said, "Would you like a cup of coffee?"

"Uh." Skye was immediately wary. Neva had never offered her any refreshment before. "Sure."

"How do you take it?"

"Cream and two packages of Sweet'N Low, if you have it, or three sugars."

Neva made a moue of distaste but rose and walked over to a sideboard that contained an elaborate apparatus. As she pressed various buttons, Skye took a seat on one of the pair of Queen Anne chairs facing the desk. She fished in her tote for her calendar, a notepad, and a pencil, then put the bag by her feet.

"Enjoy." Neva handed Skye a delicate cup and saucer decorated with tiny pink roses.

"Thank you." Skye breathed in the wonderful aroma, then took a taste. *Wow!* "This is fantastic."

"Yes, it is." Neva sat back down and straightened the immaculate leather-bound blotter on her desktop. "I'm very particular about my coffee. One needs the right machine, filtered water, and of course, the best beans to make a good cup."

"I see." Skye wondered where Neva was leading. She wasn't usually inclined to waste time chatting. "Any particular brand you prefer?"

"I usually order my beans directly from Kona, Hawaii, but these are from Tales and Treats." Neva took a sip. "Mr. Erwin suggested it, and I must say, he was correct in his assessment."

"He seems very knowledgeable about that sort of thing," Skye agreed.

"Which, in a way, brings me to why I wanted to see you this morning." Neva ran a fingertip along the rim of her cup. "I understand both you and Tales and Treats had a difficult weekend."

"Yes, that's true." *Shoot!* Was Neva also going to yell at her about being the pied piper for the dead? "The protesters on Saturday were bad enough, but finding that poor girl on Sunday was awful." There. Maybe if Skye made it clear she didn't enjoy discovering bodies, Neva wouldn't berate her for doing so.

"I imagine it was," Neva whispered. A single tear slid down her cheek, and she wiped it away, then cleared her throat. "You're probably unaware that Kayla Hines was my goddaughter."

"Oh, my." Skye swallowed hard. "You're right, I didn't know. I'm so sorry for your loss. Would you like to talk about her?"

183

"Thank you for your condolences." Neva leaned forward. "But I didn't bring you in here for sympathy or grief counseling."

"Oh?" Skye's heart jumped in alarm, but she forced an unperturbed look on her face.

"From what I've been told, the authorities are claiming that Kayla's death was a result of a break-in gone wrong." Neva's intense gaze bore into Skye. "Which means the police will use that as an excuse to limit the investigation."

"No, but—"

"You've got to find out who killed her," Neva interrupted Skye. "The murderer must be punished."

"Do you suspect someone?" Skye asked. "Was there anyone who hated Kayla or had it in for her?"

"No." Neva shook her head. "Everyone loved her. There was something about Kayla that drew people to her." She frowned. "And that's the problem. There's no obvious villain, so the police will give up after only a cursory investigation and blame it on the burglary."

"I'm sure the officials will use every means available to find Kayla's murderer." Skye hadn't asked Wally whether she should mention that he no longer considered burglary the motive. "And since I do work as the police consultant, I will offer any help I can."

"That's not enough." Neva tapped a manicured nail on the desktop. "As I understand it, the police only seek your advice if the crime was psychologically motivated."

"That's often true." Skye searched for a way to set Neva's mind at rest without revealing anything Wally might want kept quiet. "But since I found her, I'm already involved, and I will be working the case."

"Kayla's parents won't push." Neva shook her head, clearly not accepting Skye's reassurances. "My cousin is under her husband's thumb and too busy with her second family to spend any energy on Kayla. And Kayla's stepfather doesn't care what happened to her."

"I'm sorry to hear that. It sounds as if Kayla had to grow up fast and rely on herself and her friends to get by."

"Kayla had such talent and ambition," Neva explained. "But she was torn because she yearned for a real home but wanted a career that would make it difficult to settle down."

"That's a tough choice." Skye's tone was soothing.

"I'm counting on you." Neva gazed at Skye unblinkingly. "You seem to have a special talent for solving mysteries."

"Not really." Skye stood up. "The *Star* has exaggerated my part in previous investigations." She backed away from the desk, bumping into a delicate butterfly table and leaving a scuff on the ivory wall.

Neva rose, too. A line appeared between her brows as she contemplated the scrape on her formerly pristine paint, and Skye winced. That mark was undoubtedly going straight onto Skye's permanent record. The one Neva kept in her head.

"The police department does a great job," Skye babbled, knowing she should shut up. "I'm happy to help, but they don't need me."

"Be that as it may." Neva jerked the cuffs of her taupe wool suit jacket for emphasis. "My goddaughter deserves an advocate."

Skye reached the door. Tasting freedom, she put her hand on the knob, but Neva grabbed her wrist, thwarting her escape. "And I'm going to see she has two—you and me."

"I'll do what I can." She freed herself from the older woman's grasp, unsure how else to respond. The junior high principal had never shared anything personal with her before—which, come to think of it, wasn't an altogether bad thing.

Neva murmured, "It isn't right, how her parents ignored her." As Skye stepped over the threshold and started down the hall, she heard the principal mutter, "They treated her like a servant. Worse, like a ghost. Why didn't I ever do something about that?"

Skye blew out a breath of relief as she rounded the corner and was out of the woman's sight. She felt sorry for Neva, but there was no way she was

186

going to question the principal's past inaction regarding her goddaughter. At the moment, the best Skye could do was pass the information about Kayla's neglectful family to Wally and see whether he wanted to pursue it. She couldn't think of any reason her parents would want Kayla dead. Heck, it sounded as if they barely knew she was alive.

A few minutes later, Skye sat in her office staring at the brown stains on the white ceiling tiles. She often thought those blots could be used to administer a Rorschach test. Too bad that was an assessment tool rarely used by school psychologists anymore.

The windowless room was painted yield-sign yellow and was no bigger than a walk-in closet. Skye had attempted to dispel the claustrophobic effect by arranging crisp white curtains around a travel-poster scene of the mountains. The custodian had originally used this space to store cleaning supplies, and there was nothing she could do about the faint lingering smell of ammonia. The pine-scented air freshener she'd plugged into the only outlet had made her sneeze, so she'd discarded it, preferring the stench to the sniffles.

Still, she was grateful for the private office. Not having to share or beg for a room every time she came to the building was a blessing. Many school psychologists would give up both their sick days and their retirement funds to have that luxury.

Skye's thoughts were interrupted by the jangling of her newly installed telephone—a perk she still wasn't sure how she'd gotten. She stared at the blinking light, trying to remember whether she was supposed to pick up the receiver, then press the button, or vice versa.

Mentally flipping a coin, she did the former, then crossing her fingers, said tentatively, "This is Skye Denison. May I help you?"

"It's about time." Her mother's voice blared from the handset's speaker. "I've been calling since six o'clock. I tried you at home and on your cell. I finally remembered this number a few minutes ago." She paused for breath. "Why aren't you answering your phones? Is something wrong?" May didn't wait for any real troubles; if circumstances weren't exactly as she expected them to be, she made up problems.

"Everything is fine." Skye twisted the phone's cord. "Why do you always think the worst?"

"Because then I'm pleasantly surprised if it doesn't happen." May's tone was tart. "If everything is so hunky-dory, why couldn't I reach you?"

"Uh." Should she admit she'd spent the night at Wally's, which would send May into a diatribe of how wrong he was for Skye, or should she fib? She chose a middle path. "I left early this morning to go swimming," she said, which was true. She just hadn't left from her own house. "And you know I can't have my cell on when I'm at school."

"Humph." May made an unhappy noise.

"You know, Mom . . ." She paused, aware that what she was about to say wouldn't make a difference but unable to stop herself. "Being out of touch for a couple of hours does not automatically mean that I'm dead. I'm sure if I was, one of the town gossips would inform you."

"That isn't funny, missy. I've had a bad morning. First, the phone rang at three a.m., scaring me to death. Then when I answered, someone giggled and hung up."

"Well, Mom"—Skye couldn't resist giving May a little zinger—"there are worse things than getting a call for a wrong number at three a.m."

"Like what?"

"It could have been the right number."

Without missing a beat, May continued. "Next, I find out your brother's bought an engagement ring. And to top it all off, you disappear."

Yikes! How had May found out about Vince? "Are you sure?" Skye stalled, wanting to hear exactly what her mother knew about Vince and Loretta before responding. "Could Vince have just been helping a friend pick one out?"

"No." May was adamant. "Aunt Kitty's sister

saw him over in Kankakee at a jewelry store in the mall last Friday."

"Maybe it wasn't him." Skye was surprised the news had taken so long to reach her mother.

"It was him."

"Is she sure what he was buying was an engagement ring?" Skye kept trying to poke holes in the story. "Could it have been some other kind of ring?"

"It was a two-carat diamond solitaire set in platinum," May stated flatly.

"How the heck did Aunt Kitty's sister find that out?" Skye couldn't imagine someone being able to provide such detail with just a visual.

"The jeweler is her second cousin's niece by marriage on her father's side."

Holy mackerel! If Homeland Security had the spies that Skye's family had, America would never have to worry about terrorists again.

"Look, Mom, I'm sure there's some explanation." Skye thought fast. "I bet he was picking it up for someone. I think he mentioned one of the guys in his band was getting married." Which was technically true, since Vince *was* a member of the group.

"If Vince is engaged, I'd better be the first to know and not the last." May's voice held the outrage of a teenage girl being denied an iPod. "I want you to go talk to him and find out what's going on."

"Mom." She tried to figure out how to respond to May without admitting anything. "He's nearly forty years old. He deserves some privacy."

"It's not like I'm asking him for a list of the sexual positions he uses." May snorted. "I just want to know if my baby's engaged."

Ew! Skye nearly dropped the receiver. May was really upset if she was talking about sex.

"So, you have to find out," May finished saying. "I've been so worried; I couldn't get a thing done today. I'm lucky I got the bed made, the breakfast dishes washed, and the carpet vacuumed."

"Mom, it's not even nine o'clock." Skye blew out an exasperated breath. "The day is hardly over."

"Whatever." May shrugged off Skye's comment. "Just find out what's going on with your brother."

"Why don't you ask him yourself when you feed him today?" Skye continued to be miffed that her mother delivered meals to Vince at his hair salon. She never brought food to school for Skye.

"He said he didn't need lunch this week because salesmen were bringing pizza and subs a couple of days, and he'd have the leftovers the rest of the time." May's voice held disbelief that her son would prefer takeout food to her cooking. "In fact, he said he was superbusy this week and probably wouldn't talk to me until after Sunday." She paused for breath. "Which is why I can't call him, and you need to speak to your brother, then report back to me."

"I'll try." Skye poised her finger over the disconnect button. "Listen, Mom, I've got to go. I've got a lot of kids to see today."

"Whoa, Nelly, not so fast." Apparently May was far from finished. "A little bird said that you and Wally were talking to Father Burns."

"We told you, he's filing the papers to get an annulment." Skye stiffened. *Now what?*

"And how's that going?" May sounded like she already knew the answer.

"Fine." Skye silently counted to ten, then did it again. "Why?"

"I heard that they can't find that ex-wife of his." May's tone was gleeful. "What if he killed her and the body is buried in his backyard?"

Skye took a deep breath before answering; screaming at her mother would only mean she'd have to go to confession. "You know darn well Darleen moved to Alaska. Why would you even say something like that?"

May had talked herself into a corner but rallied. "You never know. Look at all those people on TV who live next door to serial killers without ever realizing it, then claim their neighbors were so nice."

"Mom, leave it alone." Skye's voice was firm. "Or do you want Wally and me to elope?" *Oops!* She probably shouldn't have mentioned the E word.

Her mother's scream was loud enough to be heard in Chicago; luckily Skye had moved the receiver away from her ear. "Now, there's someone knocking on my office door and I really have to go." Skye didn't wait for her mother to respond. "Love you. Love to Dad. Bye."

She kept her finger on the disconnect button while she tried to figure out how to have her calls sent directly to voice mail. Skye knew her mother would call back as soon as she figured out a comeback.

Skye was chewing over the fact that she and her mother could keep several psychiatrists busy well into the next millennium when the PA system squawked, "Ms. Denison, please come to the office." Ursula's voice was both formal and annoyed, which meant someone was with her, and he or she was making a request of which the secretary didn't approve.

She felt a frisson of unease. Had May decided to come in person to harangue her further? Her mother and Ursula had some longtime feud going, Skye had no idea what about.

"Ms. Denison, please come to the office."

Yikes! Ursula hadn't even given her a minute to get there before repeating the message. Skye wasn't expecting any parents, and if one had come without an appointment, that usually meant trouble.

Skye grabbed her key, locked the door behind

her, and rushed toward the front of the school. When she entered the main office, she hurried to the counter and asked Ursula, "Why didn't you use the intercom?"

"Your line was busy." Ursula clipped off the words, giving them an impatient edge.

"Sorry." Skye had long ago stopped trying to defend herself to Ursula. "What's up?"

"Her." The secretary pointed behind her to where Risé Vaughn stood in the health room doorway chatting with Abby Fleming, the school nurse.

"She"—Ursula's pause was almost imperceptible—"insisted on seeing you."

"Oh." Skye looked toward Risé. "You wanted to talk to me?"

"Is there somewhere we can speak in private?" Risé glanced pointedly at Ursula.

"Is this about one of our students?"

Risé ignored Skye's question. "I'd prefer to speak to you alone."

"Okay." Skye gestured over her shoulder. "We can use my office."

"Thank you."

Now what? This day was going downhill fast. Skye led the way and Risé followed, the only sound the squeak of the bookstore owner's tennis shoes on the worn gray linoleum.

Once they were seated, Skye behind her desk and her visitor on a folding chair, Risé said, "I hope this isn't a bad time. You seem a little tense."

"No. It's fine." Skye rubbed the back of her neck. "I just got off the phone with my mother."

"Did you two have words?" Risé's expression was sympathetic.

"Yeah." Skye made a wry face. "But I didn't get to use mine."

"Ah."

When Risé didn't go on, Skye asked, "What can I do for you, Risé? I don't have any information I can share with you about your burglary or Kayla's death."

"I'm not here about that." Risé flipped her ponytail over her shoulder. Today she was wearing blue jeans and an orange T-shirt with FICTION REVEALS TRUTHS THAT REALITY OBSCURES—JESSAMYN WEST printed on it.

"Then how can I help you?" Skye wondered what Risé was doing at the junior high. "Do you have a student here?"

"No, Orlando and I never had children," Risé stated, almost daring Skye to comment.

"I see." Skye tilted her head. Why was the bookstore owner pussyfooting around? Risé had struck her as someone who was more direct.

"Anyway." Risé cleared her throat. "I don't generally like to ask for favors . . ."

Oh-oh.

"But I'm in a bind." Risé reached into her shoulder bag and handed Skye a flyer. "Part of Kayla's duties was to lead our teen book club."

"I remember seeing a notice for the book club, and having Kayla lead it was a terrific idea."

"Thanks. I thought having someone younger would encourage the teens not only to participate in the group, but also to express themselves more freely."

"That makes sense." Skye sneaked a peek at her watch. She really needed to get to work. At this rate, she'd be up until midnight doing paperwork, trying to make up the time she'd already lost this morning. "Did a lot of kids sign up for the club?"

"I wasn't sure what to expect, but I'd say yes. We have twelve on the list and sold nearly twenty copies of the book, so more may show up."

"That's great." Skye beamed. She'd been correct in thinking the bookstore would promote reading among the teenagers. "Will you be leading the discussion since Kayla is, ah . . . not available?"

"That's my problem." Risé's shoulders drooped. "Not only haven't I read the book, but I don't have any relationship with the kids."

"But—"

Risé cut Skye off. "If they don't enjoy themselves this first time, they won't come back." She straightened. "My husband and I have put all our money into this business. We need the teens' support."

"That's true." Skye knew Risé was right. Teens

could be unforgiving if they were disappointed. "But what do you think I can do?"

"You can lead the group." Risé held up a hand to stop Skye's protest. "My new employee tells me that the kids all like you."

"I don't know about that." Skye's cheeks turned pink. She didn't handle compliments well. Changing the subject, she asked, "Who have you hired to replace Kayla?"

"Xenia Craughwell."

"Really?" Skye was shocked. Xenia didn't need the money, and it was hard to imagine the girl in a position where she would have to be pleasant to people. "How did you find someone so quickly?"

"She came to me yesterday and filled out an application. She passed my little reading and math test with flying colors and really seems to love books." Risé looked at Skye with a curious expression. "Why do you ask?

"Uh . . ." Skye thought fast, not wanting to give her real reasons. "She just never mentioned that she was looking for a job."

"Oh." Risé seemed satisfied. "So, will you take over the teen club?"

Skye wavered. "I'd really like to help you out, but my plate is pretty full right now." She hated to see the teen book club die out before it even got started. "Isn't there someone else you could ask?"

"Not at this late date." Risé shook her head. "The group meets Thursday night."

"Well . . ."

"Last Saturday, at our grand opening, you mentioned you had read *If I Have a Wicked Stepmother, Where's My Prince?*, which is our selection."

"True," Skye admitted. "But . . ."

"You'd be perfect." Risé's tone was cajoling.

"I don't know." Skye tried to avoid looking into the woman's desperate eyes.

"Maybe your friend, the school librarian, would colead with you," Risé coaxed. "She seemed really excited that Scumble River finally had a bookstore."

"Okay," Skye gave in. "But you need to find someone else for next month. I already have two jobs, not to mention a fiancé and my family to deal with, so I can't take this on permanently."

"That's all I ask. Next month Xenia can take over. We couldn't afford to pay someone on a permanent basis, but"—Risé pulled a checkbook from her open purse—"name your fee."

"A white chocolate mocha latte and some of Orlando's amazing shortbread." Skye smiled. "I know Trixie will work for treats, too."

"We'll supply you both for a year." Risé got up. "You're a lifesaver."

"How's Orlando doing?" Skye wondered whether his falling off the wagon had started him on a downward spiral.

"He's working on remaining sober." Risé's

face was hard to read. "He *says* he wants to win back my trust, but we'll see." She opened the door. "We're having one of his favorite authors for a book signing on Saturday, and that's helping him stay positive. I just hope we get a decent turnout."

"A book signing?" Skye clapped her hands. "How exciting. I'll definitely be there."

"Good." Risé smiled wryly. "Bring a lot of your friends."

Skye accompanied Risé to the school's front door. As she watched her walk into the parking lot, she thought how similar to Risé Kayla had looked from the back. Which one had really been the intended victim? The young girl whom no one had any apparent reason to kill, or the woman with a lot of enemies?

CHAPTER 15

Pride and Prejudice

B y five o'clock, Skye had secured Trixie as a coleader for the book club, had attended two Pupil Personnel Services meetings, and was eager to get off work to go talk to Wally. Her mind had raced the entire day with all the information she'd gathered, and the more she thought about it, the more she was convinced that the murderer had meant to kill Risé.

Unfortunately, tonight was the night of Wally's monthly dinner meeting with all the police chiefs in Stanley County. Along with the sheriff, they got together at Harry's restaurant to share intel. And since Skye had worked so late, she had only a half hour to discuss the case with him before he needed to leave for Laurel. But first she had to find him.

As she hurried toward the parking lot, Skye dug her cell phone from the bottom of her tote, powered it on, and dialed his private line at the police station. After four rings, it went to voice mail and she disconnected. Her next try was his cell, which also went to voice mail, and then his home phone, where the answering machine picked up.

Sheesh! Had he left for the county seat early? Unlocking her car, Skye blew out an exasperated sigh. She had no choice. Although she'd been avoiding her mother all day, she'd have to phone the PD's nonemergency line, even if May was the dispatcher on duty that night.

Skye held her breath as the call was answered, "Scumble River Police, Fire, and Emergency."

Hot damn! She had lucked out. "Zelda?"

"Yes. Who's this?"

"It's Skye." She threw her tote bag onto the passenger seat, slid behind the wheel, and put the key in the ignition. "Is the chief around?"

"Sorry. You just missed him." Zelda Martinez's low, sultry voice thrummed through the line, and Skye wondered briefly what effect Scumble River's only female officer was having on the rest of the force.

"Did he head over to Laurel already?" Skye buckled her seat belt and turned the ignition key.

"Hold on a second and I'll check." There was a short pause; then Zelda said, "According to the board, he's going home first."

"Okay." Skye backed the Bel Air out of its parking spot and headed toward Wally's house. "Thanks."

A few minutes later Skye turned into the driveway of the four-room bungalow that Wally owned. It was hard to believe that the son of a Texas oil tycoon lived so modestly, but she certainly understood why he didn't want anyone else in Scumble River to know about his affluent background. She'd been relieved Monday night when he'd told her that he didn't have a trust fund or expect to be his father's heir, but others might not feel the same way.

Skye knocked, then let herself in the back door. Hearing water running, she was glad she and Wally had exchanged keys when they got engaged. Otherwise, she'd be stuck on his doorstep until he got out of the shower.

Passing through the enclosed back porch that had been turned into a laundry room, she noticed a folding rack hung with freshly pressed navy uniform shirts, no doubt ironed by Wally's part-time housekeeper, Dorothy Snyder. As Skye crossed the kitchen, she wondered whether Dorothy would continue to work for them once they were married. And if she did, would it be awkward, since she was one of May's best friends?

When she entered the bedroom, Skye was tempted to arrange herself across Wally's king-size mattress and surprise him when he got out of the shower. Reluctantly, she discarded the idea, realizing that with so little time before he had to leave for his meeting, it would be best to greet him upright and fully clothed.

Curling up in a leather club chair in the corner, she waited for him to emerge from the adjoining bathroom. Wally strolled out a few minutes later, still dripping and drying his back with a cocoa brown towel. It took him a second or so to spot Skye, but when he did, a slow grin spread across his handsome face.

Skye smiled back, her gaze traveling from his long, sinewy legs, to his slim hips, up to the molded bronze muscles of his chest and shoulders, and coming to rest on his depthless, dark brown eyes.

"Darlin', I didn't expect to see you tonight." Wally ambled over to her, took her hands, and drew her to her feet. "I wish all surprises were this good."

Skye wound her arms around his neck and gave him a light kiss. "You sweet-talker."

He pressed her body tightly to his. "Just the facts, ma'am."

She felt a lurch of excitement and had to fight the desire to run her fingers down his naked body. "I wanted to catch you before you left for your dinner to talk to you about what I heard today."

His lips teased her earlobe, and he whispered, "Can it wait?"

A delicious shudder ran through her body, but she gathered her self-control. "Probably not."

His breath warmed her throat. "Are you sure?"

Her resolve started to melt, and she forced herself to step away from him. "Yes."

A shadow of annoyance crossed his face; then he turned toward his dresser, slid open the top drawer, and said over his shoulder, "What's up?"

As he put on underwear and socks, she told him what Neva had said to her, and Skye's own thoughts as she watched Risé walk away, finishing with, "And I really think that not only was the murder the primary intention, as we discussed last night, but that Risé was the intended victim."

Wally zipped up a pair of black jeans and threaded a belt through the loops. "Just because Kayla's godmother says everyone loved her doesn't make it true."

"I know that, but during my lunch break today I checked her school records. She was a good student, participated in activities, and never got so much as a detention for chewing gum."

"Still, you said there was a problem with her parents." He looked unconvinced as he pulled a silver-gray turtleneck over his head. "What was your impression of their reaction Sunday when we notified them of Kayla's death?"

"Well. They both appeared genuinely shocked, and the mom was certainly devastated." Skye nibbled her thumbnail. "But the stepdad seemed like he couldn't wait to get rid of us." She tilted her head. "What did you think?"

"The same."

"So unless Neva's description is absolutely the opposite of the situation, Kayla's parents were totally uninvolved with her life, which would mean no reason to kill her. Besides, she and her boyfriend were getting married in a month. She'd be completely out of their hair after that, so why murder her?"

"You have a point." Wally grabbed a black tweed blazer from his closet. "I'm still not clear on the logistics." He stuffed his wallet into his pants pocket and grabbed his keys. "Wouldn't whoever murdered Kayla have noticed it was her and not Risé?"

"This is what I think happened." Skye clipped Wally's cell to his belt for him as she explained, "I think when the murderer arrived, Kayla had her back to the entrance. Maybe she was reaching to put away a book on a high shelf."

"Wouldn't she have heard the bells over the door jingle when it was opened?"

"Yes, but she probably said something like, 'Be right there.' Or 'Sorry. We're closed,' and didn't turn around." Skye paused to gather her thoughts, then continued, "So the killer walks up to her and whacks her on the back of the head, thinking she's Risé."

"Then why was she found facedown?" Wally looked at Skye in the dresser's mirror as he combed his damp hair. "In your scenario, she should have fallen backward."

"Unless the blow didn't knock her out immediately. In that case she would have swung around to see who hit her, and then fallen forward," Skye explained. "It's my understanding that people don't always die right away from a head injury."

"Okay." Wally put his hand on the small of Skye's back and walked with her out of the bedroom and toward the door. "Say we go with your theory that the store owner, not the clerk, was the intended victim. Who wanted to kill Risé?"

"Unfortunately, there's quite a list." Skye frowned. "And about half of the names on it are my relatives'."

Wally wasn't entirely persuaded by Skye's reasoning. However, since the stolen books hadn't yielded any usable fingerprints and they didn't have any other leads, he did agree that in addition to investigating the murder as if Kayla was the intended victim, he'd have an officer look into the bookseller's background, as well.

He also approved Skye talking to her cousins Kevin and Hugo, her cousin-in-law Flip, Charlie, and Tomi. Thankfully there was no need to talk to Pru Cormorant again. The English teacher had made her peace with Risé before the murder took place.

As Skye sat in her car watching Wally drive off, she realized that once again she'd forgotten to tell him about Vince's engagement to Loretta and the couple's plans to run away and get married in Las Vegas. Was she just absentminded, or was she subconsciously afraid that Wally might suggest they make it a double elopement?

Nah. Wally knew she wanted a church wedding, and he would never ask her to give up that dream. Tucking away that positive thought, Skye started the Bel Air but didn't put it into gear. *Shoot!* Now that she was convinced Risé was the intended victim, she probably should have mentioned Xavier's investment in the bookstore.

On the other hand, what possible reason could Xavier have to kill Risé? Without her, Tales and Treats would never succeed. Even having met Orlando only twice, Skye was sure there was no way he could run the business by himself.

Next, Skye considered her list of suspects. Which person should she question first? Better yet, what excuses could she use to drop by and see them? Hugo lived in Clay Center; she'd save him for when she could catch him at his used-car dealership.

It was a little past five thirty—suppertime for most Scumble Riverites. That meant Tomi would be busy at her restaurant, and both Kevin and Flip would be eating dinner with their families. That left Uncle Charlie. Tuesday was his bowling night, and he always ate at the alley's grill before the league started.

Skye parked in the bowling alley's sparsely

populated lot. The senior men's league didn't start until six thirty, so the few cars present belonged to either bar patrons or men like Charlie —older bachelors or widowers who preferred not to cook for themselves.

The wind had picked up, and as Skye walked around to the front of the building, she held down her skirt, not wanting to flash anyone driving down Basin Street. When she pushed through the glass door, the glaring overhead lights made her blink.

While her eyes adjusted, Skye listened to Frank Sinatra crooning from the speakers. He was bragging about doing things his way—a sentiment she understood and approved of but didn't practice as often as she should.

Charlie wasn't among the half dozen men at the bar, so Skye continued into the grill. He was seated in a booth reading the Laurel paper and drinking a chocolate milk shake. She slid in across from him and flicked the newspaper with her thumb and index finger.

Scowling, Charlie lowered the paper and growled, "Dammit, I told you—" He cut himself off. "Skye, what are you doing here, honey?"

Unlike her cousins, whom she wouldn't put past committing murder, she was sure her god-father had not killed Risé. Unfortunately, he'd made his dislike of the bookstore owner clear, so she hoped he had an alibi and could be crossed off the list.

"Have you eaten yet?"

"No. I just ordered a minute ago."

"Great." Skye put her purse down beside her. "How about some company?"

"Sure." Charlie folded the newspaper and set it aside. "To what do I owe the privilege?"

"Nothing special." Skye took a menu from the metal holder that contained the salt and pepper shakers, catsup, mustard, and a bottle of hot sauce. "Wally's got a meeting, and when I drove past and saw your car, it reminded me that you eat here on Tuesdays."

"Is everything okay with you?" Charlie's voice was apprehensive.

"Yep." Skye kept her gaze on the laminated pages showing pictures of burgers and fries. "How about you?"

"Fair to middling." Charlie eyed her thoughtfully. "Talk to your mother today?"

"Yes." *Ay-yi-yi!* She'd forgotten that May had probably filled Charlie in on Vince buying an engagement ring. "She called me at work this morning."

Skye had never quite figured out how her mother and Charlie had become so close. In the past she'd even wondered if they'd once had an affair, but she'd finally realized that Charlie's love for May was paternal, and May reciprocated with daughterlike affection. Both fulfilled a need in the other. Charlie had never married or had children, and May's father had died while she was still a teenager.

Before Charlie could question Skye further, Frannie appeared to take her order.

As soon as they exchanged pleasantries and the girl walked away, Skye, hoping to divert the conversation away from Vince, asked, "Are Orlando and Risé still staying at the motor court?"

"Thank God, no." Charlie's voice boomed. "The building inspector approved their new apartment yesterday, and they moved that afternoon."

"You said you were mad that they were going to be taking guests from you with their B and B rooms." Skye took a quick scan of the grill. Two men shared a booth, and a teenager sat at the counter. No one appeared to be paying them any attention. "Why aren't you sorry to lose *their* business?"

"It dawned on me that the kind of people who would stay with them aren't the kind that rent rooms at motor courts." Charlie took a slurp of his milk shake. "Erwin told me that they're going to have murder mystery and romance weekends and that kind of crap. What the hell, they might even bring in some trade."

"Wonderful." Skye blew out an inward sigh of relief. That removed Charlie's motive; now, if he had an alibi, everything would be perfect.

From Xenia's information, Skye figured the

victim had been attacked sometime between when Risé left at eight fifteen and Xenia came looking for Kayla at eleven. Whoever killed the girl probably turned off the light when he or she left the store.

"Yep." Charlie looked at Skye a little strangely. "Everything's peachy."

They sat in silence as Frannie served their meals; then as Charlie fussed with his cheese-burger, Skye said as casually as she could, "Are you still seeing that woman over in Brooklyn?"

"No." Charlie swirled a French fry in a pool of catsup and popped it in his mouth. "She was getting too serious."

Skye poked at her chef's salad. "That's too bad." The lettuce, boiled ham strips, and cubes of American cheese were hidden by a thick layer of Thousand Island dressing. So much for eating a healthy meal. She should have had the corn dog and onion rings she really wanted. "Then you were alone Saturday evening?"

"Nope. I spent the night with my new lady friend, the animal doc from Laurel." Charlie's bland expression didn't alter, but there was a suspicious flicker in his bright blue eyes. "Why are you so concerned about my social life all of a sudden?"

"Uh." Skye really didn't want to admit she was asking for an alibi. "No reason." She hurried to change the subject. "Oh, look. There's Bunny."

The bowling alley manager was strolling from table to table, chatting with the customers. Skye waved, and the older woman headed toward them.

Tonight Bunny's outfit was subdued, and Skye wondered whether anything was wrong. The redhead wore a tight black sweater, knit pants, and medium-heeled ankle boots. Had her subscription to the Frederick's of Hollywood catalog lapsed?

After Bunny had enveloped Skye in a hug, Skye asked, "Everything going well?"

"Better now." Bunny grinned. "For a while there I wasn't sure if life was passing me by or trying to run me down."

"What changed?" Skye asked.

"I came up with a new way to make some extra cash *and* improve my social life."

"Really?" Skye teased. "Does it have anything to do with that nice-looking gentleman who saved you a parking spot at the bookstore's grand opening the other day?"

"Maybe." Bunny lowered her voice. "But I haven't told Sonny Boy, so I can't talk about it yet."

Oh-oh! Skye cringed. Were Bunny's improved love life and her new moneymaking scheme connected? That couldn't be good.

Before Bunny could say more, she caught sight of two teenagers trying to sneak into the bar and teetered off, saying over her shoulder, "I gotta take care of that. See ya later."

"I wonder what she's thought up this time," Skye muttered.

"You probably don't want to know." Charlie shot Skye a hard look. "I'd say you have your hands full trying to get everyone's alibis for the time that poor little gal was murdered."

CHAPTER 16
Les Misérables

Skye left the bowling alley at six thirty. She was thrilled that Uncle Charlie was in the clear but worried about how she would question the others. Although none of her cousins was as smart as Charlie was, they were a lot meaner. If they suspected she was interrogating them, they might kill her. Or worse, rat her out to May, who wouldn't take kindly to her daughter trying to incriminate a family member.

With that in mind, she decided to talk to the only nonrelative on her list, Tomi Jackson. Skye was fairly sure the diminutive woman wouldn't attack her or tattle to May, but she was a little afraid that Tomi would ban her from the Feed Bag—which might be the most horrible outcome of all. Other than McDonald's and the bowling alley, Tomi's was the only place in town to get a meal without cooking it yourself. Unless you counted the fried chicken from the grocery store's deli department.

Just as Skye had hoped, the Feed Bag's parking lot was nearly empty. On weeknights the restaurant closed at seven, so only a few stragglers would be lingering over their coffee. Tomi wouldn't be busy, and Skye wouldn't have to find some excuse to visit her at her home.

The last time the Feed Bag had been redecorated was 1984, and the mauve paint and brass railings showed every bit of their age. More than twenty years of hard wear had taken a toll. Most of the vinyl seats had rips that had been repaired with duct tape, and the walls were pocked with dabs of color that didn't quite match the original. The original ferns had died more than a decade ago, and the plastic plants that replaced them were faded and dusty.

Tomi greeted Skye at the door. "What are you doing here so late, honey, and all by your lonesome?" Without waiting for an answer, she seated Skye at the booth nearest the cash register, then put a hand on her hip. "You and the chief didn't have a spat, did you?"

Ah. The joys of small-town living. "Nope. Wally's at a meeting in Laurel, and since I've had a busy day"—Skye barely stopped herself from rolling her eyes at the understatement—"I thought I'd treat myself to a piece of your famous lemon meringue pie before I head on home."

"Coming right up."

When Tomi came back with the dessert, Skye said, "I'd love some company if you aren't too busy."

"Sure. Let me grab a beer." Tomi turned and said over her shoulder, "I'll be right back."

Skye watched the tiny restaurateur speak to an employee, then dart into the kitchen.

When Tomi returned, she slid into the seat opposite Skye, twisted the cap from a bottle of Corona, took a long slug, wiped her mouth, and said, "I just gotta keep an eye on the register."

"No problem." Skye searched her mind for a topic of conversation that would lead into the questions she needed to ask. "Lots of excitement in town over that new bookstore."

"Sure is." Tomi patted a strand of hair back into her blond beehive. "Especially after what happened to that poor girl working there."

"Wasn't that a shame?" Skye cut off the tip of her pie with her fork. "Who would do such a thing?"

"Wasn't it some burglar?"

"Maybe." Skye chewed and swallowed. "But I wonder if it didn't have something to do with the store." She met Tomi's gaze. "I hear a lot of folks in town have a beef with the owners."

"Yeah." Tomi straightened the name tag that pinned the handkerchief to her pink uniform. "Scumble River doesn't like change."

"Or competition." Skye ate another bite of pie, letting the fluffy meringue melt on her tongue after savoring the tart lemon filling and finally the flaky crust. "Uncle Charlie said that Risé and

Orlando had ticked off a lot of business owners."

"So I hear." Tomi narrowed her eyes. "Especially your cousin Hugo."

"Yeah. Hard to believe someone can get so mad over something like a parking space." Skye was careful not to show what side she was on in that dispute. "It seemed to work out all right for the grand opening. Maybe they can come to some middle ground."

"Hugo, compromise?" Tomi snorted. "What universe are you living in?"

"Yeah, well . . ." Skye was almost done with her pie. She needed to bring the subject around to Tomi's own gripe about the store. "So, do you think Tales and Treats' café will lure away any of your customers?"

"Nah." Tomi wiped the moisture ring from her beer bottle with her apron. "My regulars won't pay four bucks for a cup of fancy coffee or want some citified pastry instead of my good old-fashioned cakes and pies."

"I don't know." Skye dabbed her mouth with her napkin. "People can be fickle. They get tired of the same old, same old."

"Maybe for a while, but they always come back to the comfortable and the familiar." Tomi shrugged. "And money talks. Here they can have a coffee and dessert for five dollars. At Tales and Treats it'll cost them close to double that amount."

"True." Skye wondered whether Charlie's information about Tomi being mad about the store opening was wrong. But just in case, she needed to see whether Tomi had an alibi. "Wally and I came by here Saturday night for some dessert after we got back from the movie in Joliet, but the parking lot was so packed we decided not to stop. You must have been really busy."

"Whoo-ee." Tomi finished her beer and started toward the register, where an old man was tapping his foot impatiently. "We sure were. We had Rosella Bonucci's retirement dinner, and she and her husband, Joe, have so many friends, no one wanted to leave. I'm usually out of here by ten on weekends, but that night I was here past midnight helping Carlos and Wanda clean up."

After confirming with the waitress and busboy that Tomi had indeed been with them until after twelve a.m. Saturday night, Skye paid her tab and left. Another suspect was off her list. That left her cousins. How could she approach them?

Kevin was the easiest; she could claim to want to review her insurance policies. He'd been bugging her to update them, and she had been putting him off for months. With Flip, she could say she'd heard he was doing some private carpentry now and wondered if he'd have time to give her an estimate on turning one of her spare bedrooms into a home office with built-in bookshelves.

That left Hugo. She couldn't pretend to want to buy a used car. If word got back to her dad or Charlie that she was even considering replacing the Bel Air, their feelings would be hurt. Which meant it would have to be a non-work-related reason.

She and Hugo had little in common except their genes. He was nearly ten years older than she was, and although his wife, Victoria, was closer to Skye's age, they'd never bonded, either. Victoria's only interest, besides her twelve-year-old son, Prescott, was maintaining her appearance. She spent all her time at hairstylists, nail salons, gyms, and tanning booths. Not places Skye often frequented, since both the cost and the time needed were prohibitive.

For the rest of Tuesday evening while Skye relaxed at home, and on and off the next day at school, she thought about how to approach Hugo. What pretext could she use? By the end of the afternoon, she'd conceded defeat. Since she couldn't come up with an idea, she'd go see Kevin that afternoon, then Flip in the early evening, and put off Hugo until the next day. Maybe by then some excuse would occur to her.

Skye wasn't able to leave work after the final bell, as she had planned. Instead, she was pulled into a last-minute conference regarding a student who was refusing to attend school, and by the time she'd gotten out of that discussion, she decided she'd better call Wally and let him know that both Charlie and Tomi had alibis.

Wally was in a hurry—he had to get to a meeting of the police commissioners—but he told Skye he'd assigned Martinez to check out Risé's background, and the officer would let him know ASAP what she found out. He also mentioned that he was still waiting for the ME and crime scene reports.

Because of all the delays, it was close to four thirty when Skye arrived at Kevin's insurance office, and she was afraid he might already have gone home.

As she locked the Bel Air, her cell phone rang. Sighing, she dug it out of the depths of her tote, checked to make sure it wasn't her mother calling to bug her about Vince and the engagement ring, then flipped it open and said, "Hello."

The display screen said ILLINOIS CALLER, so Skye had no idea who was on the other end until she heard, "Hi. This is Simon." His smooth tenor was oddly soothing. "I missed you at school and didn't know when you'd be home, so Frannie told me how to reach you." He paused, but when Skye didn't react—Frannie had been told not to share Skye's cell number with Simon —he continued, "I was wondering where things stand on Kayla's murder."

"Couldn't you ask Wally?" Skye pushed open

the office building's door and went in. "Or talk to the ME?"

"Boyd claims there's nothing new." Simon sounded unconvinced. "And the ME has promised to e-mail me his report before he leaves work today."

"So why are you asking me?" Skye looked around the small waiting room. It was empty; even the secretary's chair was vacant.

"Because I heard that you and Boyd talked to the librarian, and she had info about the stolen books."

"How did you hear that?" Skye asked. Although she wasn't surprised, she was annoyed. They'd hoped to keep Judy's revelation a secret.

"Anthony's mother, Sally, has been doing some of the funeral home's paperwork for me lately."

"Ah." Skye didn't bother to point out that Anthony should not have shared the info with Sally. She understood how hard it was to keep secrets from mothers. "Then you know as much as I do. Judy found the books in the library return box."

"So is Boyd still treating the case as a burglary?" Simon asked.

"Not entirely," Skye admitted. "We're checking to see if anyone wanted Kayla dead."

She felt a little guilty leaving out the fact that she believed the intended victim was Risé, but until she'd cleared her own family, she wasn't willing to share that little detail with anyone other than the person in charge of the investigation. The fact that that individual happened to be her fiancé was just a happy coincidence.

"Any luck?"

"Not so far." Skye shifted impatiently from foot to foot. "Have you found out any more about whatever Xavier is keeping secret?"

"No." Simon sounded frustrated. "He's as tight-lipped as a Swiss banker."

"I'm sorry to rush you, but I really need to go. I'm late for an appointment." Skye walked over to the closed office door. "Is there anything else?"

"I guess not." There was a long silence, and she almost thought he had hung up when he said wistfully, "I suppose you're busy tonight."

"Yes." Skye wrinkled her nose. "Believe it or not, Wally and I are going to the grand reopening of the Scumble River Roller Skating Rink."

"You're full of surprises lately," Simon commented. "I won't say have a good time. I can't imagine that. How about don't break a leg?"

"Thanks. Bye." Frowning, she flipped the phone closed. Wally had said she was full of surprises recently, too. Had she been that predictable before? Vowing to be more spontaneous, she turned back to the door and knocked on the fake wood panel.

A voice yelled, "Come in." Kevin was sitting at

his desk. He looked up and said, "Skye, what are you doing here?" Apparently realizing that wasn't a very welcoming way to greet both a client and a cousin, he smiled and added hastily, "Have a seat."

"I thought we could do that insurance review you've been reminding me about," Skye answered. "Unless you don't have time?"

"Well . . ." He glanced at his watch. "Ilene is expecting me home for supper pretty soon."

"Maybe I could just update my info, and you could get back to me?"

"Sure." Kevin unsuccessfully hid his irritation. "Let me turn the computer back on and bring up your file."

While Kevin's attention was focused on the PC, Skye said, as casually as she could manage, "I hear you have some new clients. I'm glad the bookstore owners are supporting local businesses."

"Yeah." He glanced at her distractedly as he moved his mouse around waiting for the monitor to come to life. "But I don't know if they'll continue to use local people. The wife wasn't too happy with me."

"Why not?" Skye smiled inwardly. *Jackpot!* This was exactly what she wanted to talk to him about.

"She accused me of pulling a bait and switch because the premium was more than I originally quoted." He frowned at the blank blue screen and anxiously tapped a couple of keys. "But it wasn't my fault. She failed to mention they would be renting out two of their upstairs rooms as B and Bs. The liability involved in having paying guests increased the cost of the insurance."

"Did you explain that to her?" Skye crossed her legs. "Or wouldn't she listen?"

"I told her and she seemed okay." Kevin smiled as the computer monitor filled with data. "But you never know if people believe you or not. And I'm afraid she might bad-mouth me around town."

"Risé doesn't strike me as the type." Skye watched her cousin closely. "And you know it wouldn't hurt you with your other clients."

"Probably not." Kevin rubbed his chin. "Scumble Riverites know I'm trustworthy."

Skye nodded, then said, "But your company *will* have to pay for the damages from the break-in, right?"

"Yes." Kevin jotted a few notes on a yellow pad. "But since the rare books were recovered, the rest is fairly minor. It might not end up being more than their deductible, so they may decide not to even file a claim."

"That would be good for you." Skye watched Kevin's expression closely. "But how about the dead girl? Won't her family sue?"

"Maybe, but there hasn't been any hint of that yet." Kevin scratched his head. "And since she was there after hours, we might be able to argue she wasn't acting as their employee at the time of her death."

"Great." Skye forced herself to sound happy for Kevin, but she hated the thought that the insurance company might wiggle out of paying Kayla's family for her loss.

"Okay. I've got your file up. Let's get started." Kevin's voice became all business. "How many auto accidents have you had in the past year?"

Once Skye had given Kevin all her new info, he stood up and escorted her to the door. "I'll get back to you tomorrow with my recommendations regarding your up-to-date insurance needs, but offhand, I'd say there shouldn't be much change." He grinned. "Especially since you stopped totaling cars."

"None of those was my fault," Skye reminded him as they walked into the reception area. She had been wracking her brains to figure out a way to ask Kevin about an alibi. "Say, did you and Ilene go to that party Saturday night she was telling me about?"

"What party?" Kevin looked confused. "We were away for the weekend at an insurance convention in St. Louis. We drove down Friday night and didn't get home until Monday afternoon. Maybe that's what she meant."

"Yeah." Skye hated lying, even if it was for a good cause. "I must have gotten confused." She waved and left, saying, "Talk to you later."

Once she was in her car, she made a quick call to Kevin's wife, wanting to confirm his alibi before he got home and talked to her. Skye's excuse was that she and Wally were thinking of taking a few days off, which was true, and she wondered if Ilene had enjoyed her weekend in St. Louis. Ilene assured Skye she'd had a wonderful time there.

Crossing Kevin off her suspect list, Skye drove home to grab a quick bite and change for her date. She had two more cousins to go, and if she hurried, she'd have time to drop by Flip's house on the way to the skating rink. Now, if she could only figure out a reason to talk to Hugo.

CHAPTER 17

The Call of the Wild

Bingo greeted Skye as she stepped inside her foyer. Once he'd had a sufficient number of chin scratches, he turned his back on her and marched into the kitchen. She found him sitting by his food dish, staring at it as if it might magically fill up on its own.

Skye fed the demanding cat, then made herself a toasted cheese sandwich and a bowl of tomato soup. She quickly devoured her meal, while sorting the mail into bills she could pay this month and those that would have to return to the end of the line.

As she climbed the stairs to change clothes, Bingo did figure eights between her legs. She enjoyed the feel of his soft fur against her ankles, but when she nearly tripped, she ordered him to stop.

He ignored her, and she finally scooped him up and carried him with her into the bedroom, muttering to him, "How is it that you can hear me open a can of Fancy Feast from anywhere in the house, but can't hear a simple command a few feet from your ears?"

After depositing the purring feline on her bed, Skye stood in front of her closet and pondered a question she never thought she'd ask herself as an adult. What does one wear to a party at a skating rink?

Wally had explained that the owner was an old friend of his, and he wanted to show his support. Milton Leigh had owned the rink from 1988 until 1999 but sold the business five years ago. Recently, he had repurchased it and restored the interior rink to its former glory. Milton was hoping the enterprise would be profitable enough to allow him to refurbish the exterior next. His goal was to do so within a year.

Considering all the family get-togethers Wally had attended for Skye, and all he'd need to be present at in the future, she was happy to accompany him tonight. Still, that didn't solve her clothing dilemma.

As she stared at the garments arranged in neat rows by category, color, and season, she dialed Vince's cell. Skye had been trying to reach him since yesterday, but all she ever got at any of his numbers was his voice mail, and so far despite the urgency of the messages she'd left, he hadn't called back. She wanted to let him know about May's knowledge of his engagement ring purchase herself, rather than trying to explain to a machine.

Once again her call went directly to his voice

mail. Even though she knew Vince didn't answer his phone when he was working on someone's hair, and he was notoriously bad about responding to messages, this was getting ridiculous. Was he avoiding her? But why? Or was something wrong? Should she be worried?

Maybe Vince was in Chicago with Loretta, and he wasn't getting a signal. For some strange reason, it seemed that cell phones that worked perfectly fine in Scumble River didn't work at all in the city, and vice versa. Skye actually knew a few people who had two cell phones, one for around home and one for outside of town.

With that in mind, Skye decided to wait until tomorrow to worry about Vince. Now all she had to figure out was what to wear. She pushed the hangers back and forth, waiting for inspiration. The first blouse she grabbed was dirty. Why hadn't she put it in the hamper? Oh, yeah. It was marked hand wash and air dry, which meant she'd probably get around to laundering it about the same time her first grandchild was born.

As she shoved back the soiled shirt, her new black tunic sweater slipped to the floor. *Aha!* That had to be a sign. She slipped it over her head, then after pulling on black jeans and ankle boots, she looked in the mirror. Not bad, but the outfit needed something. She tried a couple of necklaces, then a scarf, but nothing was exactly right.

Finally she remembered the belt. It would be ideal. She'd been cleaning out one of the many trunks in the attic when she found it. At first she was sure it would never fit. When she held it up, it definitely looked too small to go around her. Skye loved vintage clothing, but most items were not made for a woman with curves.

However, when she tried it on, the silver links that resembled scales encircled her waist with room to spare. And as she slid the tab into the snakehead to fasten it, the belt felt as if it had been made for her. The emerald eyes looked up at her, and she could have sworn the reptile was smiling.

After flatironing her curls into submission, applying a fresh coat of mascara, and putting on a swipe of peach lip gloss, Skye checked the time. It was six eighteen. She had to hustle if she wanted to talk to Flip *and* be on time to meet Wally at the skating rink.

Skye was a little apprehensive about appearing unexpectedly at her cousin Ginger's door. They didn't get along all that well, and she wasn't sure of her welcome.

But as soon as she explained she was there to offer Flip a job, Ginger's big blue eyes gleamed, and she swept Skye inside. "Come in, come in. With J and A Builders declaring bankruptcy, he could definitely use some work. Flip's a good carpenter, but the only other box that could be marked with a plus on his report card would be 'drinks well with others.' "

Skye let her cousin's last comment go by without a response and said, "I'm happy he's free but sorry he's out of a job." She hugged Ginger. "The developer he was working for went out of business?"

"Yeah." Ginger ushered her into the family room. "A few months ago. I can't believe you didn't hear about it. It was in the *Star*."

"Really?" Skye usually read the local newspaper from cover to cover, but during the summer, when she had been working as the wedding planner for her California cousin, she hadn't had time even to glance at the front page. "I must have missed it. I'm surprised Mom never said anything."

"Sit down." Ginger nearly pushed Skye into an itchy plaid-covered chair next to where Flip was seated in his camouflage recliner. He was absorbed in solving the puzzle on *Wheel of Fortune* and didn't appear aware she was in the room. "I'm surprised too," Ginger added. "Aunt May wouldn't have ignored that nugget on the gossip circuit."

"I was sorry he wasn't available last summer when I had my master bath remodeled. I know what a good job he does." Skye settled into the cushiony seat. "So when I heard he did some work for the owners of Tales and Treats, I thought maybe J and A had relaxed their rules and he could do my office." Skye looked questioningly at Flip.

Ginger stepped behind her husband. "Pay attention. Skye wants to hire you."

Skye winced at the hollow sound as Ginger thumped the top of his head with her knuckle. Flip's hair was doing what Skye called a balder-dash—a race to the receding line.

Flip continued to ignore his wife, and before Ginger smacked him again, Skye hurriedly said, "I can wait until the commercial."

"Okay." Ginger seemed to remember her manners. "Can I get you something? Beer, wine, or I could whip us up some margaritas."

"A glass of water would be great." It was hot in the room, and Skye's mouth was dry. "With ice, if it's not too much trouble."

"No problem. We got a new fridge with an ice maker in the door. It'll just take a second." Ginger turned to leave but pointed over her shoulder. "There are photo albums on the shelf there if you want to take a look at some of the work Flip's done."

Once Ginger disappeared into the kitchen, Skye looked around. The furniture was mostly Early American, with braided rugs scattered over the scuffed hardwood floors. Hanging over the center of the room was a chandelier made of deer antlers. It rotated slowly, as if to silent music. The walls were covered with stuffed animal heads, bows, arrows, and a variety of guns, and every flat surface was plastered with pictures of Ginger and Flip's three children—Bert, Dwayne, and Iris.

Skye guessed this was Flip's kingdom. It had probably been decorated when the family had moved in fifteen years ago and not touched since.

Ginger returned just as the volume of the TV increased, indicating that the program had gone to a commercial. She shouted over the frenetic music, "Turn that thing down and talk to Skye. She has a job for you." Ginger handed Skye the glass of ice water, grabbed the remote from her husband, and muted the set. "Men."

"Son of a b—" Flip appeared to see Skye for the first time and interrupted himself. "Oh. Hi."

"Hi." Skye snuck a peek at her watch. She needed to get going soon. "I'm hoping you can turn one of my spare bedrooms into an office. You know, with bookshelves and a built-in desk?"

"I can do that." Flip leaned back and folded his hands across his stomach. "Want me to come over Monday afternoon and take a look?"

"That would be great." Skye nodded. "I usually get home about four." This was her opening, and she laid her trap. "I wasn't sure if you were finished with the job at Tales and Treats. I thought they might have some repairs for you to do after the break-in."

"Hell, no!" Flip smacked the arm of his recliner, causing the can of beer in the built-in holder to tremble. "I wouldn't work for that woman again if she paid double, triple, golden overtime."

"Risé was hard to work for?" Skye asked innocently, not letting on how much she knew. "I'm surprised her husband didn't handle the remodeling."

"He never showed his face. I guess he was too busy baking. And she was a bitch on wheels." Flip banged down the footrest of his chair. "Then after all the crap I took from her, she tried to stiff me."

"She wouldn't pay?"

"She wanted me to take a personal check." Flip was a big, hulking man, and when he marched over to the coffee table where Ginger had tossed the remote control, the floor shook. "But I told her if it's not from a local bank, I need cash."

He resembled the massive stuffed bear that guarded a corner of the family room, and Skye stared at his hands as he fondled the remote. "Did she agree?" Skye asked. His fingers were as large as full-size Snickers bars.

"No. She got all snippy, and I had to tell her I wouldn't sign off for the building inspection without my money." Flip stomped back to his La-Z-Boy.

"What happened?" Skye wondered whether Risé thought Flip wouldn't accept her check because he was planning to cheat on his taxes. The bookstore owner struck her as someone who wouldn't put up with someone defrauding the government.

"She told me to come back the next morning, which I did, and she had the dough." He flopped down on the recliner, chugged the rest of his beer, crushed the can when he finished, then turned the TV's sound back on.

"So you were paid?"

"Yeah. We're square."

"That's good." *Phew!* As long as he got his money, Flip didn't have much of a motive to want Risé dead. It wasn't as if he *had* to work for her ever again. He wasn't a complex enough person to hold that kind of grudge. Now all she needed was his alibi.

"Ginger"—Skye turned to her cousin—"your mom said you and Flip went to a big party Saturday night." She decided to try a variation of the same ruse that had worked with Kevin. "Did you have a good time?"

"It was all right for a class reunion." Ginger tucked a strand of baby-fine dishwater blond hair behind her ear. "You know how those are. Heck, we see the people we like all the time, and no one from out of town ever shows up, even though this was our big one-five."

"Yeah. That's a shame." Skye hadn't attended her ten-year reunion, and her class hadn't had another one. "Where was it held?"

"The Brown Bag." Ginger picked up an emery board and started filing her nails. "It would have been more fun at the rec club. We could have built a big bonfire and brought our own booze, which would have been a whole lot cheaper, but the committee wouldn't listen to me. They wanted it all fancy, but Jess kicked us out at two."

Jess Larson owned the Brown Bag Liquor Store, Bar, and Banquet Hall.

"Two a.m.?"

"Uh-huh." Ginger nodded. "He said something about not being able to serve drinks after that."

"And Flip was with you the whole time?"

"Yeah." Ginger scowled. "Believe me, with all those divorcées on the prowl, I never let him out of my sight."

Once she knew Flip had an alibi, Skye made her excuses and rushed to the skating rink. It was a few minutes after seven when she arrived, and Wally was already there. He flashed his lights to show her where he was parked, and she pulled into the spot next to him. The lot was packed, and she wondered how he'd saved the space. If he'd been driving one of the police cruisers, she could understand no one wanting to be beside him, but he had his blue Thunderbird—a fortieth birthday present from his father.

Wally and Skye met in front of their vehicles, and he held her at arm's length, then gave her a kiss on the cheek. "Spiffy outfit."

"Swell." Skye grinned. The skating rink must have brought the fifties to both their minds. "You know I always think you look hot."

"Why, thank you, darlin'." Wally steered them through the lot and onto the sidewalk. "I ran home and changed clothes after the commissioners' meeting. If we take a tumble while we're skating, I didn't think it would look too good to do it in uniform."

"True." Skye smiled. "But we're not going to fall." Wally didn't know she'd been roller-skating champion of her eighth-grade class.

The exterior of the skate center looked different at night. The last time Skye had seen the rink, she'd wondered whether it was about to be torn down. Now shadows hid the peeling paint and hinted at what the building could look like if Milton was able to restore it fully. A shaft of light from the fixture above the front door illuminated the entrance.

Leaves blew over the sidewalk, making it slippery, and Wally steadied Skye as her foot slid. "Did you talk to everyone who was mad at Risé?" Wally held one of the double glass doors open.

"All except Hugo." Skye stepped into the foyer. "Charlie, Tomi, Kevin, and Flip all have alibis."

"Martinez isn't finished with the background check on Risé, but so far she's clean as a whistle. The woman hasn't even had a parking ticket."

"Did Officer Martinez find anything on Kayla?" Skye asked.

"Nothing we didn't already know." Wally shrugged. "She's exactly what you'd expect of a small-town good girl. No one had anything bad to say about her, and the dean at the Chicago School of Film and Photography spoke highly of her. He said she'd already won a couple of competitions."

"I wonder if the other students were jealous." They stopped at the entrance to the rink.

"Martinez is going up there tomorrow to check that out."

Skye nodded, then looked around. Milton had refinished the floor, laid new carpet, put in a drop ceiling, and installed nightclub lighting. Tables and chairs were positioned behind the rail, and a snack bar was located in the rear.

"If you two are through making your grand entrance, maybe you could get the hell out of the way so someone else could get in."

"What's your rush?" Wally's voice was genial, but he gripped Skye's arm and didn't move.

Skye turned and saw that the person trying to

get around them was—speak of the devil—her cousin Hugo. He held his wife's hand tightly, and Victoria didn't seem happy.

"Some of us have other places to be tonight and need to keep moving," Hugo sneered. "Unlike the police, we don't get a salary if we don't hustle."

Wally patted his flat stomach. "That's right. They pay me to sit around and eat donuts." After making sure Hugo got the message, he drew Skye aside and made a sweeping gesture. "Be my guest."

Victoria muttered as she went past. "Some of us don't need to make a big deal in order to draw all eyes to us."

Huh? Skye had no idea where that had that come from. Victoria had almost sounded jealous, but that couldn't be it. She looked like a goddess. Smooth blond hair fell straight to the middle of her back, blue eyes shone from a sun-kissed complexion, and the short indigo halter dress she wore molded to her slim, toned body.

Once Hugo and his wife were out of earshot, Skye said to Wally, "I used to feel sorry for Victoria—Hugo's one of the most insufferable men I know. But she just lost a lot of my sympathy."

"Don't be too hard on her." Wally took Skye's hand and ran his fingers over her inner wrist. "It's hard for someone like her, who has always gotten along on her looks, to realize that sometimes that's not enough."

"What do you mean?"

"Victoria doesn't think you're as beautiful as she is, but you get in the paper all the time, and now that you're engaged, that's all anyone can talk about."

"Not really."

"Yes, really." Wally kissed her palm.

"You know, Hugo didn't seem quite like himself tonight." Skye frowned.

"Yeah." Wally's grin was sharklike. "I noticed the improvement right away."

"I'm not kidding." Skye bit her lip. "He's usually a lot . . . uh . . . smoother, more unctuous. I wonder what brought about the change."

"Maybe you can find out when you talk to him tomorrow." Wally placed his palm on the small of her back. "Shall we?"

They entered the outer rink area, and Skye recognized most of the group milling around. Everyone who was anyone in town was present.

"Why are all these people here?" Skye wrinkled her brow and whispered to Wally. "Most of them seem to be doing more talking than skating."

"Same reason we are." Wally cupped her elbow, and they moved toward a man standing behind a counter. "To show support for a new business in town."

"Funny they didn't do that for Tales and Treats," Skye muttered.

"Milton's lived in Scumble River for the past seventeen years." Wally raised an eyebrow. "You know how things work around here."

Milton Leigh had short brown hair that resembled the growth on a Chia Pet. He was long and lean, with full lips framed by wrinkles. Skye couldn't tell whether he was forty or fifty or maybe even older.

Wally shook hands with the skate center owner and said, "Milton, I don't think you know my fiancée, Skye Denison. Skye, this is my old friend Milton Leigh."

Skye shook hands and said, "The rink looks wonderful, Mr. Leigh."

"Call me Milton." His gray eyes were shrewd. "You must be the mayor's niece."

"Yes." Skye stopped herself from making a face. "I must be."

Milton was dressed in jeans and a cotton plaid shirt with pearl snaps. He reminded Skye of a 1960s Grand Ole Opry star, and she wondered whether he could sing.

He looked her over and said to Wally, "Big improvement over the last filly you hooked up with."

Skye narrowed her eyes. She really didn't like being compared to livestock, even if she was being awarded a blue ribbon.

"No offense intended." Milton grinned at her sour expression. "You have to excuse an old cowboy."

"Of course." Skye changed the subject. "You've got a big crowd tonight."

"Yep." Milton nodded. "But these people aren't my bread and butter. I bet you none of them will even lace on a pair of skates."

"Oh? It's nice that they're here to support you, though, right?"

"Only a few, like your fella, are here for me." Milton caressed his big silver belt buckle. "Most are like Hugo over there. He needs to keep his finger stirring the pot and riling everyone up. He's really got a bee in his bonnet this time." Milton shook his head. "Now, are you two going to skate or what?"

"Do you think he meant Hugo's problem with Risé?" Skye asked Wally as they put on the roller skates Milton had handed them.

"Maybe." Wally took Skye's hand, and they glided into the rink. "Guess you better come up with a good reason to talk to Hugo tomorrow, because it's a sure thing I wouldn't get anywhere questioning him. He'd just call his daddy and complain about police harassment."

CHAPTER 18

The Invisible Man

It was already nine thirty Thursday morning when Skye and Caroline Greer, the elementary school principal, walked into the main office. The Pupil Personnel Service meeting had gone more than an hour longer than usual because twin six-year-old boys with special needs had moved into the district the day before, and the staff had to hurry to prepare for their intake conferences.

Caroline and Skye were engrossed in discussing the complicated case when Fern Otte, the school secretary, thrust Skye aside and screeched, "Arnold Underwood is gone!"

"When was he last seen?" Caroline, a tiny woman with a cloud of white hair, was known for her unruffled demeanor and ability to keep her staff calm.

"When his class went to gym at eight forty." Fern wrung her hands. She was extremely petite, and her affinity for brown clothing made her look like a wren. True to form, today she wore a taupe sweater and pants.

"PE class is only half an hour." Caroline

frowned. "Why didn't you come and get me when his teacher first reported him missing?"

"She just this minute told me," Fern mewled. "She didn't realize Arnold was gone until the speech therapist came to get him for his session."

"I see." Caroline nodded, then directed, "Put out a PA announcement that any staff member who is not with children must report to the office immediately. As they come in, assign them to halls A and C, then the playground and parking lot, in that order. His room is in hallway B. I'll be checking that corridor." Next she focused on Skye. "You look in the gymnasium, kitchen, and stage."

"Okay." Skye headed out of the office but stopped to ask the principal, "Are you calling the police?"

"Not until we've conducted a thorough search." Caroline's tone was intractable.

"How about the boy's parents?" Skye persisted.

"No need to worry them until we're sure he's really missing, and not just hiding somewhere. You know how ten-year-olds can be."

Skye wasn't sure what Caroline meant by that. Did she think all ten-year-olds were prone to disappearing? However, Skye was willing to follow the principal's orders, at least until they'd searched the building and grounds. After that, if he was still unaccounted for, she would call 911 with or without the older woman's blessing.

When Skye got to the gym, she found it empty except for an old-fashioned physician's scale, a long Formica-topped table, and a chair. All three were positioned in the exact middle of the wooden floor. Except for those three items, the cavernous space was completely open, with nowhere for anyone to hide.

The elementary school didn't have locker rooms, so after a quick glance around, Skye moved on to the storage area under the stage, which was padlocked. Making a mental note to get a key, Skye walked the perimeter of the empty platform. Once she was sure there were no hiding places, she parted the velvet curtains at the back and went through them. This spot had been converted to an office for the PE teacher.

There wasn't anyone around, so Skye called out, "Yoo-hoo, anybody here?"

A soft rustle came from behind the stacks of athletic equipment, and Todd Grind, the gym teacher, poked his head around a tower of boxes. "Hey, Skye. What's up? Another one of your SpEd kids needs babying?"

Skye fought to keep her expression neutral as she registered Todd's use of the derogatory label. She reminded herself that he was as prickly as his brush-cut hairstyle. Still, she couldn't allow a remark like that to go unchallenged. "Todd, the students receiving special education services are everyone's responsibility." Hoping to win him with an athletic metaphor, she said, "You know, a team effort."

"A team effort is everyone doing what I tell them to." Todd stuck his hands in the pockets of his warm-up jacket and shot Skye a cocky grin.

"Which is why I hate sports," Skye muttered under her breath, then gave up trying to reform the PE teacher and explained about the missing boy. When she finished she asked, "Have you seen Arnold since that time?"

"What are you talking about?" Todd asked, then walked to his desk, flipped open an attendance book, and ran his finger down the page. "Porky wasn't in class today."

Skye started to remind him that she had asked the faculty not to call Arnold by that nickname and to discourage its use among his classmates, but she knew she'd be wasting her breath. Todd was surrounded by the Bozone—a substance that encircled clowns like him, stopping any intelligent suggestions from penetrating.

However, she would speak to Caroline once the boy was found. As far as she knew, everyone on the staff except Todd had complied with her request to use Arnold's given name. But if the PE teacher didn't stop, neither would the other kids, and Skye did not want the awful nickname following the poor kid to the junior high. If she didn't nip it in the bud now, he'd be Porky for the rest of his life.

"Do you have the key to the storage area under the stage?" When Todd nodded, she asked, "Could you check and make sure he didn't get in there somehow?"

"If it will make you happy," the PE teacher sneered. "But Porky's too lazy to have gone far."

"Notify the office immediately if you find him." Skye had to get out of there before she slapped Todd. "I'm going to keep searching."

The gymnasium also served as the cafeteria, and the kitchen was connected through a set of swinging steel doors and a large window with a rolling metal shutter. It was too early for the lunch ladies to have arrived, so the space was empty.

As Skye opened all the cupboards, refrigerators, and even the ovens, she pondered the fact that the boy had disappeared between the time his teacher had walked her class to the gym and when Todd had taken roll call. She was sure that was significant, but why?

Still no sign of the ten-year-old anywhere, and she nibbled her thumbnail. Was there anywhere else he could be in here? Her gazed scanned the walls, stopping at a square that looked a little like a boarded-up window. She stepped over to it and tapped.

It was definitely hollow on the other side. She examined the painted plywood section, trying to figure out what it could be. Finally, she remembered that there was a basement under the old part of the school that was used for storage. This must be a dumbwaiter they used to transport supplies to and from the kitchen.

Putting both palms on the wood, Skye pushed, and the panel slid up smoothly. Squeezed inside was Arnold Underwood, and he wasn't moving. She swallowed a cry, reaching out to touch the boy's hand to check for a pulse.

Arnold's eyes popped open, and he screamed. He was big for his age, barely fitting in the small compartment, but he backed up as far as he could get against the rear wall, then crouched there, panting.

"Arnold, it's Ms. Denison. Remember, I came into your class and talked about making friends. We did little plays about different situations."

He took a gulping breath and nodded. He'd had a rough life. His parents were poor and rented an old run-down house not too far from Skye's family farm. They'd moved there from Joliet when Arnold was eight, and he'd had a hard time fitting into the already established pecking order of his second-grade class. The kids in Scumble River, like their parents, were slow to warm up to newcomers.

"Can you get out by yourself?"

He nodded again and scooted to the edge but stopped. "Am I in trouble?"

"I don't know." She was unsure what Caroline

would do and unwilling to lie to the boy. "But I'll try to help you. Why did you hide?"

He sat with his feet dangling over the edge and mumbled, "Because."

"Was someone mean to you?" Skye wasn't sure what to do. They hadn't covered a boy hiding in a dumbwaiter in her school-psychology training, and she doubted it was in the *Best Practices* manual.

A tear ran down his cheek, and he wiped it away with the back of his hand.

Skye felt her throat close. She had to do something. Her mind raced, and she suddenly put together the pieces of the puzzle. "Is it because today is weighing and measuring day in gym?"

Arnold looked at her as if she had just read his mind. "How did you know?"

"I hated that day when I was in school, too." Skye touched his hand. "Do they still yell out how much you weigh so everyone hears it?"

He nodded without looking at her and began picking at a scab on his arm.

"I used to pretend to be sick that day," Skye told him, then had another thought. "Is Mr. Grind cool about the whole thing? My teacher was pretty horrible. She always made a nasty comment if she thought anyone weighed too much."

"He's not cool at all. He's mean," Arnold blurted out. "He calls me Porky and makes pig noises."

"I'm so sorry." Skye helped him out of the dumbwaiter. "He's very wrong to do that." As she escorted the boy to the office she said, "And don't worry. I'll make sure you aren't in trouble for this."

Skye sat in Caroline's office. It was nearly eleven, and the situation was finally resolved. Arnold had been reassured, his teacher had been briefed, and he had returned to the classroom.

Now Skye was filling in the principal. "I really miss our last PE teacher. She was so great with the kids. I've explained to Todd on numerous occasions that teasing children about their appearance and lack of athletic prowess is a form of abuse. He insists that it toughens them up for real life."

"And you disagree?" Caroline spoke thoughtfully from her seat behind the desk.

"Yes." Skye leaned forward, intent on convincing the principal. "Most people can get past a bad experience, but they never get over it. Humiliation like this follows them the rest of their lives."

"Judging from today's incident, not to mention my thirty-eight years in education as both a teacher and a principal, I'd say you're correct." Caroline's expression was hard to read. "Now, the question is, what are we going to do about it?"

"Do you really want my suggestion?" Skye asked, making sure the principal wasn't using the royal *we*. She'd gotten stung too many times while trying to be helpful not to be cautious.

"Yes." Caroline's expression was anything but happy. "I'm distressed to admit that I'm not sure how to deal with Mr. Grind. This is his second year with us, and my usual methods don't seem to be working."

"I'm willing to consult closely with him. But he needs to know that I'm doing so under orders from you. And if by the end of the year we don't see any improvement, since he's not tenured . . ." Skye hated what she was about to say, but her job was to be the children's advocate, not the teachers'. "I would have to recommend that his contract not be renewed and he not be given a reference."

"I agree." Caroline sighed. "He has such promise. We don't have enough young men wanting to work at the elementary level, especially in PE. I hope you can help him see the error of his ways."

"Or at least get him to do what he's told." Skye was pragmatic.

Caroline nodded, indicating their discussion was over. As Skye walked out of the principal's office, she wondered what in the world she could do to convince Todd Grind her philosophy was the correct one.

Skye headed down the hall, mentally reshuffling her schedule. She had intended to test a fifth grader that morning but needed at least a two-hour block of uninterrupted time for that. And since she was due at the junior high at twelve thirty, it was too late to start now. She couldn't do any observations, because she hadn't made appointments with the teachers. That left report writing. There was never any shortage of paper-work, and she tended to do it in dribs and drabs, whenever she had a spare moment.

Preoccupied, she didn't register that her usually locked office door was open, and as she stepped inside, she gave a tiny yelp. Sitting on one of the two metal folding chairs was Simon. As always, he was dressed impeccably, in an elegant dark suit.

He had spread the desk with a white linen tablecloth and placed a vase containing yellow roses in the center. Arranged around the bouquet were plates of fruit, cheese, French bread, and two flutes of sparkling grape juice. At least she hoped it was sparkling grape juice, because alcohol on school grounds was cause for imme-diate dismissal.

Skye sniffed. Her office had started life as a storage room for the cafeteria, and a faint odor of sour milk usually hung in the air, but today there was a pleasant floral scent. Was it the roses, or had Simon brought air freshener?

Simon had stood up when she entered, and a grin lit his handsome face. "Surprise!"

"What are you doing here?" Skye forced herself to frown even as her stomach growled at the sight of the food. "I told you to stop it."

"And I told you I wouldn't. Haven't I convinced you of that yet?" He indicated the other chair. "Sit down. What's the harm of a little brunch? It's not as if I'm going to ravish you in the middle of the grade school. Although you do look good enough to eat."

Skye ignored his compliment. He was obviously exaggerating. She was wearing a pair of old black slacks and a pink twin set that had seen better days, and she hadn't even bothered to straighten her hair, just scraped it back with a headband.

Simon's tall frame took up most of the small space, but she managed to edge past without brushing against him. She dragged the other folding chair back behind the desk and asked, "How did you get in here?" She was sure she'd locked the door. She always did because of confidentiality issues.

"Fern gave me the master key."

"Why would she do that?" Skye glared at him. "She could get into a lot of trouble."

"I helped her out when her mom died." Simon nudged a plate of fruit toward her. "Come on. Eat something. It's no big deal, and I know you won't give Fern a hard time for trying to further true love."

"You're right," Skye acknowledged. "I won't tell on her, but you've got to stop this."

"I can't." Simon was suddenly serious. "Look, when that psycho almost killed you last October, I realized that I didn't appreciate you when we were dating. That I tried to change you, when you were perfect the way you were. That the reason you're the one for me is because of who you are, not who I want to make you into."

"Simon." Skye swallowed the lump in her throat. "Don't." It was hard to hear the genuine love in his voice.

"I'm not going to say that I can't live without you, but the truth is, there *is* only one person who completes me, and that's you. I know for certain that my life would be infinitely richer with you by my side." Simon's expression was bleak. "It's like I woke up one day and finally saw that with you the world is a wonderful place full of color and adventure, and without you, it's like a black-and-white movie."

Skye sat stunned for a moment, then said, "I'm sorry. Maybe if you had realized all of this sooner, but . . ." She shook her head. The pain in his voice tore at her. "I can't do this for a lot of reasons. You have to leave."

"I will, but I'm not giving up." He smiled sadly. "And before I go, I need to tell you about Xavier."

Simon's voice was grave. "Frannie told me last night that he's been gone a lot lately. Either he won't say where he's going, or he lies to her about where he is."

"Shit!" Skye sank into her chair. Xavier loved his daughter and would sacrifice anything for her. If he was lying to Frannie, they had a major problem.

"My thoughts exactly." Simon sat down, too, as if he were suddenly exhausted. "It has to have something to do with the bookstore and his investment."

"Have you asked him about it?" Skye absentmindedly picked up a grape and popped it into her mouth.

"Not yet. I wanted to run it by you first." Simon sounded unsure.

"I don't know what to advise you. He's a tough person to figure out." Skye nibbled a piece of cheese. "Do you think he'd tell you the truth?"

"A month ago I would have said yes." Simon's shoulders slumped. "Now I doubt it."

"Then if you really want to know what's going on, you'll have to follow him."

To Skye's surprise, Simon didn't immediately dismiss her suggestion. Instead he pulled out a small leather-bound pad of paper and started taking notes. While they discussed where Xavier might be disappearing to, what he might be doing, and how Simon could tail him, between them they polished off all the food.

Finally, Skye rose from her chair. "Now you really need to leave. I have to be at the junior high in fifteen minutes."

Once he was standing, she thrust the vase of roses in his hands. "And I can't accept these."

His smile was pained. "You aren't making this 'winning you back' thing easy."

"Because it's too late." She was silent as he turned to go, then said, "Wait."

His hopeful expression nearly broke her heart, but she steeled her emotions, "Do you know when the ME is releasing Kayla's body?"

"Yes." Simon sighed, clearly unhappy with her response. "I picked it up this morning. The wake is tomorrow, and the funeral is Saturday."

"Was there anything new in his report?"

"He found bits of a hard blue plastic material in her hair."

"Hmm." What was made of blue plastic? Suddenly Skye felt warm breath on her face, and her eyes popped open. Simon was leaning forward, their noses nearly touching and his hazel eyes blazing into hers. "I'm not giving up."

"And I'm not changing my mind."

He tilted her chin up with his finger. "I hear annulments take a long, long time."

For once, Skye was able to leave work on time, which meant she could stop by her brother's hair salon before going to question Hugo. Vince still hadn't called or answered his phone.

As Skye turned into the Great Expectations parking lot, she saw Vince's Jeep in its usual spot, but when she tried to open the shop's front door, she noticed that the CLOSED sign was in the window. Alarm fluttered in Skye's chest. It was only a little past four in the afternoon. Vince never quit work until well after six on a weekday. And where could he have gone without his car? What could have happened?

Skye's initial thought was to call her mother. Nope, bad idea. First she'd check his apartment. It took her only a few minutes to drive to the complex, and when he didn't answer the door she tried her key. It didn't work.

She couldn't imagine someone as laid-back as her brother going to the trouble of changing the lock on his apartment door. Unless it had been Loretta's doing. Still, why hadn't Vince given her the new key?

As Skye wrote a note, underscoring the urgent need for Vince to get in touch with her, she had a thought. Did he and Loretta think she was as meddlesome as May? Was that the explanation for the changed lock and the unreturned calls? The idea was so appalling, she almost forgot her real worry. Had something happened to Vince that was preventing him from calling her back?

It seemed wrong, but Skye could think of no other option. She'd have to break down and call

Loretta. She hated coming off as a nosy sister, but Vince and Loretta had both asked her to keep May from finding out about their engagement, and she couldn't do that if they remained incommunicado.

CHAPTER 19
Sense and Sensibility

When Loretta didn't answer at any of her numbers, Skye decided that if she hadn't heard from Vince by tomorrow, she could call Loretta's law office and talk to her secretary. A live human versus a machine had to have some answers. And for now, that was the best plan she had.

Checking the time, Skye realized she had to get over to Hugo's before he left for the day. She had finally come up with a reason to talk to him. Her father was turning sixty-five in January, so she would claim to be having a huge surprise party for Jed. She was checking with everyone to be sure they were available on the date.

She might even ask for Hugo's help. Skye smiled. Everyone liked her dad, and Hugo owed him big-time for helping out when his regular mechanic came across a car he couldn't fix. Hugo should be happy to talk to Skye about a celebration in her father's honor.

Hugo's used-car lot was only a couple of miles from Vince's apartment, but Skye's luck was running true to form, and his manager said her cousin had already left for the day. *Great!* Who expected a used-car salesman to keep banker's hours?

As Skye pulled into her driveway, she checked her watch. It was only a few minutes past five thirty; for once she wouldn't have to rush. She had time to fix a decent meal, freshen up, and still get to the bookstore in plenty of time to lead the teen discussion group.

Skye had just begun heating a skillet to brown a salmon filet when the phone rang. She turned the flame down and checked caller ID, congratulating herself on having finally gotten it installed. It had been worth the monthly cost ten times over these past few days, when she had been able to avoid her mother's calls.

Seeing the number of Wally's private line at the PD, Skye smiled and scooped up the receiver, then froze when May's voice blasted from the earpiece. "Where have you been? Why haven't you called me back? And what's going on with your brother?"

Since Skye didn't have acceptable answers for any of those questions, the conversation with her mother was long and painful.

Skye had long since lost her appetite and put the fish back in the refrigerator when she broke under her mother's relentless grilling. "I didn't call you, Mom, because I have nothing to tell you. I haven't been able to reach Vince. He hasn't answered his phones, and he's not at the salon or his apartment."

There was dead silence; then Hurricane May broke loose. Looking back later on her mother's reaction, Skye realized she should have cut out her tongue as soon as she heard May's voice on the phone rather than talk to her. Instead, she had ended up promising that she would let her mom know the minute she located Vince.

Because of May's intense interrogation, Skye arrived at Tales and Treats less than fifteen minutes before the book club was scheduled to begin. Entering the store, she noted that all signs of the break-in were gone. The rare-book cabinet was back in position, its glass front replaced and the valuable tomes restored to its shelves.

Even the spot where Kayla had lain was undetectable. The polyurethane finish on the wood-laminate flooring had prevented the blood from soaking through and thus had been easily wiped clean. It somehow saddened Skye to think that the young girl's death had left no mark.

Still, she couldn't help but smile as she spotted Risé behind the counter. The store owner was busy checking out a huge stack of books for a woman who was chattering enthusiastically about how much she loved the selection of mysteries and romances.

Today, Risé wore a colorful T-shirt emblazoned with the words ONE GOOD BOOK DESERVES ANOTHER. Skye wondered how many different T-shirts with witty book sayings Risé owned.

Risé saw Skye and pointed to the literature alcove, mouthing, "They're in there."

Skye found Trixie and two girls arranging folding chairs into a semicircle. The desk, generally used to give the impression of a college professor's office, was shoved against a wall, and a pitcher of lemonade, a stack of paper cups, and a tray of fancy cookies were spread across the top.

Trixie walked over to Skye and whispered, "Any news on the murder?"

"Not since I talked to you at school." Skye drew Trixie farther out of earshot of the two preteens. "I still haven't questioned Hugo, but everyone else we're aware of who was angry at Risé has an alibi."

Skye hadn't meant to tell her friend about her suspicion that the store owner was the killer's real target, but Trixie had independently come to the same conclusion, and Skye had had to admit she was looking into that possibility.

"Shoot!" Trixie stamped her foot. "On one hand I'm glad that none of them is guilty of such a horrible crime, but now what?"

"Exactly." Skye made sure no one was listening, then said, "If Hugo is in the clear, which I certainly hope, then the case is pretty much at a dead end. Officer Martinez is doing a background check on Risé and Kayla, but she hasn't found anything on either of them so far, and Wally said that no one involved in the case has any warrants in the system. All we can hope for is that the police get a lead from something the crime scene techs come up with."

Trixie's expression of frustration matched Skye's, but a steady stream of girls had started to arrive, and they were forced to turn their attention to the matter at hand. Both women knew that a roomful of unsupervised teenagers was never a good thing.

While the attendees helped themselves to refreshments and settled into their seats, Skye said to Trixie, "I wonder why Risé put us in here. I hope she doesn't expect our discussion to be literary."

"Nah." Trixie grinned. "She told me this area has the least amount of customer traffic, so we'll be less likely to be interrupted."

Although Skye had a minor in English, she was relieved that she wasn't supposed to be conducting the club like a class. She didn't think the kids would enjoy treating their book as if it were Tolstoy.

Skye recognized most of the girls and was surprised by the age range. Shawna Miles and Cassie Wren, the two who had been helping

Trixie set up when Skye arrived, were only eleven or twelve, while some of the others were at least eighteen.

As soon as Skye sat down, Bitsy Kessler and Ashley Yates immediately claimed the two chairs on either side of her. Skye knew Bitsy from the high school newspaper, and she had rescued Ashley when the girl had tumbled into an abandoned basement, broken her leg in the fall, and been trapped there.

Last year Bitsy and Ashley had been enemies; this year they appeared to be friends. Maybe they were frenemies. Skye had heard that term recently but wasn't precisely sure what it meant.

The two younger girls flanked Trixie. They, too, might fall under the frenemy label, as they were rivals in the local dance troupe.

Other teens occupied the remaining seats, and once everyone was comfortable, Skye counted heads. Fifteen—not bad for the first meeting. If the girls enjoyed themselves tonight, they might bring their friends to the next session.

Trixie held up a copy of *If I Have a Wicked Stepmother, Where's My Prince?* and asked, "So, what did you all think of this book?"

The kids were silent. Their expressions ranged from eagerness to apprehension. Trixie and Skye had come up with a few questions to use to initiate the discussion, and clearly they were needed to get the girls started, but Skye hoped that once they got going, they could ditch the formalities and just talk.

Skye leaned forward. "Maybe the first thing we should ask is, did you like the book?"

All the girls nodded, some saying they enjoyed the humor, others stating they thought the romance and excitement were the best things about the novel. A few commented that it was an easy read and they were hooked from the beginning.

"How about the protagonist? Could you identify with Lucy?" Skye asked.

Again, everyone nodded.

"Have you ever felt like Cinderella?" Trixie took up the leadership reins.

Shawna raised her hand. "I was Cinderella at our last dance recital."

Everyone but Cassie tittered. She reached across Trixie and hit her friend's arm. "We shared the role, Miss Smarty-Pants. Remember? Ms. Smothers said we were both equally good, and she couldn't choose who was better."

Trixie looked at Skye, silently asking: *Should we go back to being more concrete?*

Skye nodded, and Trixie said, "What did you think of the cover? If you were browsing the shelves, would it catch your eye?"

"Well." Bitsy tossed her copper ringlets. "That sparkly star sure would have."

"Yeah," Ashley chimed in. "The color was nice,

and the poufy dress with the Converses would have definitely made me look twice."

"Because the formal and the shoes were incongruous with each other?" Skye asked.

"Nah." One of the other girls grinned. "Because the look was so cool."

Trixie waited for the giggles to stop, then said, "Reviewers have called this book a modern-day Cinderella story. Do you think they were correct? Did any of you see the similarity?"

A brunette whom Skye couldn't place stared at the floorboards as she spoke. "Lucy's stepmother made her live in a basement and sleep on an air mattress. And her twin stepsisters were mean to her and made fun of how she dressed. And she had to do all the work."

"That's a good point." Skye smiled. "I'm sorry. I didn't catch your name."

"I'm Heidi." The girl continued to gaze at the ground, shuffling her feet.

"Do you live in Scumble River?" Skye knew most of the teenagers in town. Maybe not their names, but their faces, and this girl didn't look even slightly familiar.

"We moved here over the summer." Heidi picked at a hangnail.

"So you started at a new school where you didn't know anyone, just like Lucy?" Skye hoped this group would help the girl make some friends.

Heidi shrugged but remained silent.

After a second or two, Bitsy piped up, turning the discussion back to the book. "But Lucy doesn't end up with Prince Charming."

"Doesn't she?" Skye saw Heidi sit back in relief, so she went with the thread Bitsy had started. "What makes a boy a Prince Charming? Which boy in this story is the true prince, Connor or Sam?"

The group was silent, and Skye was afraid she had lost the girls, but finally Ashley spoke. "I don't think a real prince has to be the hottest guy. I think that sometimes the real prince is the guy who gets you. Who understands you and likes what you do. The one who doesn't go along with the crowd."

As the others murmured their agreement, Skye reflected that Ashley had certainly come a long way from the girl she'd first known—the spoiled, self-centered cheerleader who'd had sex with a bunch of jocks to ensure her popularity.

That line of thinking led Skye to another question. "Why do you think it took Lucy so long to see which guy was her true Prince Charming?"

"Because everyone wants to fit in." Bitsy's green eyes hardened. "Lucy went from zero to hero, and no one wants to take the reverse route. She thought if she broke up with Mr. Popular Jock and dated the art freak instead, she'd have to give up being considered cool and her new friends would turn their backs on her."

The other girls all nodded, but Heidi said, "Maybe. Or maybe she stuck with Connor because no one else loved her, and no matter how much better Sam might seem, he wasn't a sure thing."

"What do you mean?" Trixie tilted her head. "Her father loved her."

"Maybe, but her dad pretty much abandoned her for his new family. He dragged her all the way across the country, took her away from her old friends, then left her living in an unfurnished basement with people who didn't like her. Connor and his friends were all she had." Heidi wrinkled her brow. "I don't think it was popularity she was afraid of losing. I think it was love."

Wow! Skye was impressed. She'd have to see if Heidi was interested in joining the school newspaper staff. With that kind of critical thinking, she'd be an asset to the *Scoop*, and working on the paper would give her a chance to make some friends.

Now that the girls had warmed up, the discussion took off, and the next time Skye looked at her watch, two hours had gone by.

Skye had just signaled Trixie that they should finish up when a girl who hadn't spoken the entire time said, "Didn't any of you find it a little unbelievable that Lucy was accepted so fast?

She went from being invisible to being part of the in crowd way too easily."

Skye was about to answer when Ashley spoke. "But that's how it is. One day you're nobody. Then something happens, and the next day you're in." She shook her head. "The scariest thing is that it can go the other way, too. You can wake up one morning and be out."

"Something to think about." Trixie rose from her chair. "Unfortunately, the store is closing soon, so we have to wrap this up."

The girls grumbled a little, but after a few minutes they gathered their belongings and left to go home.

Once they were gone, Skye said to Trixie, "Since you got everything ready, I'll clean up."

"I can help."

"No. Go ahead." Skye started throwing away the used paper cups and crumpled napkins. "I know Owen likes you home before he goes to bed." Trixie's husband was a farmer who was up before sunrise.

"You talked me into it." Trixie hugged Skye. "Thanks. See you tomorrow."

Skye was putting the literature alcove back in order when she saw Xenia through the archway. She called out to her, but Xenia only waved and continued on. Skye finished folding a chair and added it to the stack against the wall, then followed her.

This was her opportunity to talk to Xenia about Kayla. But where had she gone? Skye checked the mystery, romance, and science fiction rooms. Next she tried the register area. Risé was leaning across the counter talking to Xavier in a voice too low for Skye to hear.

Xavier's brows were drawn together, and he was patting Risé's hand, clearly comforting his old friend. Skye wondered whether they were talking about Kayla's murder, Orlando's fall from grace, or maybe just the strain of opening a new business in a strange town.

As Skye watched, she saw Xavier reach over and cup Risé's cheek. Skye was glad Orlando and Risé had moved to Scumble River. It was good to see Xavier with friends in town.

Smiling, Skye resumed her search for Xenia. A quick glance in the café showed it to be empty except for Orlando washing dishes. Skye shrugged. Xenia must have been getting off work when she saw her and had already left the store.

Skye made a mental note to track her down the next day, then went back to the literature alcove. Once she finished tidying the space and made sure everything was back where it belonged, Skye picked up the empty pitcher and tray and walked into the central area. She looked around for Risé, but she wasn't behind the counter.

Figuring that since the store had closed several minutes ago, Risé might be taking a break in the café, Skye headed in that direction.

When she approached the door, she stopped and put the tray under her arm in order to grab the handle. As she did so, she heard Orlando say, "If you don't stop, he's going to tell everyone."

"But it's not right." Risé's tone was stubborn.

"Right, schmite. Just lay off."

"No."

"Do you really want the entire town to know?"

Skye held her breath. What were Risé and Orlando hiding? As she leaned forward to hear better, the tray slipped from underneath her arm. It clattered to the floor, sounding like the cymbals in a marching band.

Immediately the voices fell silent.

A few seconds later Risé pushed open the door, looked at Skye, and said, "Oh, it's you. I thought you were gone. Here, let me take those." She grabbed the tray and pitcher in one hand and gripped Skye's elbow with the other. Nearly pushing her toward the exit, Risé said in a rush, "Thanks so much for helping us out. I really appreciate it. You must be exhausted, so I won't keep you. Bye."

As soon as Skye was over the threshold, Risé locked the door, pulled down the shade, and turned the sign to CLOSED.

"You should have seen her. She couldn't wait to get me out of there." Skye lay on her stomach across Wally's king-size mattress, her chin resting in both hands. "What do you think they don't want people to know?"

"More important, who is going to tell it?" Wally was running on the treadmill next to the bed. The exercise machine was a recent gift from his father, who after a health scare was on a fitness kick. "And what does Risé have to quit doing in order to stop him?"

"I wonder if it's Hugo." Skye narrowed her eyes. "The first day I met Risé, Hugo was with me, and they had that argument about parking spaces that I told you about. As we were walking away, he said something about most people having to make a living from their business and that he'd done some digging, too."

"Did you talk to Hugo today?" Wally wiped his face with the towel hanging around his neck.

"No. I didn't realize he worked such short hours." Skye played with a loose thread on the bedspread. "By the time I got to the used-car lot he was gone. But he'll be my priority tomorrow."

"Good." Wally increased the speed on the treadmill. "Call me before you go inside, and I'll have an officer nearby as backup in case there's a problem."

"Okay." She looked at Wally, admiring his

powerful, well-muscled body moving with such easy grace as he ran in place. "Any more on the security camera image or Risé's or Kayla's background?"

"The crime scene techs had to send the tape to the state, so who knows how long that will take." Wally took a swig of water from the sports bottle in the treadmill's cup holder. "Martinez is still digging, but the police from Risé's old neighborhood said they've never heard of her."

"How about her old job?" Skye asked. "Anything there?"

"There doesn't seem to be any record of where Risé worked before opening up the bookstore."

"Wouldn't her income tax records tell you that?"

"Sure, but we'd need a warrant to see them," he explained. "I told Martinez just to ask Risé for the info, but I think Risé intimidates her. I need to get on Martinez about that."

"Or ask Risé yourself."

"I will if I have to, but Martinez needs to learn."

Skye nodded. This was the young officer's first job after police training. "Anything on Kayla?"

"The students at her school seemed to have genuinely liked her. None of them mentioned anyone being jealous."

"How about those blue plastic pieces the ME found in Kayla's hair?" Skye sat up. "Do we know what they came from? I'm assuming they must have broken off of whatever hit her on the head."

"That's what I think, too, but the ME has no idea what it is." Wally scowled. "I sure wish it was like TV, where they track a speck of dirt back to the exact location the criminal got it stuck on his shoe."

"Me, too." Skye was a big fan of those shows. "Oh, I keep forgetting to let you know Vince's big news." After telling Wally about the engagement and elopement plans, she added, "But now I can't get in touch with him or Loretta, and I'm worried."

"He's probably just hiding out at Loretta's and not answering his messages, in case your mom gets wind of what's going on."

"I hope so, but you'd think he'd *want* to talk to me." Skye wrinkled her brow.

"Maybe." Wally shrugged. "I wouldn't worry too much about him. Haven't you noticed? He always seems to land on his feet."

"True." She swung her legs over the side of the bed. "Well, I'd better get going."

Wally turned off the treadmill, walked over, and stood in front of her. "Why don't you stay?" He ran his fingertips along her inner thigh. "I could grab a quick shower, and then . . ."

"I really should go home." Skye's mouth went dry, and she swallowed. He was so darn sexy. "It is a school night."

"So?" Slowly and seductively his gaze slid over her. "I'll set the alarm for six."

"But I don't have anything to wear in the morning." She fought an overwhelming desire to lie back and forget the practicalities. "All I have here are jeans, T-shirts, and tennis shoes."

"Wrong." Wally kissed her nose. "I bought you a present." He drew her off the bed and over to his closet. Pointing, he asked, "What do you think?"

"Oh, my gosh," Skye gasped. It was the emerald dress she had tried on during their last shopping trip to Von Maur's, a high-end department store near Yorktown Mall. Although it had fit perfectly, she had decided it was too expensive and had reluctantly put it back on the rack. "When did you get this?"

"When you went to the bathroom," Wally answered. "Surprised?"

"Yes. But I can't exactly wear it with my Keds."

"Look down."

A pair of matching pumps was lined up on the floor.

"You are so sweet to me." She wound her arms around his neck and kissed him. "How can I ever thank you?"

"I can think of a couple of ways." Wally's grin was devilish as he unbuttoned her blouse and kissed his way down her stomach. "Let's start here."

CHAPTER 20
Of Human Bondage

Fridays were typically bad times to try to test or observe students. Teachers often scheduled special instructional activities then, and Skye felt it was unfair to the kids to make them miss what they considered treats. So when she got to school and found a message from Dr. Wraige ordering her to attend a course on computer-form completion at the Stanley County Special Education Cooperative in Laurel, starting at nine a.m. that day, she wasn't all that upset.

During the lunch break she tried to call Vince again, and when she couldn't reach him, she phoned Loretta's law firm. Her assistant said Loretta had taken the week off and wasn't expected back until Monday. Skye tried to wheedle additional details from him, but he refused to tell her anything else. Either he genuinely didn't know where Loretta was or why she'd taken off work, or Skye was losing her touch.

The lesson lasted until two, and while Skye drove back to Scumble River after her class, she brooded over Vince and Loretta's disappearance.

However, as she turned left on Basin Street at quarter to three, she put her concern about her brother and his fiancée aside and concentrated on what she would say to Hugo.

Skye didn't know whether her cousin had anything to do with the murder, but even if he was completely innocent, Hugo tended to view information as a valuable commodity and didn't often give it away for free. She hoped he'd make an exception for her, but she was afraid he wouldn't.

As she had promised, Skye called Wally to alert him that she had arrived at the used-car lot, then waited until she saw a squad car pull up and park a couple of spots away. She noticed that the officer had a clear view through the showroom window and gave Anthony a slight acknowledging nod before going inside.

This time she was in luck. There were no customers when she entered, and Hugo was sitting alone at one of the half dozen small round tables scattered through the space.

Skye approached her cousin, who was playing a handheld video game as he drank a cup of coffee and puffed on a cigarette. The bouquet of multicolored balloons that were attached to a weight in the center of the table swayed each time he blew out a stream of smoke.

"Hi, Hugo."

He jumped, then muttered, "What are you

doing here?" His gaze went back to his game. "Did you bring another one of your juvenile delinquents to cheat me out of a profit?"

"Nope." Apparently Xenia *had* gotten a good deal. "I came to talk to you about Dad's birthday."

"Oh." Hugo's sour expression changed to something more neutral. "When is it?"

"Not until January, but I want to throw him a surprise party."

"Why do you want to talk to me about that?" he asked, his voice indicating mild interest.

"Well, first, I wanted to make sure you have the date free. His birthday is the ninth, but I want to hold the party on the eighth."

"I'll have to check with Victoria and get back to you." Hugo blew a smoke ring in Skye's direction. "What else? You could have called for that. I suppose you want me to pitch in some money."

"Not at all." Skye decided to try and shake him up. "In fact, it looks as if business is pretty bad."

"We're just slow today." Hugo's tone was defensive. "Saturday there'll be lots of customers. I'm having an exotic dancer to show that we're 'stripping down' the prices."

Ew! Skye hoped her expression didn't show her true thoughts. "Really?" She pasted a concerned look on her face. "Last Saturday when I was at the Tales and Treats grand opening, your lot seemed deserted. And I know no one moved those cars you had parked in front of the store the whole time I was there."

"Maybe you missed it when they were taken for a test drive."

"I don't think so." Even though Hugo hadn't invited her to, Skye pulled out a chair and sat down. "In fact, those same vehicles were there in the exact same spots Sunday." Skye needled her cousin a little more. "I'm sure Risé's security camera would show that I'm right."

"Dammit it all to hell!" Hugo stood abruptly, his chair tipping over and crashing to the floor. "Are you telling me that bitch is recording my cars?"

Oops! "Maybe she's taping something else, and your cars are just there." Skye hadn't realized that Hugo didn't know about the cameras. Risé mustn't have confronted him yet. Was that what she and Orlando were arguing about the night before?

"I warned her not to mess with me." He stomped over to the glass wall and peered out, apparently not seeing or not caring that there was a police car parked in front of his building.

"You shouldn't jump to conclusions," Skye soothed. "Maybe she doesn't intend to do anything with the tape."

"Of course she does." Hugo grunted. "Women like her never know when to quit. Now she's in for it. She'll learn that most people have skeletons in their closets, but I bury mine so deep they never see the light of day."

Oh, my God! Was Hugo admitting murder? "What are you going to do?"

"Tell everyone her dirty little secret."

Phew! That didn't sound too violent. "Which is?"

"Hmm." Hugo stroked his chin. "Why not? Everyone will know in a day or two."

"Maybe you should talk to her first." No matter how much she needed this information, Skye didn't want him to expose Risé to the censure of Scumble River's gossips.

"I'm through trying to reason with that bitch." Hugo extracted a monogrammed silver flask from his inside jacket pocket and took a swig. "Everyone's going to know that the investment firm she worked for swindled its clients out of millions of dollars, and her boss is in prison for securities fraud."

"That doesn't mean she was guilty of anything," Skye pointed out.

"How could she not know what was going on?" Hugo snorted. "And if she's so innocent, why didn't she lose all her money like the people who trusted her?"

"How do you know she didn't?" Skye asked. "Come to think of it, how do you know all this to begin with?" If Wally's officer hadn't been able to find out where Risé had last worked, how had Hugo? Of course, Zelda was fresh out of police training, and Hugo had years of practice being a bastard.

"It was easy. I asked around. They paid cash for the building and have no loans or investors. That's all a matter of public record on file at city hall." Hugo righted his chair, sat back down, and picked up his video game. "As to the other, who in his right mind gives up a six-figure income to open up a bookstore in Podunk, Illinois?" His voice was an insinuating purr. "I knew there was a scandal somewhere, and once I found out where she used to work, I just looked online until I found it."

Skye ran the scenario in her head. Since Risé hadn't been sent to jail, her name wouldn't have been associated with the case. Furthermore, since men like Risé's boss usually accepted a plea bargain rather than go to trial, she wouldn't have had to testify against him.

Hugo was immersed back in his game by the time Skye said, "I have one more question."

"Yeah?" He lifted his brow in a "What now?" expression.

"Did you find out who her clients were?"

"Nah." He shrugged. "I didn't care. Just the fact she was involved in such shady dealings should be enough for the old biddies to chase her out of town. Or at least give her something other than my cars to worry about."

Skye looked at him in distaste. "That's pretty cold, Hugo, even for you."

"Hush." He put his finger to his lips. "Do you hear that?"

"What?" Skye listened, but the showroom was silent.

"That's the voices of all the people who care what you think."

"You are so not funny." Skye paused, trying to figure out how to ask whether Hugo had an alibi for the night of the murder. He certainly had a motive. "It's a good thing Risé wasn't the one murdered last week. Since you hate her so much, you'd be a prime suspect."

"Hey, Victoria and I were at our church's Las Vegas night last Saturday between seven and midnight." Hugo threw back his head and laughed. "I won the grand prize, a flat-screen TV, and the drawing was at eleven o'clock, so I have hundreds of witnesses to prove I was in Clay Center during the time of the murder. Including two priests, a deacon, and the entire choir of St. Mary's."

After calling Wally and filling him in on Hugo's alibi and Risé's past, Skye headed over to Kayla's wake. It was scheduled from four to eight p.m., and Skye had a feeling she'd better be there for most of that time. Even though Kayla had been out of high school for a year, if she was as well liked as Neva had claimed, there would probably be a lot of kids attending, and emotions were bound to run high.

Skye was surprised to see that the funeral home's lot was already packed. It was exactly four thirty, and although the visitation had officially begun thirty minutes ago, small-town etiquette dictated that the family be allowed the first half hour to themselves. Then again, Kayla's friends were probably too young to know that.

After Skye had made several trips up and down the rows, someone finally pulled out and she could park. She hesitated for a moment before opening the car door. She had meant to go home to change but had run out of time. The green dress Wally had bought her was beautiful, but she preferred to wear a more somber color for a wake.

Once Skye was out of the Bel Air, she quickly crossed the asphalt and pushed through the funeral home's double glass doors. At the top of the foyer steps, she paused and looked at herself in the mirrored wall. She tugged on the fabric, a gorgeous cashmere knit that clung to her curves. Was it a bit too sexy for this situation? The V neckline and shorter-than-usual hem made her a little self-conscious, but she had vowed not to cover herself in yards of polyester just because she weighed more than *Vogue* considered attractive.

Taking a deep breath, she hiked her tote bag higher on her shoulder, straightened her spine, and walked through the archway. It was too late to do anything about her outfit now, and she had more important things to worry about than her appearance.

The overpowering scent of flowers and the hum of numerous conversations assaulted her as she stepped inside the viewing room. Stopping, she scanned the chairs. Most were occupied by teenagers and the elderly. Perhaps Kayla's parents' friends would come later, after they got off work.

After signing the guest book, Skye joined the long line of people waiting to pay their respects. From her place in the back, Skye studied Kayla's mother, Kara. She hadn't had much time to observe the woman when she and Wally had made the death notification. Kara had collapsed on the sofa sobbing, and Kayla's stepfather had immediately hustled them out the door before Skye had been able to form an impression of the couple.

Now, seeing Kara formally dressed and made-up, Skye thought she didn't seem old enough to have a nineteen-year-old daughter. Her pale oval face was flawless, and her long blond hair fell in a straight curtain to the middle of her back. Kayla's stepfather, Mick O'Brien, stood next to his wife, looking uncomfortable in a shiny navy suit.

Mick's bored expression, and the way he gripped Kara's elbow whenever she hugged someone for too long, convinced Skye that Neva had been correct about the family dynamics. It was clear that this man had not cared about his stepdaughter and totally dominated his wife.

Skye moved slightly so she could see the first row of the seating area, the one reserved for close relatives. She was curious to get a look at Kayla's extended family. Only three chairs were occupied. Neva sat in one, with twins who appeared to be five or six on either side of her.

They were cute little boys, and Skye assumed they were Kayla's half brothers. They appeared to have inherited their mother's fair hair and complexion. Seeing them made Skye wonder whether Kayla had looked like her biological father. She'd heard that he had been killed in a hunting accident before his daughter was born.

The woman in front of Skye had just walked away after speaking to Kara and Mick, and Skye hadn't moved forward yet when she heard Mick hiss to his wife, "How much longer do we gotta stand here?"

Either Mick didn't feel it was necessary to hide his impatience, or he was the type of guy who had never had to pretend and thus never learned how.

Kara's cornflower blue eyes were shiny with

tears, and she jerked her arm from his fingers. "*You* can leave anytime."

Skye saw Mick's freckled face flush an unbecoming red, and as he reached for Kara, Skye stepped between them. Keeping her back to the obnoxious man, she said, "Mrs. O'Brien, I'm Skye Denison. I was with Chief Boyd when he told you about Kayla, but I also knew her from the gifted class at high school. You have my deepest sympathy."

Kayla's mother clutched Skye's hand. "She was amazing, wasn't she? Did you know her final project at film school last year won an award?"

"No, I didn't. But I understand she was very talented. I'd like to see some of her work sometime."

Before his wife could respond, Mick put his palm on Skye's shoulder and propelled her down the line, saying, "Thank you for coming."

Skye found herself facing Neva as the older woman stood and moved into her path.

The principal's eyes were red rimmed, and it took her several tries before she was able to speak. "What have you found out?"

"Nothing I can talk about." Skye tried to steer Neva to a more private location, but she refused to budge.

Neva swallowed hard and frowned. "That's what I was afraid of. The police are giving up, aren't they?"

"Definitely not. It's only been five days since the murder was discovered." Skye spotted a pair of overstuffed chairs screened by a huge flower arrangement. "Come sit with me and I'll tell you what I can."

Once they were seated, Skye scooted as close as she could without her knees bumping against Neva's and lowered her voice. "The police are pursuing this case as if the primary objective of the crime was murder, not burglary."

"Really?" Neva studied Skye, her expression hopeful. "Who do they suspect?"

"Unfortunately, everyone on their first list has an alibi." Skye was careful to tell as much of the truth as she could without giving away the fact that they thought the intended victim was Risé. "They'll start looking elsewhere now that those people have been cleared."

"That's good, then." Neva nodded, seemingly satisfied, at least for now.

"I'm going to mingle to make sure Kayla's friends are handling their grief okay and no one gets carried away." Skye pushed the chair into its original position and got up. "I'll see you later."

As Skye moved around the floral display, a commotion at the entrance drew her attention. Standing just inside the room, arguing in loud whispers, were Xenia and Chase. Skye had thought it odd that neither Kayla's boyfriend nor her BFF were there when she arrived, but now she wondered whether it hadn't been for the best.

Skye moved toward them in time to hear Chase say to Xenia, "I told you not to show up here if you were going to dress like a freak."

Chase was wearing a charcoal wool suit, gray shirt, and striped silk tie. He looked as if he had just stepped out of *GQ*. Xenia had on ripped tights, an oversize leather coat that dragged behind her like a train, and army boots. Then again, they *were* all black.

"Hi, Ms. D." Xenia saw Skye before Chase did. "This moron thinks that the dead care about how you dress. Tell him he's wrong."

Not giving Skye a chance to answer, Chase said, "That's not what I meant, and you know it." His voice cracked, and he blinked furiously. "Of course the dead don't care, but you need to have some respect for Mr. and Mrs. O'Brien." He appealed to Skye, "Right?"

Xenia didn't wait for Skye to respond either. "Those hypocrites?" She tossed her hair, the scarlet stripe looking eerily like a vein of blood as it curled through the black tresses. "The only time they paid any attention to Kayla was when they needed her to babysit or wanted her to cook and clean."

"That's not true." Chase's handsome face was mottled with red. "They only wanted her to be sensible and act like a proper young lady."

"Just leave me alone." Xenia sniffed, then marched off, saying over her shoulder, "I refuse to star in your psychodrama."

Chase turned to Skye. "Kayla was going to, you know."

"Going to what?" Skye asked

"Be a proper young lady. She was going to quit film school and marry me. I told her my wife would never have to earn a living. I make plenty of money working at my dad's real estate agency."

"Oh?" Skye encouraged him to continue. Kayla hadn't impressed Skye as the stay-at-home-wife type.

Chase stared blankly at the casket. "I should never have let her take that job. My salary would have supported us both."

"I see." *Wow!* Skye had really read Kayla wrong. She'd thought the girl was way more independent than that.

"Everyone said we were the perfect couple." Chase nodded, as if Skye had agreed with him, then lumbered toward where Xenia had stopped to talk to a group of teenagers.

Instead of following him, Skye pondered what she had just heard. Who was right? Neva and Xenia, who were certain Kayla's folks were neglectful and used her like an indentured servant? Or Chase, who thought Mr. and Mrs. O'Brien were employing good old-fashioned values—which was just fine with him?

The remaining hours crawled by, and Skye moved through the room chatting with as many attendees as she could. Everyone concurred with Neva's assessment of Kayla. The girl had been well liked by all, extremely hardworking, and truly helpful to her friends. Those who had seen her films also agreed that she was enormously talented and would have been a famous director one day.

Feelings were more mixed about Kara. Most didn't approve of the way she had treated her daughter, but they were somewhat understanding of the woman's dilemma. When she had married Mick fifteen years ago, Kara had been a single mother of a four-year-old with no education or skills to support herself or her child. Mick had been a savior, and she was willing to do what he said.

In contrast, Mick was nearly unanimously thought to be a controlling jerk who ruled Kara with an iron fist, had no interest in Kayla, and had been happy she would be moving out completely in a month. Still, no one could think of any reason for him to kill his stepdaughter.

It was nearly seven thirty when Skye felt a wave of exhaustion hit her. She'd been on the go for more than twelve hours and had not eaten since noon. She needed a break and a candy bar. Making her way to a sofa situated off to the side of the row of folding chairs, she sat down, prepared to intervene if any of the remaining teenagers needed comforting. So far, although Kayla's friends had been sad, none had become hysterical, but it took only one to set off all the rest.

Skye settled back, relieved to be off her feet, and fished a Kit Kat from her tote bag. She had spoken briefly with Simon, but he'd had no new information about Xavier, who had the night off.

Nevertheless, as Skye bit into the chocolate-covered wafer, something was bugging her. Something Hugo had said had pertained to Xavier. But what was it? Finally she stopped trying to think of it, hoping it would come to her after she had a good night's sleep.

CHAPTER 21

All the King's Men

Saturday afternoon, Skye arrived at Tales and Treats early for the store's first author event. She was eager to meet a real live novelist, as well as intent on talking to Risé about her previous job. Wally had agreed that since Skye had established a rapport with the shop owner, she would be the best one to approach Risé regarding her past and to ask her if any locals had lost money when her employer went to jail.

A chat with Xenia was also on Skye's to-do list. She didn't believe for a minute that the girl was really working at the store to earn a salary. Xenia's true motivation had to be something more Machiavellian.

As per Skye's usual luck, both Risé and Xenia were busy with customers when she stepped through the door. Frustrated, she walked over to a rack of greeting cards near the register. From this location she could watch and seize whatever opportunity arose to speak to either woman.

Skye was giggling over a humorous birthday card featuring a black cat wearing a tiara when a commotion near the entrance drew her attention.

Curious, she looked over her shoulder, blinked several times, then froze, unable to believe her eyes.

Oh, my gosh! What were the Dooziers doing at a book signing? They weren't a family that generally valued the written word, nor did they attend many of Scumble River's social occasions. So, what in the heck were they doing here? Spelling not being their long suit, had they supposed that a store with "tales" in its name sold hunting dogs? Or maybe, because beer was the ultimate delicacy, they figured that the "treats" part had to mean a bar?

Earl Doozier, the patriarch, led his brood straight through the middle of the store. Tattoos covered most of his body, and he usually wore shorts and a tank top so everyone could enjoy them. But today he had on overalls, a corduroy blazer with leather elbow patches, and a limp fedora with a chunk missing from the brim. Skye wondered whether one of his hounds, or possibly one of his offspring, had taken a bite out of it.

Following him like reluctant ducklings were his son Junior, his nephew Cletus, and his twelve-year-old daughter Bambi. All three of the kids' sullen expressions matched that of the woman who brought up the rear.

Earl's wife, Glenda, was clad in a denim miniskirt that showed her butt cheeks with every step she took and a red T-shirt that had been ripped open and tied back together just under her breasts. Skye thought the high-heeled purple cowboy boots were a nice touch.

Glenda's chalk white skin and heavily made-up face caused her to look more corpselike than any cadaver Skye had ever seen in a casket. Topping off this fashion disaster was a head of poorly dyed-blond hair that had been styled into an elaborately teased tower that soared a good two feet in the air. By comparison, the six-inch feather earrings and daggerlike fuchsia fingernails seemed almost ladylike.

Skye had dealt with most of the Dooziers in the years she had been the Scumble River school psychologist. They had a family tree full of stunted twigs and thorny branches, but in a funny way, she counted them among her friends. Maybe not pals she'd go to the movies and dinner with, but allies she could count on.

With that in mind, and not wanting them to stumble into any trouble or get their feelings hurt, Skye replaced the greeting card she'd been reading in the rack, pasted a smile on her face, and sprinted over to the Dooziers. Better she find out right now why they were there, and be prepared, than wait for something to happen. Where Dooziers went, trouble usually followed.

"Hi." Skye popped up in front of the family, halting their march to the front counter. "Everyone recovered from the big wedding?" She had attended Earl's younger brother's nuptials last June. It had been quite a sight. A couple dozen beer cans, a wire-hanger arch, and a cement-filled kiddie pool had transformed their backyard into a chapel. The reception had been held next to a rusted-out pickup decorated with plastic flowers and NASCAR flags.

"Miz Skye. It was the bestest ever." Earl smiled broadly, revealing several missing teeth.

"How are Elvis and his new bride doing?"

"Those two are as happy as two flies in a spit cup. Mavis's gonna pop out the kid any second now."

"Great." Skye slid a glance at Earl's wife. They hadn't been on the best of terms since their first meeting, when Skye had tried to offer some parenting tips to the bleached blonde. "Hello, Glenda."

Glenda had been giving her version of the Doozier Death Stare to a trio of women whose heads were bent close together as they gossiped in low voices, occasionally sneaking quick peeks at Earl and his family. But she focused her attention back on Skye and said, "Hey." Her voice was like a squeaky hinge. "How'd your kinfolk's hitchin' go?"

"Pretty well." Skye wasn't about to go into what had happened at her cousin's platinum affair. "I'm sure it wasn't half as fun as Elvis's."

"I heard it was a hot mess." Earl snickered.

Skye opened her mouth to protest, but Glenda stepped between them.

Standing chest to nose with her husband—Earl being barely five feet and Glenda a good ten inches taller—she said over her shoulder to Skye, "Don't pay him no attention. He likes to speak his mind, which makes the conversation pretty damn short."

"Hey!" Earl wrinkled his brow, apparently trying to figure out exactly how he'd been insulted. "It ain't right sayin' stuff like that about your man."

"You can dress a pig up," Glenda said with a shrug, "but that don't make him king of the prom."

Earl snorted, chewing tobacco shooting from his mouth and spraying the front of his wife's shirt. As he continued to snigger, Glenda's face turned red.

She grabbed him by the lapels and warned, "You better pray that comes out."

Skye raised a brow. She had no idea the Dooziers were so religious.

"Don't be a dumb-ass," Earl sputtered. "You got no call to be getting so huffy. I should—"

Glenda interrupted him. "I'm goin' home now, and after I wash my shirt, I'm gonna take a nap, so you better be mighty quiet when you get back."

"You know, Glenda," Skye called after her,

"it's not a good idea to go to sleep mad."

Glenda ignored Skye and kept walking, but Earl said, "You is right, Miz Skye. I always stays awake to plots my revenge." Skye had no idea how to respond to that statement, so she didn't, and Earl continued. "I ain't got time for all this social chitchat. I needs ta talk ta that lady about my book." He pointed to Risé, who was bagging a sale for a young woman with a baby strapped to her back.

"Your book?" Skye was surprised that Earl wanted to buy a book. "Which one do you want? Is it a hardcover or a paperback? Maybe I can find it for you."

"Not one that's already wrote." Earl puffed out his chest. "The one I'm gonna write. Junior looked on the Internet and it says how anyone can write a book and publish it theyself, and make lots of money sellin' it." He elbowed the red-headed teenage boy behind him. "Right, Junior?"

"Yeah, Pa." The boy rubbed his ribs. "It said all the bookstores would be glad ta sell it for you and give you the money."

"You're planning to write a book, publish it, and have Tales and Treats sell it for you?" Skye felt a tic start underneath her left eye as she tried to find a diplomatic way to say, *Are you freaking kidding me?* She knew Earl was all foam, no beer, but this was bad even for him. "Um, what is your book going to be about?"

"Me and my kinfolk." Earl shifted around Skye and swaggered up to the counter, now devoid of customers. "All the Dooziers done did real interestin' stuff. We been around these parts since afore the Civil War."

Risé had stepped over to help Xenia with a transaction, so no one was behind the register, and Skye took the opportunity to ask Earl, "What made you decide to write a book?"

"The little girl that used ta work here afore she got herself kilt." He paused until Skye nodded. "She made a movie based on me and my kin. Only, you know, she sorta added and changed stuff ta make it more interestin' and not so apt ta git me arrested."

"Oh." Skye wasn't sure how that connected, but she waited for Earl to go on.

" 'Bouts a year ago, she came ta the house, and I told her all my family yarns and she used them ta make her picture show." He poked himself in the chest with his thumb. "We even got to be in it." He grinned. "She was real excited that it won some kinda award or somethin' that gave her a free trip ta Hollywood and a chance ta show some real important folks my story."

"She won this award recently?" Skye was distracted, still trying to figure out how Kayla's *Dooziers Through History* movie added up to Earl writing a book.

"Yep." Earl nodded, his straggly ponytail whipping around his shoulders. "She came out ta tell us about it a month or so ago." He dug in his ear with his pinkie and frowned at the substance he exhumed. "But then I seed her a coupla weeks back, and something had sure put a hitch in her getalong. She twern't happy no more, and she said ain't nobody would see our movie after all."

"So you decided to fix that." Skye finally thought she saw the light in Earl's tunnel of confusion.

"Yep." His head bobbed up and down like a balloon caught in the breeze. "At first I was gonna make a movie, too, except that turned out ta take too much fancy equipment. But you don't need nothin' ta write a book."

Skye's mouth opened and closed, but before she could think of a reply, a male voice boomed, "My reading will begin in one minute. Please take your seats."

Risé swept everyone into the literature alcove, introduced the author, and then stepped away, allowing the man to take her place behind the podium, aka the desk. Folding chairs had been arranged in rows facing him. He wore jeans, a tweed jacket, and a hat rather like the one on Earl's head, although without the bite taken out of the brim.

As Skye sat down, Earl announced, "I'm gonna go talk ta the book lady. She won't have nothin' ta do what with you all sittin' in here."

Skye opened her mouth to point out that he'd miss the talk, then thought better of it. Maybe that was for the best. With Earl, the lights were flashing, the gates were down, but there was no train coming.

"Me and the other kids'll be waiting in the café," Junior told his dad.

Earl nodded and went in search of fame and fortune.

Skye glanced at her watch. It was one o'clock. Trixie had said she'd try to meet her here, but Owen had wanted her help in buying some new clothes at Farm and Fleet in Kankakee, and she might not make it back in time. Just in case, Skye put her tote bag on the seat next to her to save it, although people weren't exactly pouring into the room. Besides herself, there were the three ladies that had provoked Glenda's ire, four or five teen-agers, a strange guy dressed in a long overcoat, and Orlando.

The author, Walker Josephson, picked up a hardback with a cover featuring a tough-looking man holding a big gun in his hand, his arm around a seminaked girl. Twenty minutes later, Skye was fighting to keep her eyes open. Josephson had a monotone voice, and she would have much preferred that he talk about the story rather than read it to them.

When the writer finally closed the book, took a sip of water, and asked for questions, Skye looked around. Who would be brave enough to go first?

Orlando stood and said, "Walker, thank you for coming to our bookstore."

"It's my pleasure." Josephson nodded his head regally.

Next, a brunette from the trio of women raised her hand and said, "It's such an honor to have you here in Scumble River."

Thank you, little lady." The author sucked in the small potbelly that hung over his waistband. "Which of my books was your favorite?"

"Oh." The brunette tittered. "I haven't actually read any. I don't have time to read. Are they available on CD?"

He grimaced and shook his head. "Any other questions?" He glanced around the small space, stroking his beard.

Silence. Then finally one of the teenagers asked, "Did you write the whole book yourself, or did you, like, copy some of it?"

"That would be plagiarism." He glared at the girl. "I would never do that."

"Sorry. My history teacher said to ask." The girl chewed, then blew a bubble with her gum. "He told us if we came to this we got extra credit and he wouldn't fail us for using papers we bought on the Internet."

"Well." Josephson seemed to be unable to think of anything else to say.

Skye felt sorry for him and raised her hand. "Could you tell us a little about your writing process?"

While he was explaining his method, Risé stepped back into the room. Once he finished, she said to him, "Thank you, Walker." There was a smattering of polite applause. When it died down, she pointed to a table off to the side. "We have cookies and coffee, and Mr. Josephson will be happy to autograph books for you."

Orlando slipped out of the room, but everyone else rushed for the refreshments, and Skye had to fight her way in the opposite direction. Once she got her book signed, she walked over to Risé and asked, "Do you have a minute to talk to me?"

"Sure." Risé raised an eyebrow. "Somehow I don't think there will be a run at the register."

"Somewhere private?"

"Okay." Risé led the way. "We can use the back room."

When they were settled, Risé in an old office chair and Skye perched on a box, Skye said, "I wanted to warn you that my cousin Hugo found out about what happened in your previous job and plans to tell everyone."

"I know." Risé shrugged. "It was never a huge secret, although it would have been nice to be able to leave it in the past." She grimaced. "I wish it hadn't happened, but I had no idea my boss was running a Ponzi scheme. The police cleared me, and I was hoping to start fresh."

"You might want to give the *Star* an interview and get your side out in the open. Maybe something on the order of the positives in starting over." Skye made a face. "I don't always agree with Kathryn Steele, the paper's publisher, but she's usually fair."

"Good idea." Risé nodded. "I don't worry about what people think—they don't do it often enough for me to be concerned—but it does bother Orlando. And right now he's struggling to stay sober, so I don't want him more stressed-out."

Skye nodded sympathetically. "Then it really would be a good idea to let people know what *really* happened versus what Hugo might say."

Risé pursed her lips. "I met Kathryn at a chamber of commerce meeting, and I think she'd be open to my story."

"Great." Skye smiled. "One other thing." She twisted the handles of her tote bag. "You know the police now think that murder was the primary intention, not burglary. So we're exploring all possibilities, which includes the chance that you rather than Kayla were the intended victim."

"Really?" Risé's face knotted with surprise. "Me? Why?"

"Well, I hate to ask . . ." Skye hesitated.

"Go ahead." Risé met Skye's gaze. "I've never

flinched from uncomfortable questions, and I'm not about to start now."

"Fair enough." Skye nodded. "I'm thinking it might be someone who lost money with your firm and blames you. Was there anyone local who invested?"

"Yes."

"Who?" Skye asked, hoping Risé wouldn't claim confidentiality.

"Troy Yates."

"The bank president?" Skye clarified, although the only other Troy Yates she knew was his son, Troy Jr., currently away at college.

"Uh-huh."

"Then we'll talk to him." Skye dug a pad from her tote and made a note. "Anyone else around here who lost money and might want to kill you?"

Risé hesitated for a nanosecond before shaking her head.

Skye watched the other woman's expression. "Are you sure?" She was certain Risé was holding something back.

"Yes." Risé got up. "Yates is the only one from this area who lost money and might hold a grudge."

"Okay."

Skye started to leave, but Risé stopped her. "Um, if I was the intended victim, do you think the killer might try again?"

"It's hard to say," Skye hedged. "It would probably be a good idea not to be alone, make sure the doors are locked after hours, and keep up your guard."

"Yeah." Risé's skin was pale, and there was fear in her eyes. "I'll do that."

Skye watched Risé head into the café, then walked over to the counter. Xenia was alone at the register, and Skye handed the girl Josephson's book and a fifty-dollar bill. "I'm curious about something."

"Yeah?" Xenia rang up the purchase.

"Let's face it. I know you don't need the money, so why are you really working here?" Skye held out her hand for the change and was a little dismayed to see it was less than twenty dollars. This was why she rarely bought hard-covers.

Several different expressions crossed Xenia's face before she settled on nonchalant. "I thought it would be an interesting experience."

"Try again."

"I don't answer to you." Xenia's posture was belligerent as she shoved the book into a bag.

"No, you don't," Skye replied smoothly. "But if it has anything to do with Kayla's murder, I really need to know."

"Why?" Xenia's voice was bitter. "Nothing will help Kayla now."

"That's true," Skye agreed. "But once you kill

someone, it's much easier to do it a second time."

"So you're worried about me." Xenia's tone was a little less hostile.

"Yes, I am." Skye stuffed her purchase into her tote bag.

"Why?"

"Because you're my friend." Skye realized that was true. She did regard the prickly teen as a friend. "And I don't want to see anything bad happen to you."

"Say I believe you. I can't talk about it here." Xenia glanced over her shoulder. "I get off work in twenty minutes. Meet me at my car."

CHAPTER 22

Lady Chatterley's Lover

"L ike everything about Xenia, there's no one clear reason," Skye said to Wally as he drove them toward Troy Yates's house. "She's making a documentary about people who have downsized and simplified their lives. She's observing Risé and Orlando to see if they're happier in their new circumstances, or if they would prefer to go back to their previous existence."

The Yateses lived in one of the new subdivisions just inside the Scumble River School District. Previously, the county sheriff's department had been responsible for patrolling that area, but it had been annexed into the city limits a couple of years ago.

"And?" Wally pulled into a paved driveway flanked by two concrete lions—one with its right paw raised in the air and the other its left.

"And she wants to find Kayla's killer." Skye craned her neck to examine the massive brick house as it came into view. It had lots of fancy shaped windows, expensive landscaping, and a five-car garage that was bigger than many homes. The Yateses certainly didn't appear to be hurting for money. "Since Xenia had no clue where to begin to investigate a murder, she figured working at the scene of the crime was her best bet."

"Not bad reasoning." Wally stopped the squad car and turned off the engine.

"She's getting bored working in the bookstore, so I don't think she'll last much longer." Skye got out of the cruiser and met Wally on the walkway. "Plus she finds it a strain to be pleasant to people she considers her inferiors."

"Don't we all." Wally grinned, then discretely tipped his head toward the house. "Let me do the talking here." Someone had drawn back a curtain and was watching them. "You gauge Yates's reactions and give me a sign if you want to ask something."

"That's probably best, considering Mr. and Mrs. Yates tried to sue me last year for printing that unflattering article about their daughter in the *Scoop*." Skye followed him to the front door. "Even after I rescued Ashley from a deranged killer, I don't think they completely forgave me."

Mrs. Yates responded to the doorbell, and when Wally asked to see her husband, she ushered them through an impressive marble foyer containing a striking curving stairway, down a short hallway, and into a huge family room. A wall of floor-to-ceiling windows displayed an in-ground pool surrounded by a brick patio.

Troy Yates lay sprawled on an enormous leather sofa in front of a mammoth TV. It took his wife several tries to get his attention, but he finally tore his gaze away from Sylvester Stallone blowing up people. He muted the set, put down the remote, and said, "Chief Boyd, what can I do for you? Is there a problem at the bank?"

"No." Wally moved so that Yates could see Skye, who had been standing behind him. "We wanted to talk to you about something personal."

"Have a seat."

Wally and Skye settled into matching club chairs that flanked the sofa.

Troy gestured to a mahogany bar in the corner. "Would you like something to drink?"

"No, thanks," Wally answered for both of them. "When I said personal, I meant your personal dealings versus the bank. We're here on police business."

Yates's demeanor changed. He straightened and looked at his wife, who had been hovering by the door. "I'll handle this, dear."

She nodded and scurried away.

Yates the genial host was gone. He said, "Maybe I'd better phone my attorney before we go any further."

Skye felt her heart race and her stomach clench, but she managed to maintain a calm expression. Had Yates killed Kayla? He was certainly acting guilty about something. Or maybe his behavior was typical of the wealthy.

"We just have a couple of questions, but if you feel you need the protection of a lawyer . . ." Wally let his voice trail off insinuatingly.

"Of course not. I'll trust you not to violate my rights." Yates's voice was jovial, but his expression was steely. "What do you want to know?"

"I understand you knew Risé Vaughn prior to her move to Scumble River."

Skye admired Wally's neutral opening.

"Yes." Yates crossed his legs. "Although I don't see how that's any of your concern."

"And I understand you lost quite a bit of money when Ms. Vaughn's boss was arrested and the firm closed down."

"So?" Yates raised an eyebrow. "What have my private financial affairs got to do with the police? I somehow doubt this is about getting my money back."

"No. That's way above my pay grade." Wally gave him a good-old-boy grin. "We're investigating the possibility that the intended victim of last week's murder at the new bookstore wasn't the clerk but the owner."

"And you think I might have killed that poor girl by mistake because I lost a few dollars in the market?" Yates asked, sounding amused.

"We have to check out all possible leads. And money is always an excellent motive for murder." Wally's face was now impassive. "Do you have an alibi for last Saturday night, from eight fifteen until eleven?"

"Actually, I do." Yates's smile was smug. "My wife and I were attending a dinner party hosted by the mayor." He addressed Skye for the first time. "Your uncle has an impressive wine cellar."

Wally shot Skye a questioning glance. She shrugged. As far as she knew, Uncle Dante only drank Budweiser or bourbon, but anything was possible.

"And FYI, I never invest more than I can afford to lose." Yates stood and escorted them to the hallway. "Unlike some people."

"Who, for instance?" Wally asked.

"I'm not one to point fingers." Yates walked back to the couch and plopped down, then turned up the volume on the TV. "I'm sure you can find your own way out."

"What do you think?" Wally asked once they were outside.

"The mayor's a darn good alibi."

"Who do you think he meant when he said some people lost money they couldn't afford?" Wally helped Skye into the squad car.

She was about to say she had no idea, when it hit her. *Hell's bells!* Skye forced her face to remain expressionless. It was Xavier. He hadn't put all his savings and his veteran's group's treasury in the bookstore, as he had told Simon. He couldn't have. Hugo said that Risé and

Orlando paid cash to open Tales and Treats and didn't have any loans or investors.

Xavier must have invested all the money with Risé's company and lost it when the firm went bust. That had to be the big secret. *Shoot!* Now Skye had no choice but to tell Wally the whole story. And he wouldn't be a happy police chief or, come to think about it, a happy fiancé.

Skye waited until they had arrived back at the PD and were parked in the garage before speaking. Stopping Wally before he got out of the cruiser, she told him the whole story. Then she waited for the explosion.

"You're telling me you knew all along that Xavier Ryan had some big secret connected with the bookstore and its owners, and you never shared this information with me?" Wally ground the words out between his teeth.

"Yes, but—"

"But nothing." He cut her off, and she didn't try to continue. Her grandma Cora always said, never miss a good chance to shut up, and this was clearly that time.

Wally ran his fingers though his hair. "It's not only that you had a responsibility as a police consultant, but you had an obligation as my fiancée not to keep secrets from me. Especially when an ex-boyfriend is the one asking you to stay quiet." He slumped in his seat and stared out the windshield. "One thing I can't handle is disloyalty."

"I know. I'm so sorry. You're right." Skye's shoulders drooped. Nothing sucked more than that moment during an argument when you realized you were wrong. "I should never have promised Simon not to tell you in the first place, and then when Kayla was killed, I should have told you everything." She put a hand on his and gazed into his eyes. "I truly am sorry, and it won't happen again."

"Well." She detected a thawing in his tone, but suddenly his voice hardened and he shook off her touch. "No. You still have feelings for Reid or you wouldn't have kept this from me."

Was Wally right? Skye examined her conscience, then took his hand again. "I'll probably always have some feelings for Simon, the same as you'll always have some feelings for Darleen. They were a big part of our lives. But the reason I didn't tell you was because of my affection for Xavier and Frannie, not because of Simon."

Wally's long silence made Skye afraid she had blown her chance for happiness.

Finally Wally let out a long, audible breath, and although his frown lingered, he said, "I believe you." He looked intently into her eyes. "But don't *ever* let this happen again."

"I won't." Skye leaned over to kiss him, but Wally got out of the car and walked toward the police station door without waiting for her.

313

Sighing, she followed him. Clearly he was still upset, and she could only hope that once he cooled off, he'd give her another chance.

Xavier wasn't easy to locate. There was no one at his house, and when they checked to see whether he was working, Simon told Wally and Skye that Xavier and Frannie had gone to dinner and a movie in Bolingbrook. Frannie had been feeling a little down since her boyfriend, Justin, was out of town due to a family emergency, so Xavier had taken his daughter to the Red Robin on Weber Road, one of Frannie's favorite hamburger restaurants, then to see *The Brothers Grimm*.

Simon seemed worried when Wally was questioning him, and as she and Wally left, Skye glanced back. Simon's disappointed gaze skewered her to the spot. Her shoulders slumped. She'd had no choice but to tell Wally, and she shouldn't have agreed to keep the secret in the first place. Still, she hated that she felt as if she had somehow let both men down.

They had gotten Xavier's cell number from Simon, and when he didn't pick up, Wally left a message for him to call immediately, as they had some questions about his connections to the bookstore.

While they waited for Xavier to phone them, Wally and Skye had dinner at the Feed Bag, then took a ride along the river. They spent the time talking about Wally's feeling of betrayal and why Skye had kept quiet. Finally Wally truly forgave Skye.

Nevertheless, she knew she was on probation and silently vowed not to mess up this relationship as she had so many others. An ex-fiancé and a string of ex-boyfriends proved she needed to make some changes in how she acted.

It was nearly ten by the time Xavier phoned. He didn't want them to come to his house, so he agreed to meet them at the police station, and they hurried back into town. Skye and Wally met the older man as he entered the PD. The three of them proceeded down a short hall to the coffee/interrogation room, and Skye took a seat at one end of the long table in the center of the room.

Xavier sat opposite her. He wore dark trousers and a short-sleeved white shirt. It was the most casual attire in which Skye had ever seen him.

Wally closed the door, then settled in the chair next to Skye and said to Xavier, "Thank you for coming in."

Xavier dipped his head slightly. "I thought it best we speak here instead of in front of my daughter." His pale blue, lashless eyes were magnified behind old-fashioned horn-rimmed glasses, making them seem reptilian.

"Why is that?" Skye asked, then shot Wally a look. Should she go on?

He nodded. They had agreed she would lead the inquiry since she had the best relationship with the suspect. Xavier kept mostly to himself in Scumble River, preferring to socialize with his out-of-town veterans' group, but he had formed a connection with Skye through her friendship with Frannie.

"I didn't want to worry my daughter. It's rarely a good omen when the police want to talk to you." Xavier ran his fingers along the scarred tabletop. "She thinks I got called to transport a body."

"That's probably best." Skye's tone was sympathetic. Frannie was Xavier's whole world, and he'd do anything to protect her. "I'm sorry we have to ask you some personal questions."

Xavier bobbed his head, as if understanding her discomfort. "Go ahead."

"Simon told me that you had invested in Tales and Treats, but that's not the truth, is it?"

"Not exactly." Xavier's hands were clenched. "When I asked him for a loan, I wasn't completely honest with him."

"Why?" So that was how Simon found out about Xavier's situation. Simon hadn't mentioned he'd loaned Xavier money. "He would have given you the cash even if you told him you had lost yours in Risé's firm's scandal. Which is what happened, right?"

"Yes. That's what happened." Xavier's expression was grim. "But I couldn't take the chance that Simon might not help me. I had to replace the funds from my veterans' group treasury. I promised them their capital would be safe. In the war, men trusted me with their lives; I couldn't let these guys down any more than I could have left behind someone who was wounded on the battlefield."

"What about Simon?" Skye was torn between understanding Xavier's circumstances and feeling disgusted that he'd used his friend. "Simon trusted you, too."

"I know." Xavier's rigid posture sagged. "One lie led to another."

"They always do." Skye spoke from experience. "But how do you plan to reimburse Simon?"

"If the store is successful, I'll be able to repay the loan with interest."

"I thought you said that you didn't invest in Tales and Treats," Wally interjected.

"Not directly." Xavier met Wally's stare. "But Risé and Orlando are giving me a third of the store's profits until I get back all the money I invested with her."

"The problem with that is that bookstores often don't last very long." Wally raised an eyebrow. "And the ones that do rarely earn enough to pay dividends."

"Risé wouldn't start a business she didn't see a way of making money from." Xavier took a deep breath and explained, "According to her plan, they'll make most of their profit from the café and retail items. There's a huge markup on the packaged gourmet foods and coffee they're selling."

"Really? Enough for them to live on and give you a cut?" Wally's tone was doubtful.

"Yes." Xavier nodded. "Because they went into the store with no debt, own the building, and live above the store, they're in a good position. The reason so many small businesses fail is that the owners have to borrow so much capital to get started."

"I see," Wally acknowledged, then asked, "Is Risé reimbursing Troy Yates for his losses?"

"No."

When Xavier didn't elaborate, Skye said, "How did Troy know you had lost money?" While Yates hadn't come right out and named Xavier, his comment about those who couldn't afford to lose their investment had to have been about him.

"Risé didn't like to do business with friends, so when she didn't want me to invest in her firm, I asked Mr. Yates to intervene for me with her boss."

Skye glanced at Wally. If that were true, then Xavier had no reason to want Risé dead. In fact, since she was giving him part of her profits, he had everything riding on her making a success of the shop.

Wally asked, "Is there anyone who can vouch for your whereabouts from eight fifteen until eleven last Saturday night?"

When Xavier didn't respond, Skye said gently, "We'll try to keep this as quiet as we can."

Xavier groaned, losing his usual Zen-like calm. "This cannot get out. We knew it was wrong, and we ended it that night." He implored Skye, "You have to make sure no one finds out. It would ruin her marriage and one of my oldest friendships."

"Oh, my." Skye turned to Wally. "Frannie told Simon that her father had been gone a lot lately, and either he wouldn't say, or he lied about where he'd been." She looked across at Xavier. "You were with Risé, weren't you? You've been having an affair with her."

CHAPTER 23
The Scarlet Letter

Once Xavier confirmed Skye's guess, Wally asked him to remain at the PD while they contacted Risé. Before leaving him alone, Skye assured Xavier that they would talk to his ex-lover without her husband being present. As she and Wally walked out of the interrogation room, Skye looked back. Xavier was sitting ramrod straight, as if waiting for the firing squad.

Once they were out of his hearing, Skye said to Wally, "Do you think it's possible that Orlando already knows about the affair? Maybe he found out recently. Maybe he intended to kill his wife and struck Kayla by mistake."

Wally thought for a moment, then shook his head. "Surely he could distinguish his own wife's backside from that of a nineteen-year-old."

"True." Skye nibbled her lip. "But we're still going to check Orlando's alibi, right?" At this point she didn't trust anyone.

"Oh, yeah. No one gets a free pass." Wally led Skye up the stairs to his office. "Orlando claims he got to his AA meeting at quarter to nine and it lasted until eleven. Since Laurel is a forty-five minute drive from Scumble River, that would jibe with him leaving the store at eight. Which would put him in the clear."

"How can we check?" Skye tilted her head. "Those meetings are confidential."

"I know the guy who's in charge of that particular meeting. If I tell him I need the information to exonerate one of his participants, he'll trust me enough to tell me if Erwin was there or not." Wally flipped through a Rolodex, then picked up the phone and dialed. A few minutes later he hung up and said to Skye, "He's in the clear. Do you want to call Risé to ask about Xavier?"

"No." Skye made a wry face. "But I will." Could this be more awkward?

It was not a pleasant conversation, and Skye hoped she'd never have to have a similar one again, but Risé did confirm Xavier's alibi.

After Wally buzzed the dispatcher and instructed her to allow Xavier to leave, he sank back into his chair.

After a couple of minutes, Skye asked, "Are there any other leads?"

"No." Wally laced his hands behind his neck and stared at the ceiling. "We talked to Kayla's people, we looked into the burglary angle, and you've cleared everyone we know who has a grudge against Risé. We'll have to expand our inquiry to nonlocal investors who lost money when her firm folded." He shook his head in disgust. "We'll also have to start over and reexamine all the evidence again." He sighed. "I sure wish the crime scene guys would hurry up. They promised me some answers by Monday about those plastic pieces found in the vic's hair."

Several more minutes of silence went by before a voice rumbled out of the intercom, "Sorry to interrupt, Chief, but there's been a multiple-car accident near the entrance ramp to I-55. Our ambulance is on its way, and I've called for backup from the Clay Center and Brooklyn EMTs. Do you want their officers, too?"

"I'll let you know. Right now, get any of our men you can locate out to the scene ASAP." Wally had already leaped to his feet. "I'm on my way." He was halfway to the door when he turned to Skye and tossed her a set of keys attached to a sterling silver disc. "Take the Thunderbird. There's no telling how long I'll be."

"Be careful," Skye called after his retreating back. "I'll come by and pick you up tomorrow after church."

Skye's head was spinning with conflicting emotions as she drove herself home. On one hand, she was relieved that Xavier had an alibi. She hadn't let herself think how awful it would be if Frannie's father was the killer. It was also great that Xavier had a decent chance of getting his and the veterans' club's money back eventually.

On the other hand, she was dismayed. With the exception of the men she'd dated in the past, Skye had always considered herself a good judge of character. But Xavier, someone she had grown to like and trust, had lied to his boss and had an affair with his best friend's wife. Apparently he had fooled her, and she worried about whom else she might have misjudged.

Then there was the little annoying fact that Kayla's murder investigation was stalled. They had completely run out of leads.

Skye parked the T-bird, wiggled out of the car, and dragged herself up the front steps of her house. When she opened the door, she heard the phone. Who in the world would be calling after midnight? As she dodged past Bingo, who had greeted her with his tail waving in the air and purring, the ringing stopped. She ran into the kitchen, hoping to catch whoever was calling while they were in the process of leaving a message, but the flashing light was already blinking.

She checked the number on caller ID, didn't recognize it, and immediately hit REDIAL, but no one answered. Skye frowned. It had been less than a minute or two since the ringing had stopped. What had they done? Drop the phone and run away?

Bingo rubbed against her shins, and she scooped him up, cradling the furry comfort device. She pushed the button to hear her messages. The first trio were from her mother, each more hysterical and demanding than the last. Essentially it was the same old, same old. May wanted to know where Skye was and why she wasn't answering her phone, where Vince was and why he wasn't answering his phone, and why her ungrateful children were trying to give her a heart attack and kill her.

Skye erased all three, feeling a little guilty, but she knew May's penchant for exaggeration and was fairly certain an unanswered call would not put her mom in the hospital. Besides, Skye had no news, and she didn't have the energy to spend an hour or more reiterating that fact or reassuring her mother that the Four Horsemen of the Apocalypse were not stampeding down Basin Street. It was too late to phone her parents anyway.

The last message, the one she had apparently just missed, was from Vince. Skye sagged against the counter in relief that he was okay. "I'm fine. Talk to you in person tomorrow night. Come to Tales and Treats café at six, and tell Mom and Dad to be there at half past, since you know they'll be at least fifteen minutes early. Make sure you arrive before they do."

Son of a gun! Skye's mood darkened. What

was her brother up to? The bookstore closed at four on Sunday, and obviously he hadn't phoned their mother, which meant Skye would have to do it. Thank goodness it was past her parents' bedtime.

Lights-out for May and Jed was ten thirty, as soon as the news was over. She could put off the call until tomorrow morning, when she was awake and alert. Skye had learned a long time ago that talking to her mom without being in full control of her faculties was never a good idea, especially when she had something to hide.

Before going to sleep, Skye needed to unwind, and she knew just the way. As she waited for the tub to fill, she stripped off her clothes, then twisted her hair into a knot on the top of her head. Looking around the newly enlarged and remodeled bathroom, she smiled contentedly.

It had been worth every cent she'd paid to bring the space into the twenty-first century—and heaven knows she'd spent a lot of pennies. Gone were the leaky pipes, dingy linoleum, and antiquated fixtures. Now there was a separate shower, oversize Jacuzzi, and built-in vanity. She had chosen shades of green for the tile and the paint, and as she slipped into the hot water and leaned back, she gazed at images of clouds rather than a cracked ceiling.

Stretching out, she let the bubbles flow through her fingers, willing her mind to stop whirring and relax. She had dozed off when she jerked awake. There, at the edge of her dream, was a clue, but as she concentrated, it slipped away. She knew she was overlooking something in the murder case, but what?

She reached out idly to stroke Bingo, who was curled up on the bath mat waiting patiently for her to go to bed. What was she missing? They had checked out all of the local people who might want Risé dead. The only ones left would be someone from her previous life, who might have tracked her to Scumble River. But was that really likely?

Risé had been cleared by the law, and her boss was in prison. Unhappy investors were more apt to go after him, weren't they? So, where did that leave the investigation?

Suddenly, Skye sat straight up, splashing Bingo, who ran away with an indignant howl. What if she'd been mistaken all along? What if Risé wasn't the intended target and Kayla was? What if the murderer had killed the woman he intended to kill?

Damn! That would put them right back where they had started. Wally's officers had looked into Kayla and hadn't found any reason someone would want to kill her. So who had done it?

Skye toed open the drain and got out of the tub. She didn't have an answer to that question, but she was pretty sure she knew where to find someone who might. Someone who wouldn't have told the police anything. As Father Burns always said, the Lord would provide.

May was glad to hear that Vince was okay, but she was extremely displeased that he'd called his sister and not his mother. May was also unhappy that Skye had not gotten any details as to his whereabouts. But she agreed that she and Jed would be at the bookstore café as per Vince's instructions. The only thing that had saved Skye from lengthy recriminations was that her mom had to get to six o'clock Mass.

Which was why she had called May at five forty a.m. Thank goodness Xenia attended a later service, since Skye wasn't sure what her priority would have been if the teenager also went to the early Mass—avoiding May or talking to Xenia.

Skye didn't know how long Xenia had been going to church, since Skye usually went at eight. But a few months ago, she'd had to attend the eleven o'clock Mass, and she'd been surprised to see the teenager there. Somehow the Goth-punk apparel didn't seem to go with Catholicism, but Xenia was anything but predictable.

Now Skye kept an eye on her as Father Burns concluded the service, saying, "The Mass is ended. Go in peace."

After the parishioners responded, "Thanks be to God," Father Burns added, "Remember, a closed mind is usually accompanied by an open mouth."

Smiling, Skye joined the congregation shuffling down the aisle toward the exit. As always, Mass had made her feel at peace, but it was time to talk to Xenia about Kayla. And this time she wasn't giving up until she got the whole story.

When Skye had tried before, she'd accepted Xenia's claim that Kayla was an angel and there was no one who would want to hurt her, but now Skye wondered whether she'd been too quick to believe Xenia. No one was that perfect, and Xenia had to know more about Kayla than she had told Skye. After all, who had more dirt on a teenage girl than her best friend?

"Wait up, Xenia." Skye caught up with the girl at the foot of the stairs, and they moved onto the grass.

"Ms. D." Xenia stopped. "I bet I was the last person you thought you'd see at church."

"Not the last person . . ." Skye trailed off, not wanting to lie. "But I thought maybe with your trust issues—"

"Hey," Xenia cut her off. "I believe God loves me. I just think he has a really, really wack way of showing it sometimes." She grinned. "Besides, I like asking Father B. questions that get him all riled up. I'm an equal-opportunity annoyer."

Skye couldn't imagine the priest "all riled

up," so instead of commenting, she asked, "How about I buy you lunch?"

"McDonald's or the Feed Bag?" Xenia challenged.

"You pick."

Xenia weighed the choices. "Since you probably want to pump me about Kayla again, McDonald's is more private."

"True." Skye was glad that Xenia seemed to be in a cooperative mood. "Then McDonald's it is."

"I'll meet you there. Get me a Big Mac, fries, and a large coffee," Xenia said, then started off to the right. "The lot was full, so my car's parked on the street."

Skye nodded and headed in the opposite direction. She hoped this wasn't Xenia's way of ditching her.

When she arrived at McDonald's, Xenia had staked out a booth in the back corner. Skye placed their order and joined the girl once their meals were ready.

Skye slid into the seat opposite Xenia and distributed the food. "Thanks for talking to me."

"Duh. Like you wouldn't have hounded me until I did." Xenia decapitated a sugar packet and poured the contents into her cup, stirred, then asked, "So, what's up?"

"I need you to be straight with me." Skye had thought a lot about how to approach Xenia and decided head-on was the best way. "I know Kayla was your friend, and you don't want to speak ill of the dead, but we need to find her killer. No one is as wonderful as you described Kayla to me last time we talked."

"True," Xenia agreed without the least bit of embarrassment. "But why should I tell you Kayla's personal business?" She fiddled with her stirrer, spattering the tabletop with droplets of coffee. "Besides, I thought you told me yesterday that the murderer was after Ms. Vaughn, not Kayla."

"Now I think I was wrong." Skye shook her head. "Something's been bothering me, and I think I figured out what. Your version of Kayla and Chase's version of Kayla are too dissimilar. It's almost as if you two were talking about different girls."

"That's 'cause he had no idea who she really was." Xenia took a bite of her sandwich, swallowed, and added, "He thought she should be like some nineteen-fifties housewife—pop out two-point-five kids, make his dinner, and clean up after everyone."

"And you thought she should pursue her art and become a famous director." Skye gave Xenia a calculating glance. "Was that her dream or yours?"

"Both of ours." Xenia sneered. "Chase is a jerk. He's just like Kayla's stepdad."

"You're sure?" Skye made a face. "One of my personality flaws, and a bad one considering I'm a psychologist, is that I'm often too quick to judge people."

"I'm right about Kayla." Xenia's voice was firm. "And about Chase."

"One thing I always try to remember is that the side a person shows you is not always representative of them as a whole." Skye stabbed her salad over and over with her fork as she considered Xenia's statements. "Kayla had to see something in Chase. They were together a long time."

"Back when they first started dating, he was what she needed—someone to love her more than anyone else. He was a way to escape from her family and for her to be number one in someone's life." Xenia twisted a skull-shaped ring on her finger. "But that was years ago. When Kayla started film school in Chicago, she got a taste of freedom and saw what life outside of Scumble River could be like. It made her think that maybe Chase wasn't the right guy for her."

"Chase said they were getting married later this month."

"True. She agreed a couple of weeks ago to marry him." Xenia narrowed her eyes. "But now that we're talking about it, Kayla said something the night before she was killed that made me wonder if she'd changed her mind."

"What?"

"I can't remember exactly." Xenia shook her head. "It was just a fleeting impression."

"Interesting." Skye thought for a moment. "Did you tell me that the night Kayla died, Chase started calling you sometime before eleven o'clock?"

"Yeah." Xenia nodded. "Way before. Maybe as early as quarter after eight or eight thirty."

"Oh." Skye's mouth dropped open and she sat up straighter. "He told me he didn't start calling you until after midnight."

"Then he lied. And I can prove it. I haven't erased his messages."

"I need to talk to Chase." Skye felt the ghost of an idea percolating in the back of her mind.

"Not without me." Xenia stood up. "Let's go. I know just where to find him."

CHAPTER 24

The Heart Is a Lonely Hunter

D on't you have to get to work?" Skye asked. Despite her attempt to dissuade Xenia from accompanying her, the teenager doggedly followed Skye to her car, plunked down in the passenger seat, and ignored Skye's commands to get out.

"I'm not missing this." Xenia whipped out her cell. "I'll call in sick. They'll be okay without me."

"You're going to make this harder," Skye argued. "He'll probably talk to me more openly if you aren't there, since you two don't get along."

"So, you'll have to work for it." Xenia crossed her arms. "Deal." When Skye glowered, Xenia asked, "Do you think he killed Kayla?"

"I don't know." Skye measured her words carefully. "I want to check on something." What the Dooziers had said about Kayla's winning film, and what Xenia had said about thinking that Kayla had had a change of heart regarding marrying Chase, were starting to add up, not to mention his lie about the timing of his calls to

Xenia. But Skye still wasn't sure she'd done the math correctly.

Part of her refused to believe that the young man who was so torn up at seeing his fiancée crushed under a bookcase could be the one who put her there. However, another part of her knew it all fit. If she was correct about the motive, Chase may even have convinced himself he didn't do it. Another thing to keep in mind was that Chase was a darn good actor. His Prince Charming in the school's production of *Sleeping Beauty* had been outstanding.

"What do you want to check on?" Xenia asked. "Do you think he murdered her because she broke off their engagement? That's pretty wack, even for him."

Skye ignored the girl's questions. "I am going to call the chief and have him on the line while we talk to Chase."

"Is that legal?"

"Yes. You told me Chase will be at the park playing baseball, so he has no expectation of privacy. Plus, I'm not recording him." Skye paused, considering what the city attorney had told her when she was hired as a consultant, then murmured half to herself, "We aren't arresting him or even taking him to the police station, plus I'm not a sworn officer so I don't have to read him his rights."

"Cool."

"I'll be back in a second." Skye got out of the Thunderbird and said over shoulder, "Don't forget to let Risé know you're not coming in." As soon as Skye was out of Xenia's earshot, she phoned Wally, explained her theory, and asked him to check something with the ME. Although Wally wasn't thrilled with her idea, he did agree that bringing Chase into the PD and formally interviewing him probably would not elicit much information.

When she pointed out that Chase was a long shot and they would be in a public place, in full view of dozens of witnesses, Wally finally acquiesced, saying, "The only reason I'm going along with this is because I know if I don't, you'll do it without me. At least this way I can be nearby to protect you."

"True. And I appreciate your being there." Skye smiled. At least he realized his limitations. "I'll call you back once we find him, and if I need you, I'll say, 'Thanks for clearing that up.' "

"Fine. I'll ask the medical examiner your question."

As Skye and Xenia drove to the baseball field, Skye outlined what she wanted Xenia to do, then asked, "Any questions?"

"Duh. What part of shut up and keep quiet do you think I might not understand?"

Skye went over the plan in her head as she turned onto the park's rutted gravel pathway.

Chase was far from the sharpest cleat on the athletic shoe, and he was easily riled up. She just needed to poke at him until he lost his temper and blurted out something incriminating.

When Skye first got out of her car, she didn't see Chase, but she finally spotted him sitting on a bench in the dugout among several other guys in their early to mid-twenties. Once she got Wally on her cell phone and reminded Xenia to keep quiet, Skye approached the young man.

"Hi, Chase." Skye waved. "Can I speak to you for a second? It's important."

Instead of answering, he glared at Xenia. "What's she doing here?"

"Actually"—Skye thought fast—"she's the reason I need to talk to you. Xenia has told me some things that don't jibe with what you've said."

"She's a liar." His face was tight with indignation.

"I know Xenia has had some issues with the truth in the past." Skye shot the girl an apologetic look, and Xenia rolled her eyes. "That's why I want to hear your side before leaping to any conclusions."

"Gee, Ms. Denison." The young man pushed back his cap and scratched his head. "I can't leave. We're in the middle of a game."

"How about we just stand over there in the parking lot so you can see when your team goes on the field?" Skye was used to coaxing teenagers, their parents, and sundry school personnel into doing what she wanted. "I only need a couple minutes of your time."

"Well, okay, but I gotta leave as soon as my team takes the field." Chase got up off the wooden bench and said to the guys sitting near him, "I'll be right back."

Skye and Xenia followed Chase across the gravel.

The three of them stopped near his SUV, and Chase jerked his chin at Xenia, asking, "What did she say?"

"Xenia tells me you started calling her as early as eight fifteen, but you said you started at midnight." Skye thought she'd begin with the easy stuff.

"I'm not a clock-watcher." Chase shrugged. "Maybe it was earlier than I thought. So what?"

"You also told me that you and Kayla were getting married later this month, right?"

"Yes." Chase opened the BMW's front passenger door, grabbed a can of beer from a cooler on the seat, and offered, "Want one?"

"No, thanks." Skye edged back as he popped the top, not wanting to get sprayed. "Xenia says that Kayla changed her mind and was going to call the wedding off." Although this wasn't exactly what Xenia had said, Skye hoped it would make Chase angry enough to blurt out something incriminating.

"That's not true!" Chase shouted. "We were going to get married, have kids, and settle down.

She was going to forget all about making those stupid movies." He gulped back a sob, then took a slug of beer. "I had it all planned out. It was going to be perfect."

"But since you didn't see her that night," Xenia interjected, "you didn't know if she was going to dump you or not."

"No!" he roared. "Kayla knew she could never leave me."

"But she had won a big award and had the chance to show her movie to lots of famous directors and producers." Skye leaned against the rear passenger door. "Xenia, wasn't Kayla going to Hollywood?"

"Yes." Xenia stared at Chase. "She showed me the airline ticket."

"You're lying." Chase jerked as if he'd been Tasered. "That was before. We talked it over and she wasn't going."

"Before what?" Could it be what she thought? Skye held her breath.

"Before she saw reason?" Chase's tone was almost a question, as if he hoped that was an answer Skye would accept.

"Could she have changed her mind?" Skye persisted. His defenses were definitely beginning to crack. "Girls do that all the time."

"No." The young man shook his head wildly. "She promised me."

"But a chance to go to Hollywood and work

for a celebrity, maybe become a celebrity herself . . ." Skye let her voice trail off. "Scumble River and her high school boyfriend might have begun to seem like settling for bronze when she had a chance at the gold."

Chase's shoulders slumped, and he choked out, "Why would you say something awful like that?"

Skye flinched. She felt a little nauseous, as if she were burning ants with a magnifying glass. But they had no other leads, and it wouldn't be fair to Kayla if her murder went unsolved.

Unable to meet his eyes, she glanced into the SUV's window. What was that in the backseat? She tilted her head. It was a half-folded, super-elaborate, heavy-duty baby stroller with a cracked blue plastic footrest. Various facts zipped through her mind in a matter of seconds.

Holy moly! The last piece of the puzzle fell into place. Earlier, when Xenia had mentioned that she thought Kayla had changed her mind about marrying Chase, Skye remembered that at the Dairy Kastle Kayla had said she hadn't been hungry the past week or so and that food wasn't appealing to her. Kayla hadn't been dieting. She'd been pregnant.

Chase followed her gaze, and his mouth tightened.

Oops! "Well, thanks for clearing that up." Time to get Xenia and herself a safe distance away and let Wally bring Chase in for a formal interrogation. Meanwhile, one of his officers could obtain a search warrant and see whether the plastic of the broken stroller matched the pieces found in Kayla's hair.

"I'll let you get back to your game." Skye took a step away. "Looks like your team is about to take the field." She gestured with her thumb to the men in the dugout rising from the bench.

"You know, don't you?" Chase's demeanor changed from sorrow to rage, and he lunged at Skye. "You figured it out!"

Skye stumbled back, but Chase grabbed her wrist in a viselike hold. "Let go of me this instant," she ordered in her firmest teacher voice.

"It's women like you who ruin everything." Anger seemed to ooze from Chase like pus from a popped pimple.

He jerked Skye toward him, but Xenia launched herself at him, landing on his back and wrapping her hands around his throat, screaming, "Leave her alone!"

Chase's gasp was an inverted howl; then all three toppled to the ground with Skye on the bottom of the pile. She pushed, but the combined weight of Xenia and Chase on her chest was too much. She couldn't get free.

Just as she was feeling woozy from lack of oxygen and starting to panic, Chase was plucked off her. Wally pinned him to the ground and handcuffed him while reading him his rights.

Xenia hopped around, pumping her fisted hands in the air and shouting obscenities. Skye wasn't sure whether Xenia was aiming the profanities at Chase for killing her friend, or at Wally for stopping her from beating the crap out of Chase. Probably both.

Skye tried to drop Xenia off at McDonald's before going to the PD, but once again the girl refused to budge. However, even Xenia wasn't able to get past Sergeant Quirk when they arrived at the station.

He blocked Xenia's attempt to get through the door, while ushering Skye in, saying, "The chief is waiting for you in the interrogation room."

Chase sat slumped in a chair with his hands cuffed to the leg of the bolted-down table. He looked up as Skye took a seat, and whined, "I didn't mean to do it."

"Sounds like she made you." Skye looked at Wally, who was leaning against the wall behind Chase, and he gestured for her to go on. "Everything was perfect until her film got that award."

"That's right." Chase nodded eagerly.

"Because when she won, she decided to leave you."

"Yes." Chase gazed zealously at Skye. "But then she found out she was pregnant. She wasn't able to take the Pill, and for the past few months, I'd been poking holes in the condoms I used."

"You figured if she had a baby, she'd have to

stay with you and could never change her mind?"

"Yes, and it worked." Chase beamed. "She was giving up her silly idea to make it big in movies."

"So what happened?"

"Saturday, after closing time, I went to the bookstore to show her the cool stroller I'd bought. It cost almost five hundred dollars and even had cup holders." Chase frowned, then looked confused. "But she started crying and told me she'd lost the baby and she wasn't marrying me and she was leaving for Hollywood as soon as she finished school."

"That must have been hard to hear." Skye hoped she wouldn't gag on the words she was forcing out of her mouth. "So, you just had to do something to stop her from going."

"Exactly." He nodded. "I told her I still loved her, even if she killed our baby, and we could have other kids. And you know what she said to me?"

Skye shook her head.

"She said that while she would always love me, she wasn't *in* love with me, and she needed her freedom." Chase slumped. "What in the hell was that supposed to mean?"

Skye shrugged. He was on a roll, and she didn't want to interrupt him by speaking.

"She kissed me on the cheek, and I grabbed her. I begged her not to go away, but she told me to leave her alone and started to walk away." Chase was silent, tears dripping off his chin.

"Then what happened?"

"I was so mad. I was still holding the stroller, and I just swung it at her. She stumbled and turned to look at me, then keeled over." He sobbed, "It was an accident."

An accident? Please. "But you pushed the bookcase on top of her." The words slipped out before Skye could stop them. And judging from the expression on Chase's face, they were a mistake.

"You bitch!" He lurched toward her, but the handcuffs pulled him up short.

Skye stood up and backed away.

"Calm down, man." Wally stepped between her and the table, blocking her from Chase's sight. "Women always stick together. I understand. Just tell me what happened after you hit Kayla with the stroller."

"I couldn't stand to see her like that." Chase heaved a sigh. "All bloody and everything. So I just sort of covered her up."

"With the cabinet?" Wally confirmed.

"Yeah. There was nothing else around." Chase hung his head. "I loved her. I really loved her. How could she do that to me?"

"You're pathetic. You killed Kayla, ended the life of someone worth a thousand of you, and you think you're the victim." Skye dodged around Wally, put both hands on the table, and looked Chase in the eye. "That's not love. That's evil. Pure evil."

Wind in the Willows

I'm so glad you were able to come with me." Skye leaned her head against the seat of the Thunderbird as Wally drove them from the police station to Tales and Treats, where Skye's family was gathering per Vince's instructions. "I was afraid you'd be tied up all night processing Chase."

"There isn't much more for me to do until the Stanley County state's attorney gets back tomorrow from his vacation." Wally pulled out of the PD's parking lot. "The ME confirmed Kayla had a recent miscarriage, the crime techs are matching the stroller to the blue plastic pieces found in her hair, and Xenia provided us with the voice mail proving he lied about what time he started calling her, so we have physical evidence."

"Not to mention the confession." Skye was proud of how she had maneuvered Chase into admitting his crime. "It's hard to believe he watched the store all night so he could pretend to arrive and act surprised when Kayla's body was discovered."

"Yep. One minute he's crying and moaning about losing the love of his life and the next he's planning his alibi." Wally parked the car a block away. "Good thing this was such a good bust, because he'll definitely try and play on the jury's sympathy."

"Is Quirk bringing Chase to the county jail?"

"As we speak." Wally opened Skye's door. "Except for testifying at the trial, my part is pretty much done."

"Thank goodness for small favors." Skye snuggled up to him. "I wish I knew what Vince is up to. I have a feeling whatever it is, he'll end up smelling like a rose and I'll be the one shoveling the fertilizer."

"No doubt." Wally squeezed Skye's hand. "But it will be good practice for you. You said you're trying to stand up to your mom more."

"True." Skye gestured to the parked vehicles. "I see Hugo still hasn't moved his inventory."

"No." Wally grinned. "But did you notice what's on the windshields?"

Skye squinted, then snickered when she saw the telltale neon yellow rectangles tucked under the wiper blades. "Uncle Dante will have a fit when Hugo comes crying to him about all these parking tickets."

"Maybe." Wally paused at the bookstore's entrance, allowing Skye to go in first. "But I pointed out to the mayor that if he wants to encourage new businesses in Scumble River, the town has to have a reputation for cooperating with them and making sure their needs are met."

"I hope you're right." Skye couldn't see her uncle taking sides against his only son.

As soon as they walked into the store, Risé rushed up to them and hugged Skye. "Thank you for calling this afternoon to let me know that Kayla's killer is under arrest."

"You're welcome." Skye patted the older woman's shoulder. "I phoned as soon as Wally gave me the go-ahead. I wanted you to know you were safe."

"It was a relief to hear that no one is gunning for me," Risé admitted. "It's such a shame that Kayla's young man thought he could change her into what he wanted, instead of loving her for who she was."

"Yes, it is," Skye said. "What he didn't realize is that any relationship is under the control of the person who cares the least, not the most."

Wally arched a brow at Skye, then said, "It's ten after six. We'd better find out what Vince has up his sleeve before your folks get here."

The first thing Skye saw as she walked through the café's door was a small wedding cake. Next to it was an envelope with her name scrawled in Vince's distinctive half-printing, half-cursive handwriting. She hurried over, snatched the long white rectangle from the table, and tore it open.

Sis,

Sorry to do this to you, but it was the only way. Loretta and I eloped last Monday—we've been in Las Vegas this past week on our honeymoon. I needed to keep you in the dark so you could be the red herring for Mom. Remember our agreement. When she and Dad get here, you need to break the news to them. We'll be here at six forty-five, so make it quick.

Love,
V

Skye handed the paper to Wally, who turned pale. "Maybe I am needed at the station after all."

"No way." Skye grabbed his arm. "You want me for better or worse, remember?"

Before Wally could respond, Skye's parents arrived. As usual, May was in the lead, with Jed trailing a few steps behind her.

May stopped, stared at the wedding cake, then at Skye and Wally, and screamed, "No!" Sinking into the nearest chair, she moaned, "Tell me you didn't elope!"

"Not me, Mom." Skye hadn't realized her mother might think she was the bride.

"Then what is that all about?" May demanded. "You scared ten years off my life."

"Maybe you should have a drink first." Skye walked toward the bottle of champagne that was chilling in a silver bucket.

"For heaven's sake, just tell me." May threw up her hands in exasperation.

Skye moved a couple steps farther from her mother, then said, "Vince and Loretta got married last Monday in Las Vegas."

May howled, "My baby!" She popped up from her seat and threw herself against her husband's chest. "My baby boy got married without me."

Jed awkwardly patted his wife's shoulder, and said, "No importance."

May stiffened, drew back, and slapped him. "It is too important, Jed Denison!" May sobbed.

Skye gasped. She had never once seen either parent lift a hand to the other. Before Skye could process what she had witnessed, the café door opened and Vince and Loretta burst into the room. May's tears disappeared faster than an ice cube in a deep fryer, and she flung herself into her son's arms.

Vince drew Loretta into the circle, and the three of them spoke in low tones for several minutes. Skye heard the words "grandchildren" and "house in Scumble River," then saw May embrace Loretta and smile.

Since all seemed forgiven, Skye popped the cork on the champagne and started pouring. After they toasted the new couple's happiness, everyone hugged, and Vince and Loretta cut the cake while Wally took pictures using his cell phone.

Once they were all settled around a table to eat, Skye asked, "Vince, why did you have us meet at Tales and Treats? A bookstore isn't your usual style."

"Exactly." Vince grinned. "I knew it would throw Mom off the trail." May whapped him on the arm, and he continued, "Besides, when Orlando came into the shop a couple of weeks ago for a haircut, he told me all about his baking, so when we decided to do this, I called him to see if he'd let me have a private function at the café after closing time."

"Why didn't you ask Maggie to do the cake?" May frowned. Maggie was one of her best friends and *the* cake maker for Scumble River special occasions.

"Because she would have told you." Vince laughed. "Same reason we didn't have this shindig at the Feed Bag. Tomi would have spilled the beans, too."

"Yeah." May's chest puffed out. "I guess I do cast a pretty wide net."

"Have you told your folks yet, Loretta?" Skye asked.

"No." The bride's expression was hard to read. "We're driving into the city later tonight to share our news with them."

They chatted for a half hour or so; then Vince said, "We've got to get going. We told Loretta's family we'd be there at nine, and even if traffic isn't bad, it'll take us at least ninety minutes."

They all followed the newlyweds out of the café, and once Skye and Wally were in his car, he suggested to her, "How about stopping at the Brown Bag for a drink? I hear they have a good fifties band playing tonight."

"Sure." Skye shook her head. "I could use something stronger than that champagne."

The Brown Bag, one of Scumble River's nicer bars, was packed. There were no free tables and only one spot at the bar. Skye took the open stool, and Wally stood behind her. While they waited for the bartender to notice them, she looked around.

Ay-yi-yi! Sitting a couple places down, with a row of martini glasses lined up in front of him, was Simon. Skye was startled. What was he doing there, and why was he getting wasted? That wasn't like him at all.

Just as she was considering telling Wally she had a headache and wanted to leave, Simon saw them.

He rose unsteadily and staggered toward them. "Well, if it isn't Dudley Do-Right."

"Reid." Wally's expression was glacial.

"I hope you're happy." Simon poked Wally in the chest. "Xavier quit."

Skye bit her lip. That wasn't good. Xavier needed a steady income. On the other hand, burying the dead was a recession-proof industry, and he'd have no problem finding a job at any of the neighboring funeral homes.

Simon interrupted her thoughts by adding, "He said he couldn't face me every day after lying to me."

"I'm sorry to hear that." Wally's tone was neutral. "Maybe once things settle down, you can change his mind."

"Like you give a shit," Simon said in a harsh, raw voice. "You want to see me lose everyone I care about."

Wally's jaw tightened. "I couldn't care less one way or the other."

"I'm not giving up on Skye." Simon straightened and seemed to sober up all of a sudden. "I hear you're having trouble getting your annulment, Boyd." His smile was predatory. "Just remember, it isn't over until the fat lady sings."

"If that's the case, Reid"—Wally arched a brow —"she's clearing her throat right now, because I've located Darleen."

Center Point Publishing
600 Brooks Road ● PO Box 1
Thorndike ME 04986-0001 USA

(207) 568-3717

US & Canada:
1 800 929-9108
www.centerpointlargeprint.com